Cover design and additional artwork by

Red Beans Press

Laissez les bon livres rouler!

A HAUNTED TIKI BAR COZY MYSTERY

MAI TAIS, MENOPAUSE, AND MAYHEM

ASHLEY DONATI

Chapter 1

"What am I drinking, exactly?" Flo scrunched up her face and swirled the neon blue liquid, the flickering light of the tiki torches glittering through the cocktail glass. "A Blue Hawaiian, you said?" She took another tentative sip, her brows furrowed in the same expression as the one worn by the huge totem statue standing guard across the room.

"You don't like it." Sunflower, though she insisted on being called "Sunny," stopped obsessively polishing the bartop in front of her, a look of betrayal on her face.

"No, no!" Flo insisted, and took an exaggerated swig from the glass to show Sunny her approval. "I love it. Really."

Sunny narrowed her eyes in disbelief before returning to her task.

"I think if you wipe down that counter any more, there won't be any counter left." Flo slid from her barstool and brought her now-empty glass to the sink behind the bar.

"I know." Sunny tossed the cleaning rag aside and exhaled loudly. "Why hasn't anyone shown up? You put those flyers on the message board at the library, right?"

"Of course." Flo had placed flyers advertising the opening of Sunny's tiki bar, The Cajun Coconut, all around town—the community center, the library, the diner, and yet, here they sat in an empty bar.

Sunny scanned the place for something to do while she waited for a customer to arrive. No luck. Everything was already perfect for opening night. The space looked like a fantasy tropical getaway, with tiki masks and totems, faux florals and palms, bamboo furniture, and velvet paintings of parrots and pirates. A new speaker system infused the room with a breezy, beachy tune. Sunny had nailed down her menu of tropical cocktails and was ready to sling fruity drinks behind the bar. *Now, if only someone would come and order one*. She sighed to herself.

At last, they heard the clacking of the seashells tied to the front door as it swung open. A man and a woman entered.

"Jeb!" Flo stood and greeted them. "Welcome to The Cajun Coconut. Thanks for coming in."

Jeb Landry simply nodded and went to the bar, his companion behind him. Sunny reached across the counter and handed them a menu.

"Let me know what I can get you." She smiled, and the woman with Jeb gave a small smile in return.

The two spent several minutes reading the list of drinks in front of them. Jeb mouthed the names of the mysterious concoctions to himself–*mai tai, pearl diver, lapu lapu*–a frown forming across his face. Eventually, his female friend took control.

"We'll have two mai tais, please," she said, sliding cash onto the bartop.

"Sure thing." Sunny nodded and got to work. The couple took their drinks to the far corner of the room and settled into two rattan peacock chairs facing each other. They sat in silence at first, sipping their cocktails from curly straws, their solemn faces bathed in the orange light of the lava lamp that hung above them.

"I recognize him from around town," Sunny leaned closer to Flo, whispering. "But who's she?"

"Not a clue," Flo whispered back, doing her best to study the mystery woman without appearing to do so. "I can tell you one thing, though. That's not his wife, and if she finds out he's spending time with another woman—" She shuddered. "His wife, Barbara, isn't someone I would ever want to cross." She wiggled one eyebrow for emphasis.

"Whoever she is, they clearly don't get along," Sunny noted. Jeb and his mystery woman had broken their silence and were now arguing, hissing at each other in angry whispers to avoid drawing attention to their quarrel.

"Hey, mom!" Danny poked his head out from the side entrance door. "Back from study hall."

"Danny, hi!" Sunny turned to rake a hand through her teenage son's black, curly hair. She kissed his cheek.

"Not the big opening night I was hoping for." She gestured towards the nearly empty bar.

"Don't worry, mom. I'm sure people will come in soon." He took an orange from the bowl of fresh fruit near the stacked cocktail glasses and began peeling and eating it. "So... you don't need my help tonight?" He gave her a pleading look, and she shook her head no. "Would you mind if I go home and play my new video game? I had a long day at school."

"Of course," Sunny nodded. After a rushed hug, her son was gone as quickly as he had come.

"If it's okay with you," Flo looked at her wristwatch and stifled a yawn, "I'm going home for a bit to check on the cats. Will you be alright?"

"Sure." Sunny tried to give her an optimistic expression, unsuccessfully.

"It's just one night." Flo reached out and patted Sunny's slumped shoulder. "I know things will pick up."

Sunny nodded, unconvinced.

"I'll go feed the kitties, let them out, and then come right back to help you close up, okay?" Flo slipped on her ratty purple cardigan and the old fishing hat she wore every day, and left.

"Is there anything else I can get you guys?" Sunny approached the couple when their drink glasses were empty. "Another drink?"

The woman whipped around, almost jumping at the sound of Sunny's voice. "No, thank you. I was just leaving." She shot Jeb an icy glare before snatching her purse from the floor and stomping out of the bar.

"I'll take another one of these." Jeb raised his glass and gave it a shake, his face lined with worry.

"Coming right up." Sunny took his empty glass

and made her way to the bar.

An excruciating hour passed. There were no new customers to the Cajun Coconut, and Sunny sat on a stool behind the bar, scrolling Instagram while Jeb slowly sipped his cocktail in silence.

"I guess I could make myself useful and put away that shipment of rum," Sunny said to no one in particular. She went to the back store room to organize the crate of Jamaican rum that had been delivered that morning. Twenty minutes later, when Sunny emerged from the back room dusting beads of styrofoam packing material from her clothing, she noticed Jeb had fallen asleep.

"Oh, great." She said, "Now what?" She thought about waking him but didn't want to seem unfriendly. Sunny and Danny were new in town, and she was already struggling to blend in with the locals. Waking up Jeb and telling him to get lost probably wouldn't help her image, so, she waited.

"Closing time is in thirty minutes anyway," Sunny shrugged. "I will wake him up then." She gathered the ingredients to mix herself a Rum Runner—rum, banana liqueur, pineapple, and lime juice—deciding that it wasn't really drinking on the job when the only customer was asleep. She rattled the cocktail shaker with extra force, hoping the noise would wake Jeb. It didn't. She pulled a tiki mug shaped like a parrot from the shelf behind the bar and strained her drink into it.

"Delicious," she cooed after her first sip. "I'll have to make Flo try this when she gets back." She looked at the coconut shell clock on the wall opposite her. Midnight— closing time.

"Alright, Jeb." Sunny walked over to where he sat

slumped in his chair. "Time to wake up, buddy." She shook his shoulder slightly. He didn't wake up. "Jeb, come on." She shook his shoulder a little harder. Jeb collapsed to the floor. Sunny gasped. The man only had two drinks. Surely, he wasn't so drunk that he couldn't be roused. She didn't know why, but the idea to check his pulse came to mind. She knelt beside him and felt his neck. Her fingers registered nothing—no flutters, no thumps. She gasped again, pulling her hand away as if she had just touched a hot stove.

Jeb Landry was dead.

Chapter 2

One Month Earlier ...

"Danny!" Sunny gasped as she walked through the door of the Minneapolis apartment she shared with her son. "Look at these decorations! You did this all by yourself?" Tears formed in her eyes as she looked at the balloons floating around their modest living room and the "Happy Retirement!" banner draped over a door frame.

"Well, you already had to buy your own party cake." Danny ducked when his mom tried to tousle his hair. "I wanted to do something to help you celebrate."

He shrugged and took the bakery box from her arms.

"Well, that was very kind of you," Sunny sighed as she collapsed into a kitchen chair. In the two years they had lived in Minneapolis, they hadn't made much headway in the friends department. Typically, Sunny was too busy to notice or too tired to care, but the empty room for what was supposed to be her retirement party put an exclamation point on one fact: Sunny had no friends. "My last shift ever as a nurse. I can't believe twenty-seven years have come and gone." She shook her head, suddenly feeling old.

Sunflower Beach had gone against her parents' wishes when she went into nursing school after college. They had wanted her to come back home to their goat farm in California and join in the family business —cheese making, chakra aligning, and reiki healing. Sunny could still see the shock on their faces when they saw her wearing hospital scrubs for the first time. She could still hear her father's disappointed words. "Our daughter, our only child, is going to be giving people antibiotics for a living!" He would have preferred she teach her patients about the benefits of the right herb or crystal. The fact that she wanted to be a travel nurse, pulling up stakes and going somewhere new every few years, made it even worse in their eyes.

"People are like plants." Her mother had fretted. "Without roots, they can't grow."

"You should be proud, mom." Danny reached over and patted her hand, snapping Sunny out of her memories. "Taking care of all of your patients, dealing with the politics of your job, and maintaining a house, all while raising me..."

She squeezed his hand and smiled. *How on earth*

did I get so lucky with this one? She thought, admiring her teenage son.

It had been challenging being a single mom and a travel nurse. Sunny and Danny had moved six times in the seventeen years since he was born. For Sunny, each move made her feel more independent and confident in herself and her abilities. For Danny's sake, it pained her to watch him make friends in each new town only to have to start all over again a few years later. Now that she was retired, Sunny was determined to find them a forever home where they could put down roots and build a community of friends they never had to say goodbye to again. The only problem was she didn't know where that forever home would be.

"Have you decided yet?" Danny asked as if reading her thoughts. "Where we're going to move?" He leaned forward in his chair, ready to start the discussion again. They had talked about this subject to death, never coming up with a good answer. At first, Sunny had considered her childhood home in Topanga, California. Her parents would be delighted to have them so close, but while she loved them dearly, she didn't know how well living next to them would go. Sunny hadn't lived there since she was a girl, and she was a different person now. She loved visiting her parents' farm for a few weeks at a time, but if she was honest with herself, it didn't feel like home.

Minneapolis hadn't felt like home either. For the last two years, she paid astronomical rent to live in a small apartment, taking the train to work every morning surrounded by strangers. The city had a constant flow of people leaving, followed by new people coming in to take their place. After the third new face moved in, she hadn't even bothered getting to know her neighbor across the hall. She rubbed her tired eyes and scanned the beige apartment—beige walls, beige carpet, beige furniture. It was time for color. It was time for risk.

"I've got an idea." She sat up and smiled. "Let's stop talking about where we're going to move. We will never reach a decision. Let's approach this in a new way." She rose from her seat and went to the hallway closet. Rummaging around, she emerged with a rolled poster.

"What's that?" Danny frowned.

"You'll see," Sunny chimed, grabbing a roll of tape. She unfurled the poster onto the bare wall before them and secured the corners with the tape. "Ta-da!" She raised her hands in triumph.

"Okay ... a map?" Danny shrugged.

"A map!" Sunny laughed. "Do you still have that dart board on your bedroom door?" she asked.

"You aren't serious." Danny narrowed his eyes when he began to catch on to what she was doing. Without another word, Sunny walked down the hallway to his bedroom, returning with a dart in her hand.

"I want you to close your eyes and throw this dart at that map, and that is where we will live." She handed him the dart.

"Mom, are you feeling okay? Maybe you should take a nap. Or maybe have a piece of cake. Your blood sugar must be low or something." Danny gave a nervous laugh and crossed his arms in hesitation.

"Oh, stop," Sunny scoffed. "Now, are you going to throw it, or am I going to have to do it for you?"

"I will," Danny said reluctantly, readying the dart in his hand. Just before he could throw it, he stopped short. "Are you actually for real? We are going to move wherever this dart lands on the map?" He looked at her as if she had lost her mind. Sunny chuckled to herself. Maybe she had.

"Yep." She nodded. Danny squared his shoulders and squeezed his eyes shut.

"Here goes nothing," he said, releasing the dart with force. It made a neat zipping sound as it pierced the map. Danny covered his face with his hands. "Where did it land? I can't even look."

Sunny moved closer to the wall and squinted to see the tiny pinprick the dart had left in the paper.

"LouLou, Louisiana."

Chapter 3

"Welcome to LouLou: population six hundred." Danny read the sign as they drove past, his voice cracking from exhaustion. The trip from Minneapolis to South Louisiana could be made in two days, but Sunny and Danny had taken three with Sunny insisting on stopping at every tourist trap along the way. They had seen the world's largest ball of twine in Kansas, the world's largest rocking chair in Iowa, and the world's largest round of cheddar cheese in Wisconsin. Danny didn't think he could take one more world's largest anything for a good long while.

"Make that population six hundred and two!" Sunny laughed as she turned her Mazda Miata into the cutest town square she had ever seen. Even late at night, LouLou, Louisiana could cast a charming spell on anyone who visited. In the warm glow of the old-fashioned street lamps that stood guard on every corner, she could see rows of small shops, each with a hand-painted sign hanging out front. She read them out loud as she drove through. "Oh, look! Bunny's Boulangerie. How adorable. And what's that one? Eddie's Hardware. What's coming next?" She squinted in the dim light. "The Hippity Hop! That looks like it's the grocery store."

"Mom! Watch out!" Danny grabbed the wheel and steered the car back onto the road, narrowly avoiding a fire hydrant on a street curb. "You need to look where you're going," he laughed.

"I'm fine." Sunny rolled her eyes. "Just got a little distracted by all the cuteness." They navigated around the square a second time to admire everything they missed their first time around. Pots of flowers were everywhere, bursting with petunias, begonias, and electric green sweet potato vines. In the center of the square stood a large Victorian house. The sign out front told them that this was the library.

"It's like something out of a Hallmark movie!" Sunny gasped as they made their way around.

"Is our house somewhere around here?" Danny asked. "I could walk to town every day to hang out. That would be kinda cool."

"I don't think the house is near the square." Sunny squinted into the screen of her phone, opening the navigation app. "Looks like we have a little further to go." Exiting the roundabout to leave the town center, they found themselves in a ritzy neighborhood, surprisingly fancy for such a small town. Hugging the shore of the vast, ocean-like Lake Pontchartrain was a long row of mansions, each oozing southern charm, with wrap-around porches and crystal chandeliers peeking out from lit windows. A sign they drove past told them the neighborhood was called Sunset Bayou.

"Is our house here?" Danny found it hard to believe they could afford one of these places.

"No...Ours is more 'charming cottage,' less 'Mercedes Benz in the driveway.'" Sunny cut her eyes at her son, hoping he wouldn't be too disappointed with their new digs. They seemed to drive for miles. The lights of LouLou got smaller in the distance behind them, the only thing in front of them wilderness. The road sliced through a darkness that seemed void of all civilization.

"Turn left for Moonlight Lane," the voice from the GPS toned, and Sunny did what she was told. Reluctantly, she pulled her car onto a long, gravel driveway leading into a scene that looked like a sinister swamp straight out of a horror film.

"Are you sure this is the way to the house?" Danny raised a questioning eyebrow as the tiny Miata struggled to navigate the potholes in the dirt road. "Who sold it to you? The Creature From the Black Lagoon?" he chuckled.

"You hush!" Sunny swatted playfully at his arm. "I'm sure this place looks great in the daylight." She wasn't actually sure about that, but she didn't want Danny to know that.

Sunny could see where her new home address got its name. Her cottage on Moonlight Lane had no neighbors with bright porch lights. It didn't even have street lamps. The only light came from the full moon that filtered down through the branches of the live oak trees, silver Spanish moss dripping from the tree limbs and swaying in the light breeze. At the end of the lane, Lake Pontchartrain spread before them, and the dazzling moon glow reflected off the water in shimmering ribbons. It was so dark that she almost ran right into her new house.

"Mom, watch out!" Danny gasped from the passenger's seat for the second time that night, and Sunny slammed on the brakes.

"Honey, I'm home." She gave a nervous chuckle and shifted the car into park. They stepped out, groaning and stretching from the long drive.

"Well, I'm *pretty sure* this is our new home." Sunny pulled at the scrunchie that held her messy bun and released her long, blonde-streaked gray hair with a shake.

"It's pitch black out. How can you tell?" Danny slipped his backpack over his shoulders and grabbed a rolling suitcase from the back seat of the car. Together, they made their way towards the little cottage by the lakeshore that Sunny had bought, sight unseen.

Had buying a house, without seeing it in person, in a town she had never visited, been impulsive? *Maybe.* Sunny shrugged to herself. The house-buying process had gone much faster than she had thought it would. On a Monday, she was looking at a real estate website that posted grainy photos of a small-but-charming two-bedroom cottage that needed a little work. On a Wednesday, she talked with an agent at LouLou Realty, who assured her with great confidence that the little house was in excellent shape and that houses at this low price with lakefront views were one in a million. On a Friday, she signed the papers electronically, and Sunflower Beach was a homeowner. She had assured herself and Danny that, while the house needed things like a new lick of paint and maybe some DIY projects in the kitchen and bathroom, it was in good enough shape to move in, and the idyllic lake views and quaint small town vibes would more than make up for its imperfections.

They stood on the porch, the wooden floorboards creaking as they walked to the front door. Sunny put the key in the lock, but before she turned it and opened the door, she looked at Danny.

"Now, remember–" She did her best to smile. "I told you this house needs a little work."

"Okay, got it." Danny shifted the weight of his bag from one shoulder to the other. "Let's go in."

"I just want to remind you of that because we've always lived in new, modern apartments your whole life, so this might not be what we're used to, and..."

"Mom!" Danny snapped. "I'm exhausted. Just open the door, please."

Sunny took a breath, gathered her courage, and reached for the door.

Chapter 4

Sunny turned the key, and the door opened with a loud, whining sound from its hinges. Before they stepped inside, she reached a hand into the darkness and felt along the wall for a light switch. The overhead light in the living room flicked on, and the two saw their new home for the first time. Sunny's heart sank. It was so much worse than the photos online. She stepped in, avoiding Danny's gaze.

The bones of the room were good—a simple square living room with two large windows that would surely let in lots of natural light once the sun was up, solid hardwood floors made from local cypress wood, and a stone fireplace that was perfect for cozy warmth, come wintertime, not that southern Louisiana had much of a winter. That was where the room's good qualities stopped. Sunny stepped further inside, Danny following behind her in silence. The photos on the real estate website had been taken strategically to avoid the piles of trash in every corner of the room, the holes in several of the walls, and the layer of filth and dust covering every surface.

"Alright," Sunny forced herself to sound cheerful. "So, it's a little more of a mess than we thought." She walked over to the fireplace. "But look how gorgeous this is! I wonder if this is a local stone." She bent over and touched the large, gray rocks that made up the hearth, admiring the craftsmanship. Something flew towards her face, the sound of fluttering wings almost inaudible over Sunny's screams.

"Oh my goodness!" Sunny shrieked, covering her head and rushing for the door.

"What was that?" Danny yelped, right on her heels. They stood on the front porch, out of breath from fright. Danny screwed up enough courage to peek back inside. A dove stood on the fireplace mantel, one wing extended to preen its feathers. "Just a bird." He released the breath.

They shooed the dove out an open window and continued the tour of their new home. The kitchen was in shambles, with cabinet doors hanging on broken hinges. The water that flowed from all of the taps was a mysterious brown color, and the bathroom looked like it was the recent home of a family of raccoons.

"What's that smell?" Danny held his nose. The hallway leading to the bedrooms smelled like more than one animal had died in the walls.

"It is quite strong," Sunny had to admit. "Which bedroom would you like to be yours? I'll give you first pick."

Danny considered for a minute, his gaze moving back and forth between the two bedrooms on opposite sides of the stinky hallway as he studied each space.

"I'll take this one." He moved into the room that was the smaller of the two but featured an entire wall of built-in bookshelves. "I can probably fit all my comic books in here." He slid a hand along one of the dusty shelves.

"That leaves this one for me, I guess." Sunny peeked into the other bedroom. It was plain, and the carpet needed a thorough cleaning, but the farthest wall featured a bay window with a cozy window seat. Some elbow grease and a few throw pillows, and that spot could be the reading nook of her dreams.

The moving van with all of their belongings would arrive in two days, so for now, Sunny could only inflate the air mattresses from the trunk of the car and go to sleep. They made beds and brushed their teeth as best they could in the dank brown water that insisted on spewing from the taps. Then, they both went to bed, utterly exhausted.

"Mom?" Danny's voice came from his room across the hallway.

"Yes?"

"Was this a mistake? This move and—" His voice trailed off. "This house?"

"Definitely not." Sunny sat up, the plastic mattress squeaking underneath her. "I know this seems bad now, but trust me, a little cleaning, some repairs here and there, and this place will be amazing." She did her best to fake confidence. "You and I have been on so many adventures together. Have I ever steered you wrong?"

"Not yet." The house was dark, but Sunny could tell that he was smiling. "Night, Mom."

"Night, Danny."

Sunny's eyes opened at exactly 5:15 the next morning, drenched in sweat. When menopause had started in earnest several years ago, it brought with it a host of fun new friends into Sunny's life including night sweats and the inability to sleep passed six a.m. She rolled off the now semi-inflated air mattress and stood, stretching her stiff muscles. Sleeping on the floor wasn't exactly good for her fifty-five-year-old back. She rummaged through her suitcase for her yoga clothes and mat, dressed, and crept out of the house as quietly as possible so as not to wake Danny.

She had started her day with yoga and meditation ever since she was old enough to walk. Her mother loved to tell the story of how a one-year-old Sunny would watch her as she did her morning vinyasa, Sunny doing her best to move her chubby little body and follow along with mountain to tree to downward dog. No matter where Sunny was in the world, whether that be at a rudimentary clinic deep in the jungle in Thailand, at a posh hospital in a suburb of Paris, or a remote clinic in the rural Arizona desert—she woke up early and did her yoga.

She pushed open the front door, wincing at the loud creaking hinges and hoping her son couldn't hear them, as she stepped onto the front porch. Looking around, she gasped.

It had been so dark the night before she hadn't been able to see anything but a glimmer of the lake when they arrived. Now, with the first rays of the sun peeking out from the treetops, she was finally able to see her new home, and it was beautiful. If the website photos had oversold the state of the cottage, they had most definitely undersold the house's surroundings. She spun around to take it all in. The cottage was ringed by a verdant forest of live oak trees, tall and skinny loblolly pines, and sweet-smelling magnolias. Black-Eyed Susans grew in clusters along the path that led from her front steps, and beyond the path was the most perfect water view she had ever seen. Lake Pontchartrain glittered in front of her, its blue waters lapping gently at the rickety dock that she guessed was hers now.

"I've got a dock!" She whispered to herself in delight. "And a porch with a lake view. And wildflowers and trees—" Her voice faltered as a tear came to her eye. Someday soon, she would be sitting on this porch in the most comfortable rocking chair money could buy. She would have a cup of tea in one hand and a good book in the other. Her heart swelled. It hadn't been a mistake to move here, after all. LouLou was starting to feel like her forever home.

She headed to the woods behind the house, walking down a pine-straw-laden path with her yoga mat under one arm. Once she found a level clearing, she unfurled her mat and sank into downward dog, groaning as the stress of packing up her life and making the long trek down South began to leave her body. Thirty minutes later, she had completed her usual routine. She was a wet noodle from the late summer Louisiana heat, but she decided not to complain about the weather. *Back in California, people pay a lot of money to get sweaty at hot yoga.* She thought. *Here in Louisiana, I get to sweat for free!* She was almost to her front porch when she heard a low, rumbling growl. Three feet from her front steps, she froze. On her porch was the longest, fattest alligator she had ever seen (not that she had seen many). It lay outstretched, basking in the early morning sunshine.

"Don't panic, Sunny," she whispered to herself, her feet frozen to the ground. "Don't panic. Don't panic." She reached for a nearby rock and threw it at the scaly beast standing between her and her front door. "Shoo! Go on now." The alligator opened its craggy jaws and gave her a warning hiss. *What did I see on the Nature Channel once? Make myself look bigger? No, I think that's for bears. Run in a zigzag?* "I get that you don't like rocks being thrown at you, but you need to leave my porch. Okay?" Sunny's whole body trembled. By some minor miracle, the alligator seemed to understand her words and agree. It slowly walked down the front steps, across the lawn, and silently slipped into the lake. Sunny made a break for the front door and dashed inside.

She sank to the floor, her heart finally slowing to a normal pace, and mopped her blotchy red face with the hem of her shirt. The house was quiet, and she guessed that Danny was still asleep. She decided to let him rest since the long drive from Minnesota had been a lot to endure. Rummaging in a duffle bag, she pulled out a jar of instant coffee and her favorite mug. After flushing the kitchen sink's tap for a few minutes, the water ran clear enough that Sunny felt comfortable using it to make her cup of joe.

"And now let's figure out breakfast," she muttered to herself. The agenda for today would most definitely include a trip to the local grocery store, but for now, the only food she had were the remnants of their road trip snacks—a box of Cheez-Its and the last few homemade granola bars she had baked for their journey. She grabbed a granola bar and her mug and returned to the porch. She hesitated before stepping outside. What if that modern-age dinosaur had decided to come back? But she told herself that alligators were a part of life here, and she would have to get used to that fact if she wanted to use her lovely new front porch. Plus, weren't alligators one of Mother Nature's children too? And she had to admit that the creatures that all the locals called "swamp puppies" were kind of cute as long as they didn't try to eat her.

Without any furniture yet, she carefully set her mug on the porch floor and lowered herself onto the front steps with a groan. She stretched her arms and legs in front of her, basking in the early morning sunshine like a happy cat.

"A cat," she thought out loud. "I bet I could finally get a cat now that I will be staying in one place." She smiled at the thought. Danny had always wanted a pet, but with her job and their mobile lifestyle, Sunny never thought it was a good idea.

Off in the distance, a skiff floated on the lake. The woman in the boat turned and waved to her, and Sunny waved back. She sat for a moment, enjoying her coffee and watching the woman cast her fishing line into the water. When she heard Danny rustling around the house, she rose from her spot. Before opening the door to go inside, she took one more look at the dazzling lake and the friendly fisherwoman. Sunny blinked. The woman and the boat were gone. Sunny shrugged and went in.

"Morning, Sunny's Little Sunshine!" She sang the words she had greeted him with every morning for the past 17 years. "Not so little anymore," she chuckled. He gave her a sleepy grin and rolled his eyes.

"So, what's the plan for today?" Danny reached into the box of Cheez-Its and grabbed a large handful. "I'm guessing we will need to start cleaning this place." He shot a look around at the filth that surrounded them.

"Clean this place, fix what we can, maybe do some painting," Sunny nodded. "Here's something fun—let's pick out all new paint colors, a different color for each room. I want the house to be bright and happy."

Danny nodded in agreement, and they spent the rest of breakfast dreaming about what colors should go where. Sunny decided the living room would look best in an earthy sage green to compliment the stone fireplace and mirror the woodland peeking through the windows. She decided on a serene lavender for her bedroom, and Danny wanted his room to be a deep royal blue.

"You know what we haven't done yet?" Danny asked through a mouthful of Cheez-Its.

"Oh, you're right!" Sunny sprung from her spot on the kitchen floor and went to her room. She grabbed the items from her suitcase and returned to where Danny leaned against the kitchen counter. "Where should they go?" She asked, holding the pink and white crystals in one hand, the Hamsa hand in the other. Without waiting for Danny to answer, she walked into the living room and placed the pink quartz and the moonstone crystals on the fireplace mantel. "That's good, I think." She stood back and studied her decision.

"And the hand above the front door, for sure," Danny said as he entered the room. "Here, I can reach it better because I'm taller." He grabbed the wooden plaque–a hand with the evil eye painted in the center of the palm–and propped it onto the woodwork of the door frame.

"We can hang it up properly when our toolbox arrives with the moving truck tomorrow," Sunny smiled.

Sunny's childhood on her parent's farm had been anything but conventional—wearing handmade clothes, eating her mom's vegetarian cooking, and living off the grid. While most kids in her class were taking violin lessons or playing soccer, Sunny spent her after-school hours wandering around her mother's lavender garden, helping her father care for his bees, and learning the magical alchemy of turning goat's milk into everything from soap to cheese.

Until she left Topanga when she turned eighteen, her parents' lifestyle was all she had ever known. Some of it was wonderful, like caring for the sweet-natured goats or the love and attention her parents gave her. Some of it wasn't ideal– she sometimes longed for a white-bread-and-turkey sandwich in her lunchbox or a pair of real blue jeans like the other kids. For better or worse, a few bits of her upbringing stuck with her well into adulthood. She was still a vegetarian, loved making her own natural cleaners and beauty products, and she couldn't quit the habit of displaying her mother's crystals.

When she first began to travel the world as a nurse, her parents had made her promise she would carry items for protection–not a gun or pepper spray, but quartz and amethyst. Sunny couldn't decide if she believed that the crystals had healing powers or that the hamsa hand really warded off evil spirits, but whenever she moved house, she had wrapped them up carefully, always to be brought out again at the next place.

It was probably a silly thing to do. She thought. *But what could it hurt?*

For the rest of the day, Sunny and Danny worked diligently clearing out the trash that littered the house, making lists of repairs to be done in the kitchen and bathroom, and washing the walls with a bucket of hot water and the peppermint castile soap Sunny had intuitively packed in her suitcase.

"This room doesn't look half bad now." She put her hands on her round hips and admired her handiwork. With the help of the soap and water and quite a lot of elbow grease, the living room looked and smelled fresh and clean.

"Well, if you ignore those two big holes in the wall," Danny smirked. "Who's going to fix those anyway?"

"We can do it," Sunny scoffed. "I bet if I watch enough YouTube videos, I could patch those up easy-peasy." She shuffled to the kitchen sink to dump the dirty water from her bucket. Danny watched her struggle with the heavy bucket, giving her a doubtful look.

"I'm starving." Sunny returned to the room, clutching her gurgling stomach. "Do you think this town has pizza delivery?"

When the veggie supreme pizza from Dino's Pizza Parlor arrived, Sunny grabbed the quilt from her makeshift bed and spread it on the living room floor for an indoor picnic. They ate in silence, partially because they had worked up a ravenous appetite with their morning work, but mainly because they had run out of things to say after three days in the car and all day together. As Sunny reached for the last slice of pizza, something swooped over their heads and flew around the room.

"Not again!" Sunny ducked, her pizza slice flying out of her hands.

"Open the window!" Danny scrambled to his feet. He grabbed the empty pizza box and shooed the dove out of the room and into the summer sunlight.

"Clearly, our chimney is home to a family of birds." Sunny put her hand to her chest and breathed deeply to slow her racing heart rate. "We need to clean that out ASAP. I can't have doves flying around here, scaring the life out of me every day." She rose and crept to the fireplace, bending and tentatively examining the flue.

After twenty minutes of Googling "how to clean bird nests from a fireplace flue," she walked outside to the front yard.

"Where are you going?" Danny called after her,

but she didn't answer. She returned several minutes later brandishing a tree branch with the confidence of a DIYer who knew just enough information to be dangerous.

"And what is that for?" Danny motioned towards the branch.

"I'll show you." Sunny smiled and walked to the fireplace. On her knees, she leaned into the firebox and stabbed the branch upwards. An avalanche of soot, dust, leaves, and empty bird nests showered down on her head. When the air cleared enough to see his mother's dirty face, Danny couldn't help but laugh.

"Oh, Mom!" He held his side and cackled. "You look like...like..." He was laughing too hard to get the words out. Silently, Sunny stood and handed him the stick, her mouth a straight line.

"Maybe it's best if you do this job," she sighed, shaking the dust from the sweaty yoga clothes she was still wearing. Danny took the branch, still laughing, and got to work clearing out the fireplace.

Chapter 5

As Sunny watched her son take over the messy work of cleaning out the fireplace, the doorbell rang.

"Who's that, I wonder?" Sunny asked, and then her dirt-smudged face brightened. "Hey, at least we have a working doorbell. That's something, right?"

Sunny opened the door to find a woman standing on her porch wearing a prim cornflower-blue sundress and a prim expression on her face to match. A large, round Tupperware container balanced in her hands. Everything about the person in front of her screamed "perfection," from her short bob of golden curls to her flawless tan to her wrinkle-free face, and Sunny had to admit that the effect of it all was dazzling. She gave herself a tiny shake to bring her thoughts back to reality —one where she stood with her dirt-covered face and sweaty clothes in front of this angelic beauty queen.

"May I help you?" Sunny asked, trying to wipe the soot from her cheeks.

"I'm Mary Kay Middleton." The woman flashed a bleached-white smile and began to extend a hand to shake. She glanced at Sunny's appearance and obviously thought better of it, quickly placing her hand back under the Tupperware."I'm the mayor's wife, and I'm also the head of the welcome committee at St. Boudreaux's Catholic Church. So, it's my job to welcome newcomers into town. I baked you a cake." She held the Tupperware out for Sunny to take.

"That is so kind of you." Sunny took the cake from her and welcomed her inside. "You know, we've moved around a lot, and not once has anyone ever welcomed us to town, especially not with something they baked themselves. What a nice thing to do." Sunny gestured for Mary Kay to come inside.

"This old cottage has been vacant for years and years, so when we heard someone finally bought it, we were so excited to have new blood here in town. So, where are y'all from?" Mary Kay asked, her nose scrunching slightly at the sight of the room's clean, but still dingy and damaged, walls, the outdated ceiling fan with sagging blades, and the strange smell that still emanated from the hallway. *What the heck is that smell??* Sunny fumed, suddenly very aware of the icy blue gaze of her visitor. She studied Mary Kay's face, unable to decide if the woman was friend or foe. Mary Kay's words seemed friendly but something about the woman's energy felt off to Sunny. It made her feel uncomfortable.

"California, originally." Sunny tried to sound polite, but found herself nervously shifting from one foot to the other. "But I was a travel nurse, so we have moved around a lot." She watched Mary Kay's eyes scan the room, landing on Danny with his head and shoulders up the chimney.

"I think I got all the nests out," Danny yelled, his head still up the flue. "But the entire inside of the chimney is covered in bird poop!"

"That's my son, Danny." Sunny gave an embarrassed chuckle. "Hey kid, stop what you're doing for a second and meet our new friend, Mary Kay."

Danny dusted what Sunny hoped was soot from his hands and said hello. She watched as their visitor took a slight step backward as he approached.

"Mary Kay has made us a cake." Sunny widened her eyes, hoping to send Danny the message to be his most polite self. Even before she came to town, Sunny knew they would be seen as a little different, but there was no point in upsetting the locals so soon.

"Wow, thank you." Danny smiled and took the cake from his mother. "I'll bring this back to the kitchen. It's nice to meet you." He dipped his head politely and disappeared into the hallway with the Tupperware container.

"What a nice and polite child you have." Mary Kay said, a strained smile on her glossy pink lips.

"Oh, he's very polite," Sunny reassured her. "We both are. Just two nice and polite people." She smiled, shifting her feet from side to side.

"So rare in teenagers these days." Mary Kay's curls bounced as she shook her head. "I can barely get mine off his cell phone."

"Indeed," Sunny nodded, wondering how long this little visit was going to last.

"Look at those." Mary Kay moved towards the fireplace mantel and reached for the crystals. "Are you a rock collector?" She held the pink quartz up to a sunbeam that shone through the window and eyed it curiously.

"Not a rock collector, per se." Sunny crossed her arms. "These are crystals, you know, for protection?" The words felt so silly coming from her mouth, but they had been said now, and there was no taking them back. *Way to blend in with the townsfolk, Sunflower.* She mentally kicked herself.

"Oh, my." Mary Kay dropped the stone back onto the mantel like it was a hot coal burning her skin. "Well, I'll be." She backed away from the spot, clearly worried that even standing near the stones might jeopardize her status as the most righteous woman in town. "Well, it's been very nice meeting you, but I really must be going." She headed for the door, and Sunny moved to open it for her. She swung the door open with such force that the Hamsa hand fell from its perch on the doorframe and landed right at Mary Kay's feet. She gasped and glared at Sunny.

"Oops, sorry about that." Sunny bent and picked up the wooden hand. "A hamsa hand," she explained. "Lots of religions use it—Islam, Judaism, Wicca—to ward off evil spirits." She shrugged.

"In this town, we are Christians." Mary Kay's crisp words shot like barbs into the space between them. Her chin raised, and jaw squared, she marched down Sunny's front path and was gone.

"That went well," Sunny snarked as she sank onto the quilt still spread across the floor, her face creased with worry. If she was going to make LouLou their forever home, she would need to fit in and make friends, and if the other people in town were built like Mary Kay Middleton, that might not be as easy as Sunny had planned.

Chapter 6

"Danny, I'm back!" Sunny called, carrying two canvas bags filled with groceries to the kitchen. When she didn't hear a response, she leaned her head from the kitchen doorway out into the hallway. The water in the bathroom was running. "He must be in the shower," she mumbled to herself as she put a gallon jug of milk into the old refrigerator. It had needed several rounds of scrubbing with hot water and vinegar, and it surely wasn't pretty. But the scratched olive-green Frigidaire kept things cold, and that was all that mattered. As she stacked two boxes of cereal on the pantry shelf, next to several cans of beans, she replayed her visit to the town's grocery store.

The Hippity Hop didn't sell tofu. It didn't sell kale either, and not one employee knew what the heck kombucha was. *No biggie,* Sunny had told herself as she perused the aisles of the quaint store. No doubt she could take a quick trip across the lake to New Orleans and find a store that sold tofu, kimchi, and whatever else she liked to eat. What shocked Sunny most about the store was not what it didn't carry, but rather what it did. She grimaced, remembering her discovery of an entire aisle devoted to preserved pig parts–feet, snouts, ears, and other unmentionables, floating in a red mystery liquid in hefty glass jars. It appeared that Cajuns really did eat the whole hog. *Right,* she winced as she pushed her cart away as quickly as possible. *Avoiding aisle five from now on.* Terrifying jars aside, she had to admit that the store had a certain simple charm, and she liked how people stopped to say hello to each other as they did their shopping. Each aisle echoed with hellos, hi y'alls, and "How's your momma doing?" *Hopefully, one day soon, somebody will stop to talk to me while I'm shopping,* Sunny wished. *Just not in aisle five.*

She put the last of the groceries away and stared into the open fridge, wondering what she should make for dinner. She had packed one frying pan, one wooden cooking spoon, a few forks, and the tin plates from her camping equipment–enough to cook and eat a simple meal until her kitchenware arrived with the moving van.

The doorbell rang. She stood for a moment in amazement. Most of the apartments she had lived in didn't have doorbells. She had owned a doorbell for less than forty-eight hours, and it had already rung twice. At least this time, she wasn't covered in whatever filth had been lodged in the chimney for the last twenty years. She looked down at her olive green linen maxi dress and

Birkenstock sandals. *Perfectly suitable for entertaining company.* She nodded.

"Coming!" she called out. The woman who stood on the doorstep could not have been any more different from the woman who had stood in the same spot that morning if she had tried. The woman's kind face was weathered, but her green eyes sparkled. She wore a tattered purple fishing hat and camouflage overalls two sizes too big. In her hands, she carried a casserole dish wrapped in tin foil.

"Hi there. I'm Flo Charboneaux. " Her voice was grizzled but kind. "I saw that somebody finally bought this old house, so I wanted to bring a little something by to welcome you."

"Thank you so much." Sunny took the warm dish. "Please come in." She moved aside for Flo to enter. The sun was setting in earnest now, its last few beams of pink and orange sinking through the trees. Sunny flicked on the room's overhead lighting. Its harsh brightness made the furnitureless living room look even more empty somehow. "Sorry, the house is so sparse. Our moving van gets here tomorrow."

"That's quite alright," Flo smiled. "What brings you to our neck of the woods?"

"A dart on a map, actually," Sunny chuckled, leading them into the kitchen. To Sunny's surprise, Flo didn't question this odd remark, but simply nodded like she completely understood, like Sunny's answer had been the most mundane, typical response she had ever heard. Sunny lifted the foil from the top of the dish—the most delicious smell wafted from the pan.

"This looks wonderful!" Sunny smiled. "Would you like to stay for dinner? We'll have to sit on the floor,

I'm afraid," She laughed.

"I would love to. Thanks for the invite." Flo gave a warm smile. She reached for the only spoon in the kitchen and heaped food onto two tin plates.

"What is it?" Sunny asked. "I've got a lot to learn about southern cooking."

"It's my jambalaya casserole," Flo nodded.

"Jambalaya?" Sunny cocked her head to one side. "I've heard of this, but I've never had it. What's in it?"

"Chicken, sausage, rice, and spices. You are gonna love it." Flo didn't notice Sunny's cheeks redden at the mention of meat as the main ingredient. She kept talking while carrying the two plates into the empty living room. "Won me three blue ribbons at the county fair over the years. My secret weapon is the andouille sausage I get from my cousin, who makes it himself."

Sunny lowered herself to the floor and sat cross-legged with the plate over her lap. She had been a vegetarian for her entire life, excluding one wild weekend in college when she rebelled against her parents by eating a Big Mac. Her palms began to sweat. She wanted to make friends and fit in, and she wasn't about to let this second meeting of a potential new friend in this town go as badly as the first social call had. *Just take one bite.* She willed the fork to her lips. *One bite isn't a big deal.* She scooped a forkful of casserole and shoved it into her mouth. She looked over at Flo and was thankful to find the woman completely unaware of Sunny's inner dilemma. Sunny swallowed hard and scooped another forkful.

"Oh, I didn't know we had company," Danny blushed as he stood in the hallway in his Pokemon pajamas–his love for Pikachu a holdover from his younger days that he secretly still harbored. He put a hand to his clean hair, damp from the shower, and brushed down the cow-licks.

"Danny, this is Flo." Sunny pulled herself to standing. "She's been so kind and brought us dinner."

"Awesome," Danny smiled. "Thank you. What is it?"

"It's a type of chicken and sausage casserole." Sunny gave him a wide-eyed glare that said *don't embarrass me.*

"Chicken?" Danny shot her a frown. "Mom, are you eating meat? You're vegetarian!"

"Danny!" Sunny hissed. "Don't be rude!"

"Oh, no!" Flo put a hand on her heart. "I had no idea. Please, don't eat that if you don't eat meat. I can make you something else. Why didn't you say anything?"

"No, no." Sunny lowered back onto the floor next to Flo, her voice rising into a panic. "This is so nice of you. I didn't say anything because I appreciated the gesture. We just moved to town. I didn't want to seem like a weirdo right away." A nervous peel of laughter escaped from her lips.

"Don't be so worried about fitting in." Flo reached over and squeezed Sunny's now trembling hands. "Take it from me. Some people in town like me, some don't. Just be yourself. I know it sounds hokey, but at least I know my friends like me for me." She stood and took the still-full plate from Sunny. "Next time, I'm making you my famous macaroni and cheese. All of my friends love it. The secret ingredient is the hoop cheddar. They make it special a few towns over from here." She paused on her way to the kitchen. "You do eat cheese, right?"

Sunny nodded sheepishly and followed behind her. Before Sunny could say no, Flo washed and dried their dishes at the sink and returned them to the cabinet, chatting happily as she worked. They learned that Flo was originally from Church Point, a small town several hours west in the heart of Cajun country, but she had moved to LouLou twenty years ago to fulfill her dream of being a shrimper. She was one of the only female shrimpers in town, but she held her own. Flo loved nothing more than taking out her trawler boat, The Sweet Pea, into the gulf to cast her giant nets and gather the shrimp that lived in abundance there. Several times a week, Flo sold her catch right off her boat in the LouLou Marina, where she docked. The boat wasn't just her means of making a living–it was her home, too. Below deck, she had a small-but-cozy living space, a tiny kitchen, and just enough space for her two beloved cats, Oyster and Boo, and her chatty parakeet Tabasco, to play.

"I must say, this visit is going much better than the visitor I had this morning," Sunny huffed and leaned against the counter while Flo dried the last fork and put it away.

"From that coconut cake on the counter there, I can see you got a visit from Miss Mary Kay," Flo smirked and gave a mischievous chuckle.

"Did I ever." Sunny tried to stop her eyes from rolling without success. "Now you see why I ate meat when I'm a vegetarian. I want LouLou to be my home, and if everyone in town is like her, I'm in trouble."

"I'm not going to sugar-coat it. That lady is a piece of work, and there are more than a few people in town who are just like her." Flo dried her hands on the dish towel and looked into Sunny's concerned face. "But there are also plenty of people in LouLou who are kind, caring, and good. It's going to work out just fine." She grabbed her casserole dish and headed for the door. "By the way, I go fishing on the lake most weekend mornings. I'd love to have you and Danny join me sometime."

"Wait a minute!" Sunny slapped her hand on her forehead when a thought dawned on her. "That was you this morning. You were the fisherman I waved to while I was sitting on my porch."

"Fisherwoman," Flo winked. "Let me know when you want to go out on the lake." She waved goodbye and walked out of the door.

Sunny stood on the porch and waved until the tail lights of Flo's old blue pickup were out of sight. She paused for a moment before going back inside. The full moon had waned slightly, a little less circular in the cloudless sky. She listened as the forest echoed with a chorus of cicadas buzzing and tree frogs chirping in the humid night air. A sprinkling of fireflies danced along the edge of the lake.

"Magical," she whispered and stepped back inside.

Chapter 7

It took a week of nonstop work for Sunny and Danny to get the house the way they wanted. Four layers of filth were polished away from the cottage's original cypress wood floors, and now they gleamed a warm honey brown. Each room was painted in happy and soothing colors. Their furniture arrived and was put into place, and they had even managed to hang a few pictures on the walls. Sunny had watched enough YouTube videos to figure out how to complete some of the home's most urgent repairs, like patching the holes in the living room walls and rehanging the doors on the kitchen cabinets. Flo had stopped by every afternoon bringing a pan of some (meatless) Southern goodness and her endless knowledge about home repairs. Now, the kitchen looked as good as new with a fresh coat of butter yellow paint on the walls and a happy mint green on the cabinets. Sunny even went to the local thrift store and found the perfect mint green gingham plaid curtains for the window over the kitchen sink.

In Sunny's opinion, the best part of the whole house was her bedroom. Before they left Minnesota, she sold her worn-but-functional metal bed to a college student on Facebook. She had carted that old bed from place to place for over twenty years, so when the time came to furnish her new space, she wanted a change. She had scoured furniture websites for hours, looking for what she called "her sanctuary." Sunny wanted the most beautiful, comfortable, luxurious bed she could find. She almost cried the first time she saw it–an antique wooden sleigh bed with ornately carved roses in the center of the headboard all made up with tons of fluffy pillows, the softest light gray duvet, and the quilt her mother had made her draped across the end.

It was eight o'clock in the evening now, and Sunny was performing her new favorite ritual. Fresh from the shower, she donned one of her new cotton nightgowns and her fuzzy pink robe. She went to the kitchen, fixed a quick mug of chamomile lavender tea with plenty of honey, and headed back to her room. With a sigh of contentment, she slipped under her blankets and nestled between two big pillows before grabbing her book in one hand and her tea in the other.

Bliss, she thought, turning the page to the next chapter.

"Night, kiddo," Sunny called when she saw Danny pass by her open door. "Don't stay up too late playing that video game. You've got school tomorrow."

"First day," his voice cracked with nerves.

"You're going to knock 'em dead," she smiled. "Trust me."

The week passed, and Sunny sank into a familiar rhythm—yoga in the morning, followed by making Danny breakfast before school, a bit of light gardening, which mainly consisted of pulling weeds because she had no idea which plants grew in southern Louisiana, lunch in front of the TV, waiting for Danny to come home from school, cooking their dinner, and then more TV-watching followed by an early bedtime. In other words, Sunny was extremely bored.

It was Monday morning, and the sunlight filtered through the cottage windows filling the kitchen with dappled, dancing light. Danny had needed convincing to go to school earlier that morning, and Sunny worried about him having a hard time making friends as she lowered herself into a kitchen chair, coffee cup in hand. She glanced at the clock on the wall above the stove, her hand drumming nervously on the kitchen table. It was only ten a.m.

So much day to fill, she thought, resting her head on the tabletop. Sunny had known that retirement was going to be an adjustment for her. She had spent so long on hyperspeed–working, parenting, and working some more, all on her own, with no one to rely on. She remembered the long nights of wishing she had more freedom to live life at a slower pace, and now, here she was, free to do whatever she wanted. If she was honest with herself, the freedom she had always longed for was now a terrifying prospect.

"Right," she said to the empty kitchen, rising from her seat and slipping on her sandals. She headed to the hallway mirror and examined her hair and face. *I'm a bit of a wild woman today.* She patted at her frizzy French braid. *But it will have to do for now.* She grabbed her purse and headed out the door. If the life she wanted wouldn't come to her, she would go to it. She jumped into her car and headed for town.

She drove in indecisive circles around the square several times. Every time she came *to town,* as locals put it when they went to the square, Sunny felt like she was living in a real-life fairytale. Everything in LouLou was just so picturesque and quaint. The square was lined with local shops. Sunny couldn't wait to browse in Jethro's, the local record shop, or try one of the French patisseries displayed in the shop window of Bunny's Boulangerie. The town only had two restaurants–Dino's Pizza Parlor and a diner called Gary's. The diner sat off to one side of the square right next to The Hippity Hop, which she had learned from Flo was simply referred to as "The Hop," and an ample empty green space where the farmer's market met every Saturday. She passed what served as the town's social hub for nightlife–Buzz's. It was the kind of hole-in-the-wall bar that had giant TVs blasting sports games at all times and always smelled like stale beer. Sunny wrinkled her nose. It wasn't exactly her kind of place. She pulled her car into a parking spot in front of the library.

The LouLou library was housed in a behemoth of a Victorian mansion that looked even taller because of its spot on the hill in the center of the town square. The outside was clad in pink wooden siding that had paint peeling in places. The inside smelled of paper and dust, and the ancient wooden floor creaked the way old houses should. Sunny had fallen in love with the place the first time she stepped inside. It helped that the librarian, Marian Hammersmith, was friendly and intelligent, seeming to Sunny like perfect friendship material.

"It's easy to remember my name." She had chuckled, her brown eyes twinkling from behind her tortoiseshell glasses. "Marian rhymes with ..." She pointed at Sunny to respond.

"Librarian!" Sunny laughed. Since their first meeting, Sunny had returned to the library almost daily. She pushed the heavy oak door open and sighed as a wave of cool air met her face. *How did anyone live in the South before air conditioning was invented?* She stopped in the library's entryway. On one wall was a large bulletin board where locals could post flyers about town happenings.

"Book club ... hmmm ..." She scanned the leaflets and posters for something that piqued her interest. "Knitting club? I don't know how to knit. What about Zumba? I'm not exactly Miss Twinkle Toes." She felt a tap on her shoulder and turned around.

"Good morning." Marian stood behind her, a warm smile on her face. "Looking for something?"

"Actually, yes." Sunny glanced back at the bulletin

board. “Honestly, I am in desperate need of something to fill my time, but I don’t know what yet.” She blushed, her hands fidgeting with the wooden bangles on her wrists. “I’ve spent so long being a working single mom, and now that I finally have free time, I have no idea what to do with myself. I know that probably sounds silly.” Sunny’s gaze shifted to her sandals in embarrassment.

“Not silly at all.” Marian put her arm around Sunny’s shoulders. “Let’s see …” She pushed her glasses further up her nose. “Tennis league?” She cut her eyes at Sunny’s face to gauge her reaction. “Hiking club? Quilters circle? Well, you simply must come to our book club. We meet every month–sometimes in a club member’s home and sometimes here at the library. It’s fun to talk about books, and you will meet a ton of people in town.” She turned to see what Sunny was thinking.

“Right,” Sunny nodded. “I think I’ll do all of it.”

“All of it?” Marian raised an eyebrow over the rim of her glasses.

“Yep.” Sunny squared her jaw. “Thanks, Marian!”

Sunny stopped at the office supply store on the square, which also served as the town’s post office, DMV, and ice cream parlor. She bought a new spiral-bound planner and a scoop of mint chocolate chip on a waffle cone.

“This’ll be all for you?” The cashier, a young girl with a disinterested face, pressed buttons on the register and reached for Sunny’s dollar bills.

“That’s all, thanks.” Sunny looked around at the store’s shelves stuffed to the brim with a hodgepodge of items–stamps, envelopes, books about the best fishing spots, bubbling tanks of live bait, car registration forms, license plates, ice cream cones, and bottles of rainbow sprinkles filled every free space.

"Jennie, you got any Tylenol?" A boy emerged from the back of the store. "I got a ragin' headache." He pressed his temples with one hand.

"Sure. Aisle Six." The cashier pointed towards the left side of the store.

"You know what else is good for a headache?" Sunny couldn't help but interject. The boy stopped and looked her way. "Mugwort. It works like a treat without all the nasty side effects of chemical medicine."

"Mug-what?" The boy and the cashier said in unison, their faces screwed up in confusion.

"Mugwort. I bet you could find some growing outside if you don't have any in stock. It's very prolific, and it grows pretty much anywhere."

"Thanks," The boy eyed Sunny with suspicion. "I think I'll just stick with Tylenol."

Sunny scooped up her new planner and headed for home.

For the rest of the afternoon, she sat on her front porch in her new rocking chair, filling her calendar with every activity she could manage—tennis on Monday mornings, zumba on Monday afternoons. Kayak Club met every Tuesday for outings on the lake. The knitting club got together in the community center on Wednesday nights. The little matter of her not being a knitter could be sorted out later. On she went, filling each day with nonstop commitments.

"Let's just see you try to be bored now, Sunflower." She bit the end of her pen. If she wanted to make friends, she wouldn't meet them sitting at her kitchen table alone. A full calendar would cure that.

"Hi there!"

She turned at the sound of Flo's gravelly voice.

"Good morning!" Sunny slammed her planner shut. Today, Flo wore her signature faded purple fishing hat, a turquoise button-down, and a khaki skort. Without missing a beat, she eyed what was in Sunny's lap with suspicion.

"Whatcha got there?"

"This?" Sunny feigned ignorance. "Oh, nothing. Just got a new planner, so I can keep my dates straight. That's all." She gave a nervous laugh as Flo eyed her suspiciously. *How did Flo always have the ability to read my mind like a book?* "Oh my goodness! Flo, watch out!" Sunny stood and pointed as her newly-made alligator acquaintance slowly crept his way up her porch steps. Sunny screamed.

"Oh, him?" Flo chuckled at Sunny's panicked expression. "That's just Billy. He's kind of a local celebrity around here. He's nothing to worry about." She stepped closer to the alligator and tapped him on the nose. "G'on git, Billy." She put two fingers in her mouth and let out a sharp whistle. The alligator obeyed and slunk back towards the water's edge.

"Nothing to worry about?" Sunny's voice cracked, and she sat back down in her rocking chair. "That thing wants to eat me for lunch!"

"Nah," Flo waved a dismissive hand but then reconsidered her position. "Probably not anyway. Besides, this house has been vacant for so long, he's been coming up on this porch for a lot longer than we have."

Sunny wasn't convinced.

"I've been thinking, and I know retirement has not been easy for you to get used to." Flo lowered herself onto the other rocking chair next to Sunny. "Come fishing with me tomorrow morning. It will be fun."

"Thanks for the invite." Sunny shifted in her seat. "But I'm a vegetarian. I can't catch fish and kill them, even if I don't plan to eat them. In a way, that's almost worse!" She ran a hand over her long braid.

"I've already thought about that, and I've got a solution." Flo raised her hands, staving off any of Sunny's potential protestations. Sunny laughed. Of course, Flo already had an answer. In the short time that they had been friends, she always did. "Just catch and release," she shrugged. "It doesn't hurt the fish at all."

Sunny scrunched up her face in thought.

"Okay," she nodded. "Let's do it."

"Just to warn you." Flo stood and stretched her knees. "I get up at the crack of dawn. You have to, for the best fishing."

"That's fine with me." Sunny pushed her rocker back and forth. "Thanks to my crazy hormones and all my years as a nurse, I'm up that early anyway. See you tomorrow."

When Flo left, Sunny reopened her planner and coordinated her new routines with the precision of a military operation. She didn't look up from her calendar pages until she heard feet crunching on gravel. She saw Danny trudging down the driveway from where the school bus had dropped him. His shoulders sagged.

"Sunny's Little Sunshine!" She did her best to sound cheerful. "How was it?"

Danny didn't answer. Instead, he delivered an intense scowl before stomping inside and slamming the door behind him. Sunny sighed. Danny had been in high school for a little more than a week, and it already wasn't going well. She shook her head. Her son had been the new kid at school so many times before and had always managed to make friends. Why was this time around going so badly? She rose from her chair and followed him in to do damage control.

When Danny refused to talk, Sunny gave him some space, but when he refused to come out of his room for dinner, she brought in the big guns–her famous hot chocolate. After warming milk on the stove, she added a combination of dark and white chocolate to the pot along with a few splashes of heavy cream and a generous pour of Mexican Vanilla. She stirred until the concoction moved around her wooden stirring spoon like chocolate velvet. With two piping hot mugs in her hands, she made her way to Danny's room.

Even though he refused to talk when she first stepped into his bedroom, the hot chocolate soon did the trick as it always did, and Danny told her everything–how the other kids at school had been friends since they were in diapers and weren't looking to add anyone to their already well-established cliques. Sunny shook her head. They had to find some way to connect with the people in town. But how?

Chapter 8

Early the following day, Sunny rubbed her tired eyes as she stood on the LouLou Marina dock, waiting for Flo to gas up the tiny fishing skiff that would take them out for Sunny's first-ever fishing expedition.

She yawned as she looked out at the lake. Boat traffic would churn the water into shimmering blue ripples by midday, but, for now, it was a calm and smooth, muted-green glass. She inhaled deeply, enjoying the air while it was still cool and fresh. It would be hot and sticky by the time they made their way to shore again. The drilling of a woodpecker at work sounded overhead, and a welcome breeze danced through the cypress and pines. The first rays of the sun attempted to light the early morning sky, creating a lavender light, and Sunny almost regretted bragging to

Flo about how early she liked to wake up every morning. Sipping coffee in pajamas as the sun rose was one thing, but standing on a boat dock with dead fish wafting towards her nose was another. All regrets faded when she spied Flo, her face smiling and her hands at the rudder as the skiff putted along in the marina waters.

"Mornin'!" Flo yelled over the rumbling of the boat's motor, pulling the skiff next to the dock so that Sunny could climb on board. "I'm kind of surprised you made it out this early," she laughed.

"I told you I get up early. Now, teach me how to fish!" She cheered, shifting a large tote bag from one shoulder to the other. The weighty sack was filled with snacks, water, and a natural sunscreen she had made herself from zinc paste and baking soda, and the bag straps dug into her skin.

"Looks like you packed enough food for a week's expedition," Flo chuckled. "We're only going to be out there for a few hours."

"I'm a girl scout," Sunny shrugged. "I'm always prepared. So sue me."

"I'm pretty sure that's the Boy Scouts' motto, not the Girl Scouts'. Now, let me help you on board." Flo reached a hand up to Sunny and guided her onto the boat.

Out on the lake, Flo was a master at her craft. She had her process down to a science–where to anchor for the best fish, the best rods and reels, and the most effective bait.

"Oh, no!" Sunny looked down into the small netted cage where Flo kept her favorite fish bait– live brown shrimp. "I forgot about the whole bait thing. We aren't going to kill the shrimp, are we?" She winced.

"Turn your head, and let me bait your hook." Flo rolled her eyes, and Sunny did as she was told.

After teaching Sunny the right way to cast a line, they sat in pleasant silence for a while, watching the water and waiting for their lures to dip with the bite of a fish.

"Who's that over there?" Sunny asked, keeping her voice quiet. She pointed to another skiff with two men out in the distance.

"That would be Jeb Landry and Earl Hebert." Flo reached into Sunny's bag of snacks and pulled out an apple. She polished it on her purple overalls and took a bite. "They are out here every weekend in the summer."

"Where are their fishing poles?" Sunny asked, puzzled. She squinted at the men to get a better look. They were clearly dressed for a morning's fishing on the lake with the exception of that one key item.

"You noticed that, too." Flo raised her eyebrows. "Now, in all my time out here, that's a mystery I have yet to solve." She shrugged and changed the subject. "How's life now that you are more settled in? The house is looking great."

"Thanks. It is starting to feel like home, but ..." Her voice trailed.

"But?" Flo reeled in her line and cast it again.

"But I haven't made any new friends yet, present company excluded, and to be frank, I'm no good at the slow life. I'm kind of losing my mind."

"Give it time." Flo took the last bite of her apple. "Just be patient. You'll find your way."

"I wish I was as sure as you are," Sunny shrugged.

After several hours on the water and one speckled trout caught and promptly released, they headed to the marina. Flo pulled the skiff up to the back of the Sweet Pea and secured it to the boat's side with a thick rope.

"This was fun," Sunny smiled as she climbed onto the dock. "My spirits have been thoroughly lifted. Thanks, Flo."

"Any time." Flo adjusted the brim of her bucket hat. "Oh, I almost forgot. I made more of that sweet potato casserole that Danny likes. It's in my kitchen. Do you have time to come in and get it?"

"Sure." Sunny had yet to see inside Flo's shrimp-trawler-turned-houseboat, and she had to admit that she was curious about what it was like inside. She had lived in some pretty cramped apartments during her travels, but even she thought life on a boat would be far too cramped for her liking.

"Welcome home!" squawked the green bird on a perch on the boat's top deck. He flew over to Sunny and landed on her shoulder.

"Aren't you a pretty birdy?" Sunny cooed, reaching out to pet the bird's smooth, green feathers.

"Tabasco, why don't you give our guest a little space?" Flo took the bird from Sunny and made a kissing sound as she placed him back on his perch.

"Wanna see some magic?" the bird crowed. "Magic? Magic?"

Sunny cocked her head and gave Flo a questioning look.

"That's the last time I let him watch Harry Potter," Flo chuckled and reached into her pocket, pulling out a birdseed cracker and raising it to the parakeet's beak. "Here, birdy, have a cracker and quit yapping." She handed him the treat before heading inside.

When Sunny stepped inside the boat's cabin, she

was surprised to find that it was nothing like she had imagined. The boat's operating deck occupied one end of the space–a dashboard littered with maps of the Gulf, several small fishing radars, and an ancient-looking marine radio. In the center of the deck was a large wooden steering wheel that faced a window overlooking the bow. The rest of the cabin featured a small floral sofa with several crocheted blankets in bright colors, a bookshelf that looked like it was about to buckle under the weight of the romance novels stuffed on every inch of shelf space, and in one corner, an easel with a half-completed watercolor on canvas. In another corner, a kitchenette with a small oven. A tiny hallway led out of the main living space towards a small bedroom and bathroom.

"I didn't know you were a painter!" Sunny moved towards the easel.

"I dabble," Flo shrugged.

"Flo Charboneaux, you are quite the Renaissance woman," Sunny smiled and shook her head. "I want to be you when I grow up."

"Ha!" Flo laughed as she headed for the kitchen. "Be careful what you wish for." She reached for a casserole dish wrapped in a tea towel.

"Danny will be thrilled. He loves this stuff!" Sunny took the dish and placed it on a side table for her to bring home after her visit. "I do, too. Thank goodness I also love yoga." She laughed and patted her ample hips.

From inside a cozy plush cat house next to the sofa emerged two adorable cats–one calico, one shiny black. They stretched their legs and kneaded their paws on the braided rug on the floor before welcoming the humans home, rubbing against Sunny's and Flo's legs and purring. Flo reached down and patted their heads.

"Oh, these must be the kitties!" Sunny cooed and bent down to pet them.

"This boy is Oyster." Flo patted the calico on the head, "And this little lady is Boo. She's going to have kittens in a few weeks." She picked up the black cat and cradled her like a baby.

"I've been wanting a cat," Sunny confessed. "And now, seeing these cuties, I want one even more."

"I better get those cookies I baked for Rachel ready," Flo said, half to herself. She gently placed Boo on the sofa, hurried to the kitchen, and began rummaging around for a Tupperware container to pack the snickerdoodles that were cooling on a baking rack on her small kitchen counter. A knock sounded from the front door of the boat cabin, and before Flo could get to it, a woman opened it and stuck her head inside.

"Flo?" She called. "Oh, hi. I didn't realize you had company. I'll come back later."

"No, Rachel," Flo opened the door wide. "Come on in. Meet my friend, Sunny. She's new to town."

"Now, how did you know that ..." Sunny's words trailed off. *How had Flo known Rachel would be stopping by?* Sunny swore that her friend was a psychic or something.

Rachel Stickler was tall and lanky, with strawberry-blonde hair that fell to her waist, and hazel eyes that were beautiful but sad. She held out a hand.

"Nice to meet you." Her eyes briefly met Sunny's before shifting to the floor.

"Rachel lives in town with her two kids, Tommy and Jennifer." Flo continued her introduction. "And she works as the receptionist for our doctor."

"Dr. Greg Day," Rachel nodded, and Sunny noticed the slightest blush on the woman's cheeks. "Flo, I came by to ask a favor." She fidgeted with the gold locket around her neck. "Could you possibly watch the kids tomorrow afternoon? I've got an errand I need to run, and my babysitter can't make it."

"Sure," Flo smiled. "Bring them over whenever you need. I know Tommy loves helping me around the boat, and Jennifer's getting pretty good with the watercolors." She patted Rachel on the shoulder, and Rachel exhaled gratefully.

"Flo's been kind enough to give my daughter art lessons," Rachel explained to Sunny. "And she won't even let me pay her." She gave Flo an exasperated look and shook her head.

"No way, Jose," Flo laughed. "Oh, before I forget–I made you some cookies to bring to work tomorrow." She handed Rachel the Tupperware container.

"Mmm, these are my favorite!" Rachel lifted the corner of the lid and inhaled the warm, cinnamon scent. "Why should I bring them to work?" She lifted one puzzled brow.

"Because I hear snickerdoodles are Dr. Day's favorite too," Flo grinned. Rachel blushed, suppressing a giggle. She nodded goodbye to them both and left quickly.

"It's almost eleven." Flo adjusted her wristwatch. "Want to stay for lunch?"

"Eleven!" Sunny exclaimed. "Oh, shoot. I've got Zumba in ten minutes. Could you drive me back to my place? I walked here this morning."

Sunny grabbed the casserole dish on the side table and scurried out of the boat and down the dock to

Flo's truck.

"So...Zumba, huh?" Flo gripped the pickup's steering wheel and cut her eyes at Sunny in the passenger's seat as they bumped along the dirt road.

"Zumba at eleven, then book club this afternoon, and possibly chess club this evening if I have the energy." Sunny conceded, tired of trying to hide her schedule from her friend, who obviously knew she was up to something. "Oh, you should come to the book club! We're meeting at Julia Donahue's house. Do you know her?"

"I do. Very fancy." Flo's voice had a hint of teasing to it. "That sounds like a busy day."

"The only way to fit in and make friends is to get out there and participate." Sunny clenched the air with determined fists.

"Hmmm... ..." Flo turned the pickup onto Sunny's gravel drive. They bumped along the path, chatting about how adorable Flo's cats were and how meeting them made Sunny yearn for a feline friend of her own. When they pulled in front of Sunny's house, she jumped out of the truck and waved goodbye before hurring inside. It was time to get ready for Zumba.

Sunny hurried up the steps of the LouLou community center, late for her first-ever Zumba class.

Nestled in a thick mix of live oaks and pine trees, the community center was an unexpectedly modern, boxy concrete building with floor-to-ceiling windows overlooking the lake. If Sunny wanted to meet people in town, she decided this had to be the place to do it.

She followed a maze of closed doors down a twisting hallway, and when she finally found the room for Zumba, the class had already begun. As she opened the door, a blast of reggae music hit her in the face.

"Welcome to Zumba!" The class instructor shouted a greeting as she shook her booty to the beat. Sunny gave a small half-wave and headed for the back of the room. She joined the last row and tried to catch on.

One, two, left hand to the right, oh wait, it's supposed to be right hand to the left. Shoot... ...How is everyone here so good at this?? Sunny began to feel flustered. Every woman in the room bobbed and weaved her hips and arms to the music in perfect unison. Every woman in the room except her, that is. She watched the instructor closely. Barbara Landry must have been Sunny's senior by at least twenty years, but she somehow had the figure of a Barbie doll and the energy of a bouncy teenager. Not a hair from her teased brunette bob was out of place as she shimmied her way through the exercise dance routine.

"Good job, ladies!" The song ended, and Barbara daintily dabbed sweat from her forehead. "Now, don't stop moving!" She began to march in place. "You don't achieve perfection without a little discipline and a whole lot of work. Now let's go!" The next song blasted from the speakers, and the whole group broke into a hip-hop routine. Sunny caught a glimpse of herself in the mirrored wall in the front of the room and couldn't help laughing.

I bet Danny and Flo would pay money to watch me do this.

By the end of the class, Sunny was a red-faced, sweaty puddle. She grabbed her water bottle from her tote bag and took a long gulp.

"New in town?" Barbara's voice came over her shoulder. Sunny jumped a little before turning around. "I don't believe we've met. I'm Barbara Landry." She motioned to a blonde woman with sharp features. "And this is my friend, Suzy." Suzy gave a quick, tight smile, her eyes boring virtual holes into Sunny.

"Hi, Barbara, Suzy. I'm Sunny." Her legs felt like jello, but Sunny did her best to sound peppy. "My son and I just moved here a few weeks ago." A thought flashed in Sunny's head. "Hey, I was out fishing with my friend this morning, and I think I saw your husband out on the water. Jeb?"

"That's him, alright." Barbara let out something between a laugh and a choke, and Sunny caught the tiniest flash of disdain in the woman's eyes.

"And I bet my hubby was out there with him," Suzy smirked. "You know men. All they want to do is fish and hunt, hunt and fish." She rolled her eyes. Sunny gave a polite chuckle. She had been single most of her adult life, so she didn't know.

"Throw in a Saints' game or two, and that's all they're good for." Barbara shook her head, her hairdo unmoving.

How much hairspray does she use? Sunny took another long drink from her water bottle to avoid having to figure out what to say next.

"Sunny, Sunny... ..." Suzy tapped a finger on her

pointed chin. "Are you signed up for the book club meeting this afternoon? At Julia's?" She flicked her eyes down and up, making Sunny feel uncomfortably examined. Sunny was suddenly keenly aware of the differences between her and the women in front of her, with their perfectly fitted spandex leggings and brightly-colored crop tops, and she tugged self-consciously at the legs of her hand-sewn linen harem pants.

"Yes," Sunny smiled politely. "I'll be there."

"I thought I saw your name on the guest list." Suzy's smile didn't reach her eyes, and she tossed a lock of bottle-blonde hair from her shoulder. "I'm the book club committee chair, you see. I practically run the whole thing." She gave a haughty laugh.

"Well, we look forward to seeing you there," Barbara nodded. "Let's go, Suzy. We've got a spin class in five minutes." Barbara walked away with Suzy obediently following her lead.

"Great," Sunny called after them. "See you there!" Her eyes followed them as they left the room, unsure if she had just made new friends or met new enemies. *I'm sure with time, those two will turn out to be perfectly lovely people,* she reassured herself and rushed home to read the book before the book club meeting.

Chapter 9

Sunny stood on the grand wrap-around porch of Julia Donahue's Queen-Anne-style stunner of a home, the afternoon sun shining into her tired eyes. She had spent the last several hours speed-reading the pages of this month's featured book–a romance novel with enough steamy moments to make Lady Gaga blush. The last thing she wanted was to attend the book club meeting unprepared, without anything intelligent to say. Having finished the book with minutes to spare, she took to the internet to read online reviews, writing down several solid talking points on notecards. With the book under one arm and the notecards in her pocket, she confidently pulled at the brass knocker on the polished mahogany door.

"Well, hello, honey." An elegant woman in her

seventies wearing a feminine pink and white gingham blouse, expertly tailored white trousers, and enough diamond jewelry to sink a ship answered the door. "Come on in. I'm Julia." With her gentle Southern drawl, her name floated in the air between them as "Joo-ya."

"Thank you for having me in your beautiful home." Sunny stepped into an entryway that was as big as her whole cottage. The ceiling was crowned with gleaming, dark wood molding, and the hardwood floor was accented with antique Persian rugs. A round table stood in the center of the space with a glorious cluster of hydrangea blooms arranged in a vase that looked so expensive Sunny tiptoed past it so as not to somehow knock it from its place and break it.

"You are quite welcome, dear." Julia followed her inside. "Everyone is gathering in the sitting room." She gestured for Sunny to enter a door on the right side of the hallway. "I don't think I got your name." Her diamond bracelets clinked as she touched Sunny's shoulder.

"Oh, silly me!" Sunny slapped her forehead. "Sunny Beach. Well, it's Sunflower, but that's always seemed like a bit much. You know how it is–hippy parents. So, I just go by Sunny." She clamped her mouth closed, suddenly realizing that she was babbling. Julia paused momentarily to take her in, her judging eyes resting on Sunny's strappy hiking sandals and unpolished toenails for a few moments longer than Sunny would have preferred. Finally, she broke her silence.

"Oh, I'd go by Sunflower if I were you. It's got real pizzazz."

The sitting room was a din of chatter, and Sunny

looked around to see if she knew any of the women who gathered in clusters, talking and drinking wine. She spotted several people she recognized from around town but didn't know their names. Mary Kay Middleton was in the corner, eating cubes of cheese from little toothpicks and chatting to Barbara Landry in hushed tones.

"Let's just avoid that area for now," Sunny muttered.

"What's that, honey?" Julia raised her eyebrows.

"Oh, nothing," Sunny smiled and made her way further into the room. Like the entryway, the sitting room was a beautifully-appointed space. Two large cream-colored sofas flanking a marble fireplace, and above the mantle hung an oil painting of Julia decked out in a purple dress and jewels like a queen.

"Sunny, hi!"

Sunny winced a little at the sound of Suzy's voice but then reprimanded herself. *That woman was perfectly nice to you this morning. You play nice and make friends.* She plastered a smile on her face.

"Suzy! Hello."

"I'm so glad you could make it." Suzy wore a breezy white button-down shirt and a blue mini-skirt that perfectly accentuated her long, tan legs. She gave Sunny another one of her down-and-up appraising looks, and Sunny felt for the first time that her typical style of hemp, handmade clothing, and hiking sandals might not be the height of fashion in LouLou social circles. She pulled at the skirt of her purple dress and felt her face grow hot.

"Got my book, and I'm ready to talk about it." Sunny tried to sound cheerful.

"Oh, we don't actually talk about the book at these meetings." Julia appeared over Suzy's shoulder and let out a peel of laughter. Sunny looked confused.

"We do, too," Suzy bristled. "Sometimes."

"Mostly, we just use the book club as an excuse to get together and day drink." Julia winked. "Speaking of which, Sunny dear, can I get you a glass of Chardonnay?"

"You wouldn't happen to have any kombucha, would you? Or maybe some herbal tea? It's a little early in the day for me to start drinking," Sunny blushed.

"Kom-boo-chay?" Julia puzzled. "Is that like Perrier? I can check in the kitchen."

"Actually, Chardonnay would be great. Thank you," Sunny nodded shyly.

Sunny spotted Rachel, the young mom she had met at Flo's house earlier that day. She was sitting in an armchair in the back of the room, staring at her smartphone.

"Rachel?" Sunny walked over to her. "Hi, I met you at Flo's house this morning?"

"Oh, hi." Rachel's voice was quiet but friendly. "It's good to see you again. Was it Sandy?"

"Sunny." She smiled and took the seat opposite Rachel.

"Sorry." Rachel shook her head. "I'm the worst at names."

"Oh, me too!" Sunny reassured her.

"I really should put this up." Rachel lifted her phone from her lap. "Just looking at some pictures the babysitter sent of the kids playing in the backyard." She attempted a laugh, showing Sunny a picture of a blonde boy who looked to be about six and smiling, rosy-cheeked girl who looked to be about four. "I'm supposed to be out meeting people and getting a bit of a breather from the kids, but all I want to do is look at pictures of them. What's wrong with me?"

"I totally get it!" Sunny laughed. "You know, I'm a single mom too."

"Really?" Rachel's eyes brightened.

"Mine is older now, so some things are a bit easier," Sunny nodded. "But it's still tough to do the mom thing alone. Feel free to stop by my house if you ever need anyone to talk to. Bring the kids if it's easier."

"I would appreciate that." Rachel's eyes grew misty. Sunny patted her on the knee. She knew how hard it was to be the sole provider for a family. When Sunny discovered she was pregnant after a one-night stand with a guy she had no intention of seeing again, at least she had a solid career to support them financially and two parents who were excited to be grandparents. It seemed like Rachel didn't have anyone.

Sunny spent the rest of the meeting chatting with Rachel. Despite their fifteen-year age gap, they realized they had so much in common. When the meeting was over, they made plans to meet with Flo for dinner one night soon.

After spending several hours at the book club meeting, and never once talking about the actual book, it was time to go home. Sunny walked onto Julia's grand front porch, the hostess on her heels.

"Sunflower!" Julia called to her back, and Sunny turned around. Julia took a business card from her pants pocket. "Don't take this the wrong way–" The Southern belle leaned in and began to whisper. "But I think you could use this. Might help you feel more comfortable if you spiff up your clothes a bit." She handed a confused Sunny the card. Without looking at it, Sunny quickly slipped the card into her bag and gave Julia a motion that was half nod, half embarrassed shrug before walking as fast as she could to her parked car.

Once in the safety of her car and away from the prying eyes of the women of LouLou's uppermost social club, Sunny retrieved the card and held it up to read it.

La Boutique Jolie ~ The Latest Fashions for the Sophisticated Southern Woman ~ Located on the LouLou Town Square

Sunny slapped the card onto her dashboard. Where did Julia Donahue get off telling her that she needed new clothes? She liked her clothes just fine, thank you very much. Looking down at her linen maxi dress, she saw for the first time the tiny moth holes on one side of the skirt and how she had rushed sewing the hem, leaving it to lay wonkily in rippled bunches. She looked at the card again and sighed. Maybe a makeover was exactly what she needed–new town, new look. She shifted her car into drive and headed to the square.

La Boutique Jolie was a tiny brick building positioned between Pinky's Nail Salon and Pelican Bay Outfitters, a fishing supply shop that always seemed to be packed with people buying rods, reels, and everything else needed for a day out on the lake or the nearby Gulf. She reached for the door of the clothing shop and paused. Places like this always made her uncomfortable–snooty salespeople, polyester clothing, high prices. Should she go in? She hurried inside before there was time to talk herself out of it.

"Welcome to La Boutique Jolie. Can I help you with anything?" An impossibly cool, bird-like woman called from the sales counter in the back corner of the room.

"I'm looking for some new clothes," Sunny answered. She gave a slight cough. There were several scented candles lit, causing the store to smell strongly of sickly-sweet candy. The saleswoman stepped around the counter. She wore a red puffy-sleeved sundress that floated around her, draping over perfectly tanned knees. Gold bangles clinked on her wrists, and her makeup and hair were flawless. Sunny shrank inside herself. What was she doing here? She fought the visceral urge to run out of the door and never come back.

"I can certainly help you, but..." The saleswoman studied Sunny with calculating eyes. "I'm afraid I don't sell anything that looks like...*this...*" She motioned to what Sunny was wearing. Sunny fought the urge to tell the woman just where she could stick her nasty attitude, but instead, Sunny took a deep breath and did her best to remember why she was in this awful little shop in the first place. If new clothes would help her make friends, then, new clothes were what she was going to get.

"Oh, no!" Sunny reassured her. "I want a makeover. Give me a whole new look." She gave a determined nod.

"Let's get started." The saleswoman clapped her hands with gleeful satisfaction.

An hour later, Sunny walked out of La Boutique Jolie carrying two heavy shopping bags. She swung them with considerable effort into the trunk of her car and headed home. When she got to her cottage, she found Danny's bedroom door locked.

"Danny?" She knocked and waited, but there was no answer. "You okay, sweetie?" Still no answer. "I know you're home from school because I saw your backpack on the sofa."

The door to his room opened slowly, revealing Danny sitting in the dark, staring at the wall with angry eyes.

"You want to talk about it?" Sunny asked quietly. Danny shook his head no without saying a word.

"I know this hasn't been the easiest transition." The springs of his mattress creaked as she sat on the foot of his bed. "Just hang in there. It's got to get easier." She waited for a minute or two, hoping he would open up to her the way he used to when a kid on the playground had called him a mean name, but the wall he placed between them stayed up. She patted his knee and went to the kitchen to make supper.

Chapter 10

Another week zipped past.

"Time flies when you're having fun," Sunny said to her reflection in the mirror. She smiled, but the words felt hollow. In the span of seven days, she had tried chess club, hiking club, rowing club, Zumba, step aerobics, book club, and the knitting society, and aside from Flo, she couldn't say that she had made any real friends yet. The people she met were polite. They smiled and shook her hand when they were introduced, but nothing ever came of it. No invitations to dinner parties or cups of coffee at the diner. No suggestions that they meet for a swim at the lake or at the library to browse the shelves together. She thought she had made progress with Rachel, but every time Sunny suggested a time for Rachel to come over for dinner, the young mom was always busy. She shook her head, unable to think of a solution to her social woes.

"I'm not letting that get me down," she muttered as she dressed in one of her new outfits for the evening meeting of the LouLou quilters circle. "If at first you don't succeed… …" She slipped into a pair of khaki capris and a bubblegum-pink polo shirt.

The doorbell rang.

"Hello, stranger." Flo stood on her front porch with her ubiquitous casserole dish and what looked like a basket of freshly-baked rolls. "Haven't seen you all week." Flo eyed Sunny's strange new outfit but said nothing.

"Come in! It's good to see you." Sunny moved aside for her to enter. "I know I've been busy. Looks like you came bearing gifts. That smells wonderful."

"I do, indeed." Flo walked through to the kitchen and set down the dish on the counter. "I thought I would bring you and Danny dinner."

"Oh, I would love to stay and eat, but… " Sunny started to protest as she reached for her purse and slung it over her shoulder.

"But what?" Danny was standing in the kitchen doorway, his arms crossed over his chest. "You haven't been home for more than ten minutes this week. I'm the teenager here. Aren't *you* supposed to be complaining about never spending any time with *me*?" He gave Flo a hug hello and peeked under the tin foil that covered the casserole dish. The buttery aroma of Flo's famous mac and cheese wafted up from the pan.

"I'm with him." Flo put her arm around Danny's shoulders. "It's great that you're getting involved with stuff in town, but I haven't seen hide nor hair of you."

She moved towards the countertop and began to divvy up the pasta onto plates.

"You guys know I'm just trying to find my place here." Sunny let her purse slip off her shoulder and hit the floor with a thud. "It hasn't been easy being retired, not knowing anyone, but I didn't mean to neglect you guys, especially not Sunny's Little Sunshine." She reached up and pinched one of Danny's cheeks. He swatted her hand away.

"We forgive you." Flo handed her a plate and a fork.

"Let's eat!" Danny smiled.

Chapter 11

The following day, Sunny woke to someone knocking on her front door. Her eyes shot open. She reached for her phone charging on the nightstand and squinted at the time. *4:50 a.m.? What on earth?* She rose from bed, wrapped her fuzzy robe around her body, and padded down the hall toward the living room. The wheels in her head began to turn. *Who would be at my door this early in the morning? What if it's an emergency? What if something awful has happened?* Her heart raced as she opened the door.

No one was there. Whoever had been banging on her door was long gone. She looked down, and on her doorstep sat a large box.

At first, Sunny thought the box on her porch must have been delivered to her by mistake. She liked her online shopping as much as anyone, but she certainly hadn't ordered whatever was in the three-foot-tall crate before her. She bent at the waist and squinted at the address label.

Sunflower Beach
44 Moonlight Lane
LouLou, Louisiana

So this was actually meant for her? How could that be? She read the return address. Somewhere in Gnome, Alaska. *Who do I know in Alaska?* She shook her head. She knew no one in Alaska. It took considerable effort to heave the box over the threshold. Panting from exertion and perhaps a little excitement, Sunny pried open the lid.

The contents of the mystery box provided more questions than answers. The first thing she pulled from the jumble was a large, hand-carved statue with fierce eyes and curling snarled lips–a tiki totem.

"What on earth?" Her eyes were wide as she set the statue down and returned to rummaging through the box. She lifted out item after item, each more puzzling than the next–blue and green glass orbs wrapped in rope netting that she knew to be Japanese fish floats, ceramic mugs shaped like volcanos and parrots, a pair of lamps with hula girls for bases. The box was seemingly bottomless. She held up a tiki mask and looked into its cheerful face carved from driftwood.

"Who are you?" She felt ridiculous in hoping the mask could give her an answer, but Sunny didn't know what else to do. Who had sent her what looked like a tropical vacation in a box? Was this some weird joke? She continued unpacking everything, pausing every few minutes to gape at the sheer amount of stuff now spread around her living room. When she lifted the last item from the bottom of the crate, a wall clock made from a coconut shell, she saw what she hoped was the answer to the morning's riddle–an envelope with her name on it.

"This better be a letter telling me what the heck is happening here." Sunny ripped it open as fast as she could.

"Dear Ms. Sunflower Beach ..." She read aloud. "Your great-aunt Edna has passed away. This crate contains the personal effects left to you in her will. If you have any questions, please contact my law firm." It was signed at the bottom by a Mr. Thomas Tinwell, Esquire. "This doesn't answer anything at all!" She shouted into the cluttered room. The letter had, in fact, given her even more questions than before. Who was great-aunt Edna, and why had she sent her this junk? She had never heard her parents speak of an Edna. She had never met an Edna. So, how did Sunny wind up in this mysterious aunt's will? She needed to call her parents. Surely, they could tell her what was happening here. She looked at the time on her phone screen–5:30 in the morning. It was way too early to call them, especially since they were on California time and two hours behind her, making it the wee hours of the night. They were probably still asleep.

"Whoa, what's all of this?" Danny stood in the hallway, wiping the sleep from his eyes.

"Danny!" Sunny jumped. "What are you doing up so early?"

"I could hear you banging around in here." He yawned. "So?" He motioned around, needing an explanation as to why their living room suddenly looked like the Jungle Cruise in Disneyland.

"I'm sorry I woke you up, dear." Sunny wrapped her fuzzy robe more snuggly around her shoulders. "And I wish I had an answer to what this stuff is, but I'm just as confused as you." She shook her head, words just out of reach. Instead, she handed him the unhelpful letter from the attorney's office.

"Who's Aunt Edna?" He raised his gaze from the letter and frowned.

"Your guess is as good as mine." Sunny shrugged. "Now, let's get some breakfast and then box this stuff back up. It's going in the attic until we can figure this out."

"I don't know. I think it's all kind of cool." Danny leaned over to examine a faux parrot housed in a bamboo bird cage.

"Attic," Sunny insisted, handing him a bowl of frosted flakes and milk. She had only just gotten her new house the way she wanted it. The last thing she wanted was all this junk messing it up.

After breakfast, Sunny carefully packed everything back into the crate and hoisted it into the attic with Danny's help. She rechecked the time, itching to call her parents but not wanting to wake them. 6:30 Louisiana time meant 4:30 California time. Still too early. She decided to hop in the shower and get ready for another busy day in LouLou–a pickleball lesson followed by chess club at the library.

"What are your plans for this fine Saturday?" Sunny popped her head into Danny's room.

"Dunno," he shrugged. "Play some World of Witchcraft, I guess."

"Again?" Sunny cocked one eyebrow. Ever since his unsuccessful start to the school year, Danny had shut himself in his room, doing nothing but playing video games. She was starting to worry. "Don't you think it would be good for you to get out a bit? Find something to do that doesn't involve casting spells and trapping hobgoblins?"

"Like what?" He rolled his eyes.

"Would you be up for a round of pickleball?" She smiled persuasively.

"What the heck is pickleball?" He grimaced.

"It's like tennis, I think." She cocked her head to one side. "I'm not one hundred percent sure, come to think of it, but it's going to be fun."

"I'll pass."

"I'm heading up to the library later. Why don't you come with me?"

"Library?" Danny sighed. "No thanks."

"I could drop you off at the community center," Sunny offered. "I've seen some kids your age hanging around there."

"Nah." Danny got up from his spot on the bed, pressed his console to life, and sank into his bean bag chair. Sunny closed his door in defeat.

Wrapping her wet hair in a towel turban, she padded into her closet for the tennis dress she had bought online the other day. It was white spandex with a polo collar and a pleated skirt. When she caught a glimpse of herself wearing it in the bathroom mirror, she did a double take. *Who was that Stepford Wife in the reflection?* She sighed. Her ensemble, topped with a white sun visor and accented with thick white sweatbands on her wrists, couldn't have made her feel less like herself. She straightened the pleats in her skirt and stared at herself with determination. She was making inroads with the natives. She just needed to stay the course. Dress like them, act like them, and eventually, fit in with them. Just last week, a woman from her quilting circle almost invited her for coffee. She was so close she could taste the friendships. She slung her racket bag over her shoulder and headed out the door.

Driving through the Sunset Bayou neighborhood with its well-manicured lawns and Mercedes-Benz-lined driveways on one side of the road and the glistening blue-green lake on the other, she reached for her cell and dialed her parents' landline. They never got cell phones because "that's how they track you." It was time to get some answers about dear old Great-Aunt Edna.

"Hi, you've reached the phone of Gary and Donna Beach. We are currently at our annual silent couples Bikram retreat in Santa Cruz. Leave a message, and we will get back to you when we return." The machine beeped, and Sunny paused for a second, deciding whether or not to record a voicemail. She almost ended the call. Whatever or whoever this mysterious family member was, she had a sneaking suspicion that her parents might have a hard time talking about it. Why else had she never heard of Aunt Edna until today? Before she lost her nerve, her curiosity got the best of her.

"Hi, Mom and Dad, um, I got something in the mail today from an Aunt Edna? Give me a call." She did her best to sound casual.

As she pulled her car into the community center's

parking lot, she spied a group of pickleball enthusiasts warming up on several of the center's tennis courts.

"Here goes nothing." She straightened her sun visor and made her way over.

"Sunny!" Rachel lifted her floppy straw sunhat and waved it to get Sunny's attention. "I'm so glad you decided to come."

"Wouldn't miss it!" Sunny smiled, setting down her racket bag on a courtside bench.

"Is that Sunflower I see?" The honeyed drawl of Julia Donahue lilted through the air. "It's so good to see you, honey."

"Julia, I didn't know you played pickleball." Sunny leaned in as Julia extended one arm in a side hug. Today, the Southern belle wore a white pleated tennis skirt, a white polo top, and her ubiquitous plethora of diamonds.

"Can't say I'm very good, but I do like to prance around in tennis whites," she laughed.

The pickleball players were divided into teams and set out on the courts to start doubles match play.

"Sunny," Rachel pulled her to one side. "I don't think you've met my boss, Dr. Day."

"I'm her partner." The tall, handsome man with short, salt-and-pepper hair put out a hand for Sunny to shake, his straight, white teeth gleaming as he smiled.

"On the pickleball court," Rachel was quick to add, her cheeks flushed. "I thought you could play with us today, as long as you don't mind that I already picked your partner for you." She motioned for a man to join them.

"Mind?" Sunny watched as the man walked towards them, his straight, jet-black hair shining in the sunlight, his white polo shirt contrasting with his deeply-tanned features. "Of course, I don't mind," she blinked, suddenly very aware that she was staring at him. *Was he walking in slow motion, or was that just her imagination?* She bent to the ground and pretended to tie her sneaker laces so no one could see her blush.

"This is Police Chief Antonio Perez." Dr. Day clapped him on the back with a hearty slap.

"Please, call me Tony." The police chief smiled at her, and Sunny stood, nodding a shy hello.

The game was uneventful. No one would have accused Sunny of playing well, but she didn't flat-out embarrass herself either. The best part of the game was chatting with Police Chief Perez in between points. She learned that they were both West Coast transplants. He had moved to LouLou from Los Angeles several years ago after his divorce. She had done her best to subtly eye his very important ring finger. *No ring,* she noted before swiftly reminding herself that she wouldn't have a clue what to do with Police Chief Perez, wedding ring or not. Sunny hadn't been on a date in almost two decades. It wasn't that she liked being single and alone. She didn't, but with raising a son on her own and working around the clock, the years had gone by so quickly, without much time for dating.

"It was nice meeting you, Sunny." Tony placed a hand on her shoulder and smiled. "Hopefully, I will see you around town."

"You, too." Sunny self-consciously wiped the sweat from her forehead. "And I'd like that."

Several hours later, she returned to the house, drenched in sweat and cursing the person who had devised the idea of outdoor sports in the sweltering

Louisiana summer. Her tennis dress was so sweaty that it looked like she had decided to swim in the lake after her pickleball game. She limped across the threshold of her front door and dropped to her knees, lying spread-eagle on the blessedly cool floor.

While her body revelled in the cool air of the living room, her mind turned again to the mystery box, her thoughts now whirling with questions. With her parents out of commission for the next few days, who else could give her answers about her mysterious morning delivery? She sat up with a bolt.

"The attorney!" Scrambling to her feet, she pulled her phone from her wet pocket and wiped the sweaty screen before reaching onto the fireplace mantel for the attorney's letter. She dialed the number on the letterhead.

"You have reached the office of Thomas Tinwell. The office is now closed." She put down the phone. *Drat.* She sighed. It was Saturday, after all.

"Well, you are a mystery, Aunt Edna, and a mystery you shall remain...until Monday morning, that is."

That night, Danny barely touched his dinner, even though Sunny had gone all out and made his favorites–goat cheese and herb biscuits, extra-tart lemonade, and his favorite childhood broccoli dish. Magical Broccoli Forest was a cheesy rice casserole topped with broccoli florets standing upright in the dish to look like trees. Sunny would never forget the first time she made this for him. He had laughed, clapping his hands in delight. She wished making him happy was as easy now as it was then, but as her mother always said, bigger kids mean bigger problems. Her heart ached as she watched him push his food around with his fork, his shoulders stooped and eyes sullen. Was moving him here a mistake?

For the first time since building her bed nirvana, she spent the night tossing and turning, unable to get comfortable. As she lay awake, staring at the ceiling, she could swear she heard a rustling sound from the attic. Was she imagining it? She turned from her right side to her left and gathered the blankets around her shoulders. Shutting her eyes tight, she willed her body to sleep.

There it was again. Sunny opened one eye. Should she go up there and see what was making those scratching noises? She decided against it. There was probably a squirrel or a raccoon, which meant it was time to call the pest control company in the morning, not investigate in the dark and end up with rabies. She shut her eyes again and finally found sleep.

The following day, she slipped on her yoga clothes and tiptoed into the kitchen to make her coffee as usual. She stopped in the hallway. The ladder that led up to the attic was down, and the attic door was open.

"Danny?" She called up into the gloom. "Are you up there, sweetie?"

"Yep."

"Well, whatcha doing?" Sunny chuckled, a little annoyed at his short response. When he didn't answer, she hoisted a foot onto the ladder and climbed up. A wave of heat hit her in the face as she stepped into the dark, musty space. Ducking to avoid hitting her head on the roof beams, she found Danny sitting on the plywood floor, some things from Aunt Edna's box spread around his lap. She navigated through boxes of holiday decorations and lots of spider webs to where he sat.

"I don't know why, but I couldn't stop thinking about this stuff." He shrugged, looking down to examine one of the round fish floats, its turquoise glass giving a faint glow despite the shadowy room's lack of light. "I get this nagging feeling that it shouldn't be shut away up here."

"You know, it's funny that Aunt Edna, whoever she is, sent me tiki stuff." Sunny picked up one of the masks with a friendly face and crooked smile. "When I was a little older than you, I loved going to tiki bars with my friends. I was obsessed! You might not know this, but California is the home of the tiki bar. We would get into someone's car, drive the hour or so to L.A., and spend all night going from one tiki bar to the next."

"Sounds like fun," Danny nodded a little wistfully.

"It was." Sunny's eyes grew distant. Those old days felt like forever ago. "My absolute favorite was this one called the Bamboo Lounge. The whole place was decorated like a tropical jungle. It even had a fake volcano that erupted throughout the night! It was amazing."

"Mom?" Danny's face took Sunny by surprise. He had a sparkle in his eye for the first time in weeks. "Let's open our own tiki bar. Here in LouLou."

"What? Oh, Danny, I don't know. That sounds like a nice dream. Maybe one day." She began to pack the things back into the crate. Danny stood to stop her.

"Come on, Mom. Think about it." He held up a volcano-shaped tiki mug. "You've been looking for a way to feel more a part of this place. You said yourself that you were bored out of your mind. Plus, we could do it together!"

Sunny paused and chewed a fingernail. She had been ready for her son to beg for a puppy or a driver's license, but a tiki bar? That had not been on her teenager bingo card. She took a deep breath in and out. Every fiber in her being said no, so even she was surprised by the answer that came out of her mouth.

"Okay. This is absolutely insane, but okay." What on earth had she gotten herself into now?

Chapter 12

Sunny's Monday morning started even earlier than usual with a ringing phone. She blinked her eyes into focus as she stared at the lit screen in her dark bedroom. Her heart gave a jolt.

"Mom?! Dad?!" She gasped. "Are you okay? What's wrong?"

"Wrong?" Her mother's calm voice sounded on the other end of the line. "Why would anything be wrong, dear one?"

"Because it's 4:30 in the morning my time, which makes it …" She struggled to calculate the time difference, still half asleep.

"2:30 my time." Her mother's voice was much too casual for a middle-of-the-night call, and Sunny didn't buy it. Something was wrong.

"Is Dad okay?" She probed.

"Of course, he is. Our weekend retreat was truly transformational–the way the mind turns inward when forced into a silent meditation!" she swooned. "And the reiki session I attended was nothing short of life-changing."

"Mom," Sunny interrupted, a bit impatient in the wee hours of the morning. "Why would you call me in the middle of the night? It can't be just to have a chat."

"Oh, Sunflower." Her mother sighed a weary, deep exhale. "You were always so perceptive. It's the intuition training I gave you as a child. You were a natural."

"Mom, please. Just tell me what's going on."

"It's about that voicemail you left on our machine."

Sunny's heart raced. Here it was. She was finally going to get some answers.

"About Aunt Edna." Her mother's voice was drawn out like every word she said was against her will. "Hold on a sec." There was a pause on the line, and then her voice returned. "I wanted to make sure your father was still asleep. He hasn't heard your voicemail, and frankly, starlight of my life, I don't want him to."

"Why?" Sunny wished her mother would come out with it.

"It would deeply upset him and would ruin all the mind palace progress he made this weekend. I will tell him about it in time, but not yet."

"Mom, what's going on?"

"It all started back before you were born." Her mother sighed again. "You know how your father was the black sheep of his family, right? How his parents wanted him to take the family track–Stanford, then UC

Berkeley Law, followed by a position at the family firm?"

Sunny nodded wordlessly, and her mother took her silence to mean in the affirmative.

"And when he decided to be a goat farmer and have a common law union with me instead, his parents cut him out of the will and disowned him, never to speak again? Well, the one member of that awful family that stood up for your father was his Aunt Edna. She had been a bit of an odd-woman-out in the family as well, studying family law instead of criminal law, which got their whole clan in an uproar. Ugh, those people." She grew momentarily flustered before returning her focus to the subject. "She was your father's only connection to his own flesh and blood, and he loved her like crazy. He always said she was like a mother to him. That was until the day she up and disappeared. Simply packed a bag and left. No explanation, no note, nothing."

Sunny couldn't see her mother, but she was sure the woman was standing in her California kitchen, with its chocolate-brown walls and avocado countertops, lips pursed and head shaking in disapproval.

"So, where did Aunt Edna go?"

"No one knew. Then, a decade later, she wrote your father a letter saying she had left to follow her heart and was living all the way up somewhere in Alaska. She had done it for love. The man she had married was a salmon fisherman she had met at a San Francisco nightclub. She knew the family would never approve, so she did what she had to do."

"Did Dad ever hear from her again?" Sunny frowned. "I never once heard him mention her. He never talked about anyone on his side of the family."

"By the time he read her letter, it was too late. Ten years of hurt had hardened his heart." She paused for a beat. "I never asked. Why do you want to know about Edna anyway?"

Sunny told her mother about the weekend's events–the box's delivery, the strange tiki items, and the attorney's unhelpful letter explaining nothing.

"That has to be the wildest story I've heard in a while." Her mother gave a small laugh. "And I spent the weekend with an organic crystal farmer who runs a llama yoga studio."

Sunny wondered if it was a yoga studio for llamas or a studio where people did yoga with llamas, but at five a.m., she decided it wasn't necessary to know.

"Can anyone tell me more about Aunt Edna and why she put me in her will?"

"Donna? Are you up, honey? Who's on the phone?" Sunny heard her dad calling from a distance.

"It's Sunflower, dear," her mother called back. "Go back to bed."

"Sunflower? Is she okay? Is Danny hurt?" His distant voice rose in panic. Sunny could hear his footsteps grow closer. He gripped the phone receiver.

"I'm fine, Dad," Sunny reassured him. "Nothing to worry about. I don't want to wake you; I'll call you later today."

None of them knew whether to say good night or good morning, so they just said goodbye and hung up their phones. Sunny sank back into her pillow. Now she knew who Aunt Edna was, but she wasn't any closer to discovering why her attic was filled with enough tropical decor to outfit a Margaritaville. Would she ever know?

Chapter 13

"Now, I know this place looks a bit run down."

"A bit?" Sunny raised one eyebrow. Flo had brought her to what she had called "the perfect place for the tiki bar." Sunny looked down at the real estate flier in her hand advertising "a unique investment opportunity in a prime location" and looked back up again at the building in front of her—an old, barely standing barn on the edge of the town square next door to Buzz's Bar. The only thing unique about the place would be the unique dosage of anxiety meds she would be prescribed if she signed the rental agreement.

"Let's take a look inside before you cast judgment." Flo turned the rusted knob of the front door. Instead of opening on its hinges, the whole door came out of the frame. "I'm sure the landlord would fix that for you." She placed the door to the side, and they cautiously stepped in.

"I don't know, Flo." Sunny shook her head and looked around. The floor beneath her feet wasn't a floor at all but compacted dirt. The wooden walls were clearly rotten in places, with sunlight shining through cracks and holes. "Does this place even have electricity? Plumbing?" She turned back to the open space where the door had been, ready to leave.

"Already talked to the landlord." Flo put up her hands to stop Sunny from exiting. "She had plumbing put in last year and is willing to get it wired up to the town electrical grid as soon as a tenant signs the lease." She walked over to a dirty window and polished one of the glass panes with her shirt sleeve. "A little bit of elbow grease, and this place will be perfect."

"I don't know about perfect," Sunny moved another step towards the exit. "But it does have a great location so close to the square." She had already taken Danny to look at several potential tiki bar spots, but none were this close to all the town action, and all of them had been way over their meager start-up budget. *Maybe this could be the place? Surely, the rent here would be affordable.* She shook the thought out of her head. *What am I thinking?* She looked at the planked ceiling heaving down on them in bowed sections. It gave the impression that it could all tumble down on their heads at any moment. *This place won't be standing upright in a week's time, let alone be turned into a tiki bar.*

"I know what you're thinking," Flo interjected. "You're thinking that this place won't be standing up for much longer, let alone be turned into the tiki bar of your dreams."

Sunny smirked to hide her complete

astonishment that Flo could read her mind with such startling accuracy. *How the heck does she do that??*

"Well," Flo continued, seemingly oblivious to Sunny's shock. "I talked to the landlord about that, too. She had the whole place inspected before she listed it, and it's as solid as the ground we're standing on. All its problems are only skin deep."

"Speaking of the ground we're standing on," Sunny crossed her arms. "You might have noticed that the floor is dirt. Not dirty, but actual dirt. The health department would shut us down in an instant if our bar had a dirt floor."

"I'm not sure you realize how good a deal this is." Flo sighed and put her hands on her hips. "I've known the landlord for a long time. She's been wanting to fix this place up and cash in on the fact that she owns property so close to town. She's willing to do whatever you need to get this place up to snuff. Plus," She pulled a folded piece of notebook paper from her jeans pocket. "This is what she wants to charge in rent." She handed the paper to Sunny.

"That's all?" Sunny's eyes grew wide. It was a fraction of what the other places had wanted. "And who is this mythical landlord who will fix all this place's problems–and trust me, there are many, many problems here–and practically charge me nothing in rent?!"

"Me," Flo shrugged and grinned from ear to ear.

"You!?" Sunny let out a loud guffaw. "I can't believe I'm saying this." She covered her eyes with her hands. "But, okay. Let's do it."

Chapter 14

The following month was a blur of meetings with contractors and construction crews, plumbing, flooring, sawdust, and paint fumes. With Flo being good on her word as a landlord and Sunny putting up a bit of the savings in her rainy day fund, the place was no longer an old barn barely held together by rusted nails and a prayer. Now, it had a solid poured concrete floor, insulation and drywall, running water, and electricity.

When Sunny wasn't helping the work crew, she spent every free minute drawing up business plans and budgeting, not to mention working on a killer cocktail menu. She watched YouTube videos late into the night with mixologists showing step-by-step how to make tiki drink classics like mai tais and zombies. Every evening, once Danny finished his homework, they sat at the kitchen table and scoured the internet for the best cocktail napkins, tiki mugs, and umbrella straws. Danny put together a playlist of tropical tunes to play over the new speaker system they had installed.

Finally, the day had come. The construction was done, and all that was left to do was add the tiki room flair. Sunny stood at her new bar made from a lacquered piece of live edge wood and looked at the room around her. She blinked with disbelief, hardly able to wrap her head around the fact that this clean and tidy space with its freshly-painted turquoise walls didn't exist a month before. She grabbed an icy cold mai tai in each hand and headed for the bar's new front patio.

"Drinking on a weekday before noon?" Flo chuckled as Sunny placed the tiki drink on the bistro table where she sat.

"It's not day drinking. It's business research." Sunny lowered herself into the empty seat beside her and took a big swig from her glass. "Delish. What do you think?"

Flo took a sip through her umbrella straw. Her lips mouthed words, but all sound was suddenly drowned out by the ear-deafening rumble of a souped-up pickup truck's muffler. Its oversized tires screeched to a halt on the curb in front of where the ladies sat on the patio. The driver's door opened, and a stout man clad in a fringed leather Harley Davidson vest and ripped jeans jumped out. He sauntered over to them, his gait casual but decidedly unfriendly.

"Ladies, how do'?" He drew saliva from the back of his throat and spat on the grassy median between them.

"We do just fine, Buzz," Flo said, a sprinkle of sarcasm in her tone. "What can we help you with today?

Come to be the first to welcome a fellow barkeep to town?"

"I most certainly did not." Buzz owned the only other watering hole in LouLou, an eponymous dive bar with sticky floors, football blasting on every TV screen, and servicing the town's rowdier crowd. His bar was right next door to Sunny's, and the two bars shared a common back alleyway. Sunny had hoped that she could count on her fellow bar owner to be a good neighbor. From the way Buzz was acting, those hopes were fading fast. "So the rumors are true then? Y'all are gonna open a bar?" He shook his head and grimaced.

"Hi, Buzz. I'm Sunny. I guess we're neighbors now." She stood, forcing a tone that matched her name, and extended a hand. "I don't think we've met. I'm the one opening the bar here, but don't worry. I won't be encroaching on your territory. My tiki bar is going to be totally different from your, um, *establishment.*" She did her best to imbue the word with positivity but failed.

"Scared of a little competition?" Flo stood and crossed her arms, a devilish grin on her face. Sunny looked over at her. *She's enjoying this.* Sunny widened her eyes, willing her friend to stop taunting the hairy, barrel-chested caveman in front of them. She looked down at his clenched fists, wondering what they were capable of and not wanting to find out.

"Here," Sunny turned and picked up her cocktail glass. "Try this. It's a mai tai."

"What competition?" He jeered at Flo before turning back to Sunny. "A mai what? Do you actually think folks in this town are going to drink whatever's in that orange concoction you've got there?" He let out a bitter laugh. "This is small town Louisiana. Ain't nobody gonna want some foreign drink in some foreign bar." He turned to his truck and walked away. "Good luck. You're gonna need it."

"Should we be worried about him?" Sunny squinted as she watched the rear of Buzz's pickup speed off, kicking up clouds of red dirt as he rode away from town.

"Nah." Flo took another sip from her cocktail glass. "You know, this drink is pretty good. What's it called again?"

"Mai tai," Sunny said weakly, her distracted mind working a mile a minute. "Do you think what he said is true? That no one is going to want to come to the tiki bar? I mean, everyone in town already thinks I'm weird. Why wouldn't they think my bar is weird too?" She plopped down in her patio chair.

"First of all, it's not true that everyone in town thinks you're weird. Just some people think you're weird."

Sunny shot Flo a surprised look.

"Second of all," Flo ignored the daggers coming from Sunny's eyes. "What's wrong with being weird? I'm weird." She shrugged and took another swig of her mai tai.

"But I don't want to be weird," Sunny whined like a toddler. "I want to fit in, be normal. Ever since I was a little girl, I have always been the odd one–the weird girl with handmade clothing and strange vegan, gluten-free sandwiches in my lunchbox at school. I didn't even get to trick or treat on Halloween because my parents thought the candy had too many chemicals. Then, as an adult, I worked hard and got good at my job. I devoted all my time to spreading my love between my sick patients and my son." Sunny sat up a little straighter at the mention of her old life. "It didn't matter if I was weird or not then because I was good at something, and when you are good at something, people tend to accept you for who you are. But now… …" Her words trailed off.

"You're still that person." Flo patted her on the hand.

"But I'm not." Sunny stirred her drink as it melted in the afternoon heat. "I don't know who I am right now."

"I know who you are." Flo stood. "Be right back." She slipped inside and was gone for several minutes. "I was going to give you this later, but I think you need it now." She held a large circular item covered in brown paper. She placed it on the table between them and gestured for Sunny to open it.

Sunny ripped off the paper to reveal a beautifully painted sign with the words "The Cajun Coconut" in turquoise and gold script flanked by palm trees swaying in a tropical breeze. Sunny began to cry.

"Like it?" Flo asked.

"Like it? This is the nicest thing anyone has ever done for me." She wiped the tears from her eyes and gave Flo a hug.

"It wasn't just me that should get the thanks," Flo smiled. "Danny helped design it, and I helped do the lettering."

"Hey, Miss Sunny," one of the construction crew poked his head from the front door. "We just finished our last job. Everything is done." He beamed, and Sunny proudly shook his hand. Her tiki bar was coming together.

"Not everything is done." Flo lifted the large sign.

"Could you help hang this on the front of the building?"

Now that the construction was complete, the inside needed to be transformed from bare walls to a tropical paradise.

It was midnight on the day before her grand opening. Sunny looked around the room with bleary eyes but a happy heart as she watched Flo and Danny rush around, filling the space with everything from Aunt Edna's box, plus some extras Sunny had found on eBay.

"How about I put this over here, Mom?" Danny called from one corner, where he had just placed a large faux palm plant in a woven basket planter.

"That looks perfect!" Sunny walked over and surveyed his work. "Let's get those flamingo string lights over here and hang them above the palms."

Sunny beamed as she studied the space. It was exactly how she envisioned it in her mind. One corner was like a cozy jungle getaway with vintage peacock chairs positioned at conversational angles and surrounded by as many fake palm plants as she could fit in the room. Another area featured Aunt Edna's two tiki masks–a small circular one with a green and white striped face and a long, oval mask made from worn, gray driftwood. Next to the masks stood a large, wooden tiki totem with a fierce expression. Above their heads hung exotic lanterns shining in a rainbow of colors and two faux parrots on bamboo perches. By the time they were done decorating, the entire tiki bar felt stuffed to the gills with layers upon layers of fish floats, string lights, fish traps, nets, parrots, jungle plants, and tiki faces.

"Well, I'm exhausted," Flo collapsed into one of the purple velvet booth seats. "And I can honestly say that I don't think there's room for a single item more on these walls," she laughed.

"You guys have done such a good job!" Sunny's eyes welled up with tears. "I don't know what I would do without you." She hugged both of them in turn. "Now, go home, you guys! I know you are all about to drop dead." She laughed, and her chuckle turned into a yawn.

"Aren't you coming home too, mom?" Danny asked, rubbing his tired eyes.

"I am in a minute," Sunny nodded. "I want to check on a few more things before the big night tomorrow."

"I'll take you home, Danny." Flo patted his shoulder.

"Thank you, Flo," Sunny smiled. "Danny, I'll be home in about thirty minutes or so."

Danny and Flo filed out of the front door. Sunny walked over and stood behind the bar, pretending it was opening night, and she was mixing drinks for the whole town. She smiled at the thought before leaning her elbows on the bartop and rested her tired head in her hands.

What was that? She slowly raised her head. From out of nowhere, Sunny had felt the slightest breeze. She looked at the front door. It was closed. The windows were closed as well.

Probably just the AC kicking on, she thought as she ducked behind the bar to double-check that she had everything stocked for opening night. *Rum, lime juice, almond syrup ...* She felt another breeze. This time, the current was strong enough to blow her hair back from her shoulders. Even though she was frozen with terror, she registered a scent. *Salt.* The room began to rumble and shake like a volcano about to erupt. Sunny screamed and gripped the bar.

"What's happening?!" she yelled. Was it an earthquake? Did Louisiana have earthquakes? Was she having a stroke? The shaking stopped, and everything was quiet except for Sunny's heartbeat pounding in her ears. This time the heart palpitations weren't from her hormones. A booming voice rang out.

"Sunflower!"

Sunny raced from the bar as fast as she could, not stopping until she was standing outside in the safety of the quiet late-night town square.

What on earth had just happened? Her chest heaved, and she worked to slow her panting breath. *Had that tiki totem spoken to me?* She would have sworn on a stack of bibles before a jury that she had seen that tiki totem's mouth move.

The longer she stood there, the less she believed that what she had seen was real. She was tired, after all. Exhausted, in fact. What she needed was a warm cup of chamomile lavender tea and her comfiest pajamas. She walked to her car and reached into her pocket.

"My keys are inside the bar." She groaned. "It's fine. Everything is fine. I will walk in, get my keys, lock up the bar, and go home." She walked cautiously towards the Cajun Coconut and gingerly opened the door. She poked her head inside. There were her keys lying in the center of the bar. She scanned the room. Everything was quiet, normal even. Not a magical breeze, mystery earthquake, or talking tiki mask in sight.

"It's now or never." She took a deep breath and dashed inside as fast as her feet would carry her, grabbed her keys in one desperate swipe of the countertop, and ran like the dickens out the door.

Chapter 15

For the first time in twenty-five years, Sunny skipped her morning yoga. She slept through her first alarm at five a.m. and her second alarm at 5:15.

"Mom?"

She woke with a jolt to Danny's voice in the hallway.

"Mom? Are you still in bed?" Danny poked his head into her room. "You never sleep in. You aren't sick on the bar's opening day, are you?"

Sunny wiped the drool from her mouth. She had been up all night, too nervous to sleep, and once she finally drifted off, she had been dead to the world.

"Not sick." She sat up in bed and yawned. "I didn't sleep so well last night. Must be opening day jitters." *Or a mid-life crisis where I hallucinated a magical tiki bar coming to life.* She winced, doing her best to forget the incident of the night before. She had been tired. Her imagination had played tricks on her–end of story. "Since I skipped my yoga, why don't I drive you to school?" Sunny slung her feet over the side of the bed and slipped on her fuzzy slippers.

"Sure, thanks." Danny padded down the hallway to the living room to put on his sneakers. Their conversation as they bumped along the country roads to LouLou High was centered around the grand opening of the Cajun Coconut. They had spent the previous week plastering flyers advertising the big night all over town. There would be door prizes, drink specials, and a round of tropical trivia with the chance to win complimentary tiki cocktails for a year.

"See you soon, Sunshine!" Sunny rolled down her window and waved as Danny stepped out of the car. She watched as he reluctantly trudged up the stone steps towards the school's double doors. Two kids that looked to be about his age were sitting on the school's front stoop. Her heart broke when they sneered at Danny as he passed them. Two months into the school year, her son was still struggling to make friends. *Like mother, like son.* She sighed, admitting to herself that it wasn't just Danny who had difficulty fitting in. The tiki bar would change all of that. The Cajun Coconut would be their time to shine. She was sure of it.

After showering and dressing in navy twill shorts, a tropical-print floral T-shirt, and the uncomfortable, but cute, espadrille wedges she had bought at La Boutique Jolie, she headed straight for the tiki bar. There was no point in waiting at home for opening time to roll around. Her nervous energy would never allow that, so she might as well go to the bar and find something to do. Pulling her car into one of the parking spots on the square, she turned off the engine and paused. Was she going to walk into the bar all alone? What if it happened again? *Maybe I should wait for Flo to come in with me.* Flo had said she would be in to help Sunny set up around three in the afternoon. She looked at her phone screen to check the time–*10 o'clock. I guess I could wait until three.* She bit her lower lip. Sure, she could avoid being alone in the bar today, but what about tomorrow? What about the next day and the next? She squared her jaw. *I'm an adult. I'm a nurse. I've given birth, for goodness sake. Surely, I can handle whatever is going on in my own business.* She marched to the front door and unlocked the deadbolt.

Stepping tentatively inside, her eyes registered nothing out of the ordinary. Everything was as it was left the night before. She let out the breath she had been holding, and her shoulders began to relax. *You silly goose,* she chuckled to herself, shaking her head. *Now, let's get ready to open this tiki bar.*

There was nothing important left to do for opening night, but Sunny found enough small, busy work to steady her nervous hands. She loaded the chest freezer under the bartop with enough ice to fill one hundred tiki mugs. She sliced enough limes to cure an entire pirate fleet of scurvy. The work was soothing, with only the tune of the gentle tiki music playing from the speakers above her and the thud of the knife hitting the wooden cutting board as she carved a whole pineapple into spears. The rhythmic sounds and motion had her so much in the zone that a knock on the door made her almost jump out of her skin.

"Coming!" she called, putting a hand to her chest to calm her racing heart. Rachel stood on the other side of the door, holding a bouquet of daisies.

"Rachel!" Sunny smiled. "Come on in!"

"I can't stay long. I'm on my lunch break at work." She shuffled in and handed Sunny the flowers.

"These are so beautiful." Sunny took them behind the bar and reached for a glass vase on a high shelf. "This is so thoughtful of you. You shouldn't have."

"I wanted to get you something not only to celebrate opening night but also to make up for the fact that I can't be here for the big party. My kids' school has a PTO fundraiser, and I promised them weeks ago that I would volunteer." She smiled and rolled her eyes in annoyance.

"I totally get it," Sunny reassured her. "The bar isn't going anywhere. There will be plenty of time to hang out later." Rachel smiled and hurried back to work across the town square.

Sunny took the vase of daisies and set them on the bartop by the cash register. She stood back and examined them. Thinking better of her decision, she moved the vase to one of the high shelves on the wall behind the bar that practically heaved under the weight of the many rum bottles and tiki mugs displayed there. Before she had even stepped away to survey the tableau, she snatched the vase from the shelf. It still wasn't right.

Sunny, the over-thinker, coming through, she laughed at herself. *Just put the flowers somewhere and walk away,* she chided, setting the vase in a bookcase featuring some of Aunt Edna's tropical trinkets. As she placed it on the bookcase shelf featuring a collection of porcelain hula girls, her hand knocked one to the floor, pottery smashing into bits.

"Oh, no!" Sunny cried, bending to pick up the pieces. The face and torso of the figurine had splintered into a powdery rubble, but the lower portion of the statuette had remained intact. She picked up the headless Hula girl and frowned. Walking to the trash bin behind the bar, she was about to toss it in but stopped. There was something inside the figurine. A piece of paper. She carefully pulled the scroll of purple paper out and unrolled it.

"A letter!" She exclaimed to the empty room and quickly reached for her reading glasses.

"Dear Sunflower, I am sure you are wondering why a relative you have probably never heard of sent you such mysterious contents or even put you in their will at all." Sunny's eyes scanned the scrawled cursive writing as fast as she could.

"I made the grave mistake of abandoning your father, my nephew, when he needed me most. It's been the biggest regret of my life. When I learned he had a child, I knew I would bestow upon that child–you, my dear–my greatest possessions on this earth."

Sunny looked around at the tiki bar, one eyebrow cocked. The tiki decor was nice and all, but *her greatest possessions?* That felt like a stretch. She kept reading.

"My love and I ran a tiki bar in Gnome, Alaska, for over thirty years. You can imagine how very much the locals of such a chilly place might need a little tropical escape. The tiki bar brought me and my community more joy than I ever could have imagined. I feel as though I am entrusting my greatest friends to you. Treat them well, dear, and they will do the same to you."

Sunny raised her head, the last line of the letter tingling in her brain. She didn't know why exactly, but the words made her feel as if Aunt Edna was hinting at something. *Had Aunt Edna seen the magic, too?* She stopped her thoughts from going any further. There was no magic.

"Oh, there's more." She pushed her reading glasses up the bridge of her nose and focused on the bottom of the page.

"P.S. When it happens, just let it. Don't fight it or be afraid. Once it happens, these words will make sense."

It? What was *it?* She couldn't have been referring to whatever happened the night before. There was no way. Right?

"Alright! Who's ready to party?" Flo burst through the front door, a loaded box of door prizes in her arms. Sunny snapped out of deep thought and quickly stuffed the letter in her shorts pocket. She would deal with that when she had more time.

"Ready as I'll ever be!" Sunny gave a nervous smile. She had been obsessing over this opening night for weeks, and she wanted more than anything for it to go well.

"Then, let's get the show on the road." Flo walked over to the neon "OPEN" sign hanging in one of the bar's front windows and flipped the switch. The blue and pink letters flickered to life.

"It's official!" Sunny clapped her hands. "The Cajun Coconut is now open!"

Chapter 16

Nine Hours Later...

Standing over the dead body of Jeb Landry, it took Sunny several beats to react. She froze, her mind thick like TV static. *There is a dead body on the floor of my bar. A dead body. Dead.*

Sunny had seen many people get sick and die in the hospitals where she worked, but this was different. She knelt, the fogginess in her brain clearing. “CPR.” She bent over Jeb and rolled him onto his back to begin the procedure.

“Sunny?” Flo’s voice sounded over her shoulder, but she didn’t stop what she was doing. “Sunny? What’s happened? Is that Jeb?”

“Call an ambulance!” Sunny said while pumping

his chest. "I don't know what's happening, but we need help."

Within minutes, the LouLou EMTs arrived. Sunny didn't stop her CPR attempts until a paramedic was by Jeb's side. The bar was flooded with emergency staff, so Sunny and Flo moved to the outside front patio to get out of their way.

"What happened?" Flo asked.

"When no other customers showed up, I went to the back and busied myself organizing the storage area. I came back to the front of the bar, and Jeb had fallen asleep. At least I thought he was asleep." Sunny shivered despite the muggy night. "I decided not to bother him, but he hadn't woken up at closing time. I went over to wake him, and ..." She started to cry. "He fell to the floor. Flo, I think he's dead!" Her shoulders began to shake as she wept harder.

Chapter 17

Minutes after the EMTs entered the bar, the police arrived with sirens blaring. Three blue and white squad cars pulled to a stop in front of the Cajun Coconut, and four police officers exploded from the doors of each vehicle.

"He's in there." Sunny's voice was weak from crying. She pointed towards the tiki bar entrance. "I don't know what happened. One minute he was okay, the next ... I thought he was just asleep at first." Her mind raced, and she suddenly realized that when she thought he was sleeping, she had wasted precious minutes that could have been used to give him CPR. Was she responsible for his death? Was there more she could have done?

"We will take care of this, ma'am." An officer

stopped her from following them inside. "Y'all stay here. The chief is on his way to take your statements."

After what felt like an hour but was probably only a few more minutes, another police car arrived, and Police Chief Tony Perez stepped from the driver's seat. His face was serious, but Sunny noticed his eyes sparkled like they had on the pickleball court. Her heart fluttered, and she silently scolded herself. *A man has died, and you are over here making goo goo eyes! Get a hold of yourself.*

"Hello, Flo." Tony dipped his head politely. "Sunny," he smiled. "It's nice to see you again." Quickly returning to the present moment, he corrected his tone, his smile fading. "Although, not like this, of course."

"Of course," Sunny agreed, looking down at her wedge sandals.

He guided them to sit at one of the patio tables and pulled a notebook and pen from his pants pocket. Flo didn't have much to say, but she told the Chief everything she could. She thought it was strange that Jeb came into the bar with a woman who wasn't his wife, and the conversation between Jeb and his mystery woman looked tense. Sunny told him how Jeb seemed to fall asleep, and she didn't want to be rude by waking him. He wrote down their words and flipped his notebook closed. He thanked them, asking them to stick around for a while he went inside to inspect the scene. Sunny and Flo waited silently, not knowing what to do next. Finally, Police Chief Perez returned and sat back down at their table. Behind him, a stretcher with a white sheet covering Jeb's body was carried by two EMTs into an ambulance.

"From what my team is telling me, Jeb shows all

the signs of having a heart attack."

"You mean, it wasn't something I did wrong? Like something spoiled in the drink I made him? Or I don't know ... murder?" Sunny was talking too fast.

"The autopsy will tell us more," Tony placed a hand on Sunny's trembling shoulder to calm her down. "But there's nothing to show it was anything like that. It was well known that Jeb had a heart condition. He refused to stop eating fried shrimp po' boys, and he never took his medications. With respect to Jeb, he was a ticking time bomb." The Police Chief stood to leave. "Besides, this is LouLou, not L.A. There hasn't been a murder in LouLou since, well, ever. We will need the keys to the bar to finish our investigation, and you'll probably need to close for the next twenty-four hours while we inspect the scene."

Sunny nodded and handed him her bar keys.

"Flo, could you drive Sunny home?" Tony shot her a look of concern.

"I'm fine." Sunny's voice still trembled, and her legs felt like she was standing under a volcano close to eruption, shaky and unnatural, but she did her best to look calm. "I'll drive myself home, Flo, no worries." She took her car keys from her back pocket and walked towards her Miata parked in the back alley between the Cajun Coconut and Buzz's bar.

"I think having a friend with you tonight is best," Tony said. "You've just had a very traumatic event. It's normal to feel a bit shaken up."

"He's right, Sun." Flo moved to stop Sunny from walking away. Sunny admitted defeat and came back to the front of the tiki bar where Flo's pickup was waiting.

"What about my car?" Sunny asked wearily.

"Hand me the keys, and I will have an officer drive it to your house in a few hours." Tony reached out a hand, and Sunny handed over her car keys dangling from the palm tree keychain. On the way to Flo's truck, they heard a familiar laugh.

"What happened over there?" Buzz leaned against the open doorway of his bar, country music blaring behind him from the stereo inside. "Your weird drinks kill somebody on opening night?" He doubled over, the only one who found his joke funny. Sunny burst into tears and ran the short distance to Flo's pickup.

"Way to go, Buzzy," Flo spat. "Why don't you mind your own darn business!" She ducked into the truck's driver's seat and slammed the door.

They quietly rode to Sunny's house, bumping along the pitch-black Moonlight Lane with the new moon dark in the sky. When Sunny spotted her little house, the gas flames flickering from the new porch lamp, she felt relief wash over her. She exhaled a tense breath as Flo's truck pulled to a stop, never more happy to be home.

"Let me fix you a nice cup of tea, and we can talk," Flo said as they stepped inside.

"That sounds good." Sunny kicked off her shoes and placed them, facing out, by the front door. "Thank you." It was two in the morning by now, the latest Sunny had stayed up in years, but she wasn't sleepy. In fact, she was convinced she would never sleep again. She tiptoed down the hallway and peered into Danny's room. Ducking her head into his doorway, she could hear his gentle snores. Satisfied, she returned to the living room and plopped into her favorite armchair by the window overlooking the forest. As Flo set the kettle on the stove and scooped two spoonfuls of loose lavender tea leaves into Sunny's worn and cracked polkadot teapot, Sunny couldn't help but replay the scene in the tiki bar over and over again in her mind. She cringed. When she had thought Jeb was sleeping, she had scrolled Instagram and made herself a cocktail. Had she been sipping a drink next to a dead man? The thought sent a shiver down her spine.

"And here we are." Flo emerged from the kitchen carrying a tray with the teapot fitted with its crocheted blue and white cozy cover, two mugs, and a tiny bowl of sugar, the smell of lavender wafting through the air as she walked. "Let me pour you a cup."

"This is just what I need." Sunny closed her eyes after taking a deep sip of tea. "Thank you, Flo."

"So, do you want to talk about it, or would you rather not think about what happened right now?" Flo examined Sunny over the rim of her mug as she sipped.

"I want to pretend it never happened, drink my tea, and go to bed," Sunny sighed. "But that's not going to work. The thought of it all is going to keep me up all night. Poor Jeb." Her bottom lip quivered, and she quickly took another long drink from her tea to stop the tears from flowing.

"You heard the chief," Flo shook her head. "There was nothing you could do. Jeb had a heart condition."

"That's not what everyone in town is going to think." Sunny replaced her mug on the tray and crossed her arms.

"What do you mean?" Flo frowned.

"I'm already the town weirdo," Sunny stood and started to pace the room. "A stranger moves to town, opens a bar, and one of the only people to try their drinks drops dead! I'm pretty sure people are going to think I'm a murderer!"

"Now, let's not rush to conclusions." Flo motioned for Sunny to sit back down. "Everything is going to be okay."

"I wish I was as sure of that as you are." Sunny did as she was told and returned to her chair. She wrapped the fuzzy throw blanket she kept in a basket by the fireplace around her lap and again took her mug in hand. She looked over at Flo, who was letting out her third yawn in the last ten minutes. "You're exhausted, Flo. Why don't you go home and get some rest?"

"Rest might be a good idea–" Flo stood and stretched her arms over her head. "For everyone here." She shot Sunny a stern look before walking her empty mug to the kitchen sink. Sunny nodded in agreement but knew she wouldn't be sleeping that night. Every time she closed her eyes, she saw Jeb's pale, slack face, his blue eyes open but lifeless. She wrapped the blanket more tightly around her legs.

"Night, Sunny." Flo opened the door. "I'll come check on you tomorrow."

"Night, Flo." Sunny tried to smile. When Flo was gone, Sunny stood from her comfy chair and decided to get ready for bed. She threw her Hawaiian print shirt into the laundry basket. She had a brief urge to throw it in the trash can, not sure if she would always think about this horrible night every time she wore it. Pulling a cornflower-blue cotton nightgown over her head and slipping her feet into her wooly slippers, she brushed her teeth with the baking soda toothpaste she had mixed the day before and splashed some rose water on her face. When she stood at the foot of her bed and began to pull back the covers, she stopped. Instead, she grabbed the book from her nightstand and headed back into her living room chair.

Sunny opened her book, the latest in a knitting mystery series that she had been devoted to for years, but after ten minutes of staring at the same page without actually reading the words, she tossed the book to the floor. She leaned back in the chair and looked out the window. The sky was cloudy, and no stars shone through the mossy oaks. But she could hear the tree frogs singing their nightly tune, and it was comforting. *Jeb had a heart attack,* she repeated to herself. *There was nothing I could do. Nothing I could do.*

She didn't know if the good people of LouLou would believe that, especially since she was having trouble believing it herself.

Chapter 18

Sunny was still sitting in her living room chair when the sun finally peaked its face over the trees. She rubbed her dry, tired eyes and padded quietly to the kitchen to brew the morning coffee. Warm coffee mug in hand, she stepped out onto her front porch, hoping the fresh morning air would chase away the fog that had filled her brain. Thankfully, when she walked onto her creaky porch floorboards and into the gentle morning sun, her reptilian friend, Billy, was nowhere to be seen. She sighed in relief and lowered herself onto the porch swing, moving it slowly back and forth with her feet. The lake was already dotted with early morning fishermen, and in the distance, the hum of a boat motor mixed with the usual morning birdsong of mockingbirds and thrashers.

Sunny could hear another noise, too–car tires crunching on the gravel of her long driveway. Perhaps Flo was coming to check on her already. She stretched her neck to see the approaching vehicle. But it wasn't Flo's blue pickup. Instead, a police car trundled slowly down Moonlight Lane. Sunny sat straight on the edge of the swing, the hairs on the back of her neck standing up in prickly tingles. Were they coming to give her more bad news?

Tony Perez stepped from the car, holding a white paper box. He smiled when he saw her perched on the porch swing. Sunny smiled back, but inside, she was dying. *"Oh my lord, here I am in practically my underwear, and my hair! Oh, my hair must look like Halloween has come early."* Self-consciously, she patted down the wild, frizzy locks that sprung from her head like palm tree fronds.

"Chief," She called out as he approached. "Good morning."

"Mornin'." He stepped onto the porch and tipped his suede uniform hat. "I'm surprised to catch you at home. No book club, rowing club, or pickleball today?" He shot her a teasing look.

Sunny gave her head a slight shake.

"I come bearing sweets." He opened the box, and Sunny could smell the sugary aroma of fresh donuts even from a distance. Tony handed her a sturdy pastry that looked like a sugar-coated cannonball. Sunny examined it before taking a bite.

"Am I supposed to eat it or put it in a slingshot and lay siege to a neighboring village?" She wondered if Tony would find her joke funny and was relieved when he laughed.

"It's called a buttermilk drop. A local delicacy in town." He lifted a donut from the box with two fingers and took a big bite. Sunny took a bite of hers, too. Her eyes grew wide with delight. The donut was sweet from the sugar coating, rich from the fried exterior, and tangy from the buttermilk in the dough. It was heaven.

"So, I'm guessing you aren't just here to deliver breakfast," Sunny said between bites. "Although I have to say, these buttermilk drops are worth the trip."

"No." The police chief shook his head and sat on the porch swing next to her. Sunny blushed a little as the side of his leg brushed hers. "Unfortunately, your donut delivery comes with a side of sad news." As they slowly rocked on the swing, Tony told her how preliminary reports showed that Jeb did indeed have a heart attack and that his wife and his doctor had confirmed the fact that he had been on statins for years.

Sunny let out a sad sigh.

"I hate to think of myself at a time like this–" She looked out at the lake, avoiding Tony's chocolate-brown eyes. "But everyone in town is going to think that I caused Jeb's death in some way. I've barely made any friends as it is. Who's going to want to be friends with a murderer?" She turned back and stared him straight in the face.

"Hold on, now." He held up his hands in protest. "Who said anything about murder? Jeb died from a heart attack, and unless you have been the one serving him up all of those fried shrimp and hush puppies, I don't think his death had anything to do with you."

"I'm worried that people in town won't see it that way."

Tony said nothing, and they swayed forward and

back on the swing in silence for a moment. Without a word, he reached into his pocket and took out the tiki bar keys. She opened her palm, and he placed them in her hand.

"We are done going over the scene, so the Cajun Coconut is free to open." His lips formed a gentle smile. "I wouldn't mind coming in for a drink sometime. I've never had a tiki drink before." He stood.

"I think we will be closed tonight out of respect for Jeb and his family," Sunny decided, "but I would love it if you came in for a drink when we open again tomorrow." She felt like a middle school girl, and for the first time in a long time, she found herself enjoying the first flushes of a crush. When Sunny had her son, she set aside any interest in dating, feeling like that season of her life could wait until he was older. Now that Danny was in high school and not a toddler tugging at her skirt hems, was it time to think about a relationship again? She wasn't sure.

"Guess I better go," he said, but his feet didn't move.

"Yeah, me too." Sunny stood from the porch swing and put the tiki bar keys in her robe pocket. "Let me know what you hear about Jeb's autopsy. I'll never forgive myself if something he drank at the bar caused this, even though I can't think what possibly could have." She shook her head sadly.

"I will, but try not to think about it, okay?" He tipped his hat and walked to his car.

Back inside, Sunny found Danny sitting at the kitchen table eating a bowl of the homemade granola Sunny had baked the day before.

"Was that a police car I saw outside?" he asked

through a mouthful of cereal.

"It was." Sunny reached into the cabinet for a bowl and poured herself some granola. She sat down and explained to Danny what had happened the night before. His eyes grew wide.

"Mom, that's awful!" Danny wiped milk from his mouth and stood to put his bowl in the sink. "Is everything going to be okay at the Cajun Coconut?"

"Police Chief Perez said we can open again whenever we want. There is nothing at the Coconut that is dangerous," she shrugged. "I think we should stay closed tonight out of respect for Jeb and his family."

"Oh, really?" Danny's shoulders sank. "It's just that ... never mind." He turned to walk down the hall to his room to get ready for school.

"What is it?" Sunny held up a hand to stop him.

"Well," Danny shifted on his feet. "When some of the kids at school heard about the tiki bar, they asked if we could all go together to see it tonight. Not to drink!" he quickly added. "Just to hang out, and it's just a few guys that I've been playing World of Witchcraft with online after school. I'll tell them we can't. It's fine." He turned to leave again.

Sunny wanted Danny to have friends in their new town more than anything. It broke her heart to see him struggle to find his people. She also didn't want to seem like a callous jerk for opening for business only twenty-four hours after a man had died in her tiki bar. She let out a deep sigh.

"You know what?" She said at Danny's retreating back. "Let's do it. Let's open the Coconut tonight."

Danny turned and let out a cheer. He thanked his mother profusely before disappearing into his room to get dressed for school.

Sunny waved goodbye to Danny as he sprinted down their long driveway to where the school bus picked him up every morning. After rushing inside to dress in a new blue and white seersucker sheath dress and nude ballet flats that cut into the sides of her feet, she grabbed her keys and climbed in her car. If the tiki bar would open for the night, she needed to pick up some fresh fruit for drinks. A few minutes later, she pulled into a parking spot in front of the Hop, grabbed a shopping buggy, and went inside.

It was an average day at the Hop. Shoppers filed down the aisles, placing cans of peas, cartons of eggs, and jugs of milk in their buggies. The butcher was helping someone decide between the redfish filets or the speckled trout. One of the cashiers, a woman in her sixties with thick cat-eye glasses and an even thicker Louisiana drawl, was chatting away as she rang up a shopper's items. Sunny was relieved that things were as they always had been in the grocery store. That meant people in town hadn't heard about Jeb yet, or at the very least, weren't gossiping about how he died or, even worse, *where* he died. When she navigated her shopping cart towards the produce section, she learned that she was wrong. It only took her one or two shifty glances her way to make her realize she had misjudged the situation.

As she gathered up a handful of limes and placed them in her cart, she heard two women whispering in loud hisses behind her.

"That's her," one woman murmured to the other.

"The one they say killed Jeb?" The other gasped.

"Yep. That's her, alright." They pushed their

buggies past where Sunny stood, frozen and flushing red.

"Excuse me." Sunny whipped around to face them, making the two women jump. "I did not kill Jeb Landry. He died from a heart attack. I had nothing to do with it." She hadn't realized that she had been shouting, but she realized it now that she could see the entire store had turned to listen. Her palms grew sweaty as she felt all of the eyes in the room bore into her. Sunny put down the limes and walked out of the Hop, her pulse racing. Hadn't she told Flo and Police Chief Perez that this is what would happen? The entire town thought Sunny was a murderer.

Chapter 19

Sunny ran to her car and put it into drive, but she decided against going back home. Instead, she turned in the direction of the marina. There was a chance that Flo was out shrimping for the day, but Sunny desperately needed to talk to a friend. The rain clouds that had gathered in her heart cleared slightly when she saw the Sweet Pea moored in its usual boat slip in the LouLou Marina. Without even announcing herself, she climbed aboard and burst through the front door, tears in her eyes.

"Flo? Oh, Flo, everything has gone wrong. All I ever wanted was to fit in, but now... ..." She stopped. "Flo, what are you doing?"

Flo stood in the middle of her small living quarters, lit candles set in a circle flickered around her, a mirror with the glass painted black in her hand.

"Me?" Flo quickly put the mirror between the wall and her sofa. "Just setting up a scene for my next painting. You know, a still life." She blew out the candles one by one. "Everything okay, sug? You look stressed. That police chief isn't giving you a hard time about all of this, is he?" Flo moved to her tiny kitchen stove and set a worn copper tea kettle to boil. Sunny followed behind her.

"No, as a matter of fact, he's been really kind." Sunny sat down on the sofa and wrung her hands. Oyster climbed onto her lap, and Sunny began to stroke his fur absentmindedly. "He says we can open the bar up tonight, by the way. I felt weird about opening so soon, but Danny really wants me to, so I think I will."

Flo handed her a cup of steaming earl grey tea, and Sunny accepted it with thankful hands. She took a slow sip before continuing.

"What's bothering me is that everyone in town thinks I'm a murderer, that I had something to do with Jeb's death." She burst into tears.

"Now how do you know that?" Flo sat down next to her and placed a comforting arm over Sunny's shoulders. Sunny recounted her unfortunate trip to the Hop, and Flo listened thoughtfully.

"The universe can teach us many lessons, Sunny." Flo spoke slowly and carefully. "Maybe the universe is trying to teach you that fitting in isn't so important after all. Just be yourself, and the friends you are meant to have in your life will come to you."

"You sound like my mom and dad with all of that universe talk." Sunny rolled her eyes. "If the universe wants me to be a weirdo, I'm not going to go down without a fight. I'm going to fit in if it's the last thing I do. At least that's what I thought before a man died in my bar." She took another sip of tea to stifle a sob that was rising in her throat. "Now, I don't know what I'm going to do."

"Look, I'll admit that I'm not the poster child of social niceties. I've never really cared about fitting in. When I first moved to LouLou, people called me a witch! Can you believe that?" she laughed. "But now, the people that are going to like me, like me. The people that aren't, don't. Just give it time. Things will get better. I promise."

"I don't want to give it time," Sunny huffed. "Will I see you at the Coconut tonight?" She rose from her seat and walked towards the door.

"Yes indeedy." Flo stood to walk her out. "I'll be there."

"You know," Sunny turned before she left and looked over at Flo. "I should be paying you for all your help at the bar. You have been doing just as much work as me to get it going. Maybe more."

"Nah," Flo brushed a hand in the air. "I like helping, and being at the Coconut is fun."

Sunny nodded and walked back to her car, thinking the whole while how much Flo gave to others. She wasn't kidding the first day she stepped into the Sweet Pea. Sunny really did want to be Flo when she grew up, and she would start tonight by helping Danny's hang out at the Coconut with his new friends go well.

Chapter 20

Sunny arrived a few hours before opening time to make sure the bar and tables were wiped down, the bathroom was fresh and clean, and the fruit was sliced and put in the refrigerator. She hesitated for a moment before flicking on the neon open sign in the bar's front window. Should she really be opening the Cajun Coconut so soon?

"In for a penny, in for a pound, I guess." She flipped the switch, and watched as the word "OPEN" illuminated, not knowing what the night would hold.

Danny was the first to walk through the door with a tall, lanky shy-looking boy with red hair and freckles on the bridge of his nose and another boy who looked at his shoes when he was introduced to Sunny. Both boys waved a timid hello, and she set to work making them virgin Jungle Birds—a mix of pineapple juice, orange juice, lime juice, and bitter red Italian soda. She placed the drinks on their table and lingered.

"Thanks, Mom." Danny tried to signal with his eyes that she should go away. Sunny got the message and made herself busy behind the bar. She didn't care if he was acting like a teenager that was too cool for his mother. She was just happy that he was making friends.

By the time Flo arrived, the Cajun Coconut was packed wall-to-wall with people. She looked around, a shocked laugh escaping her lips, and pushed her way to the bar where Sunny was mixing drinks as fast as her hands could manage.

"Sunny!" Flo exclaimed, hopping behind the bar to help out.

"Flo, can you believe it?" Sunny laughed as she shook a cocktail shaker over her shoulder. "I think the entire town must be here tonight."

Sunny beamed with pride. *Maybe people don't think I'm a murderer after all.* She thought, her optimism returning for the first time all day. She loaded six Bahama Mamas onto a tray and headed for a table in one of the bar's back corners where Julia Donahue was holding court.

"Thank you, suga." Julia gratefully accepted the fluted glass of bright red cocktail and took a swig from the straw. "This is delicious. Have you met everyone here?" She motioned to the other women who sat around the table.

"I don't believe I have." Sunny finished passing out the cocktails and put her serving tray under one arm. Julia introduced each of the five women in their group, but Sunny immediately forgot their names. She blinked several times, thinking her eyes must be playing tricks on her. Each of the women look almost identical to the other—the same sleek, bottle-blonde bob, the same expensive-looking, crisp, white button-down shirt with the collar popped and the sleeves rolled high enough to show off their massive amounts of diamond bracelets, the same red lipstick and tasteful brown eyeshadow.

"We all know each other from the club," Julia explained. "Oh, you should join! The Sunset Bayou Country Club is simply fabulous! And they have the best crawfish boils on the weekends."

"That sounds lovely." Sunny eyed the bar, worried that Flo couldn't keep up with the crush of drink orders being slung at her. "I'm not so sure that I'm country club material, but I'll keep it in mind." She turned to walk away.

"Oh one more thing, honey." Julia held up a hand to stop her. A devious look spread across her thickly made up face, and when she leaned in to whisper, Sunny got a whiff of Chanel Number Five. "Have the police determined what killed poor old Jeb yet?"

Sunny was stunned. Why would Julia or anyone else think that Sunny would know anything about that? The women at the table scooted their chairs closer to Sunny as she struggled to think of a way to respond.

"Um, well, um," she stammered. "Not yet."

"We heard that the circumstances were, shall we say, dubious." One of the women commented, raising one eyebrow on the word "dubious." The entire table began to twitter with gossip.

"Actually, that's the exact opposite of what the police said." Sunny felt her face grow hot. "They told me Jeb had a heart condition and probably died from a heart attack. I had nothing to do with it."

"Oh, we're not saying you did, suga," Julia feigned shock, putting a hand dramatically to her chest. Sunny turned and walked back to the bar. She took a deep breath in and exhaled it slowly. Instead of letting her thoughts about Jeb, Julia, and rumors spiral her anxiety to the point of no return, she busied herself mixing drinks, slicing fruit, and loading her brand new industrial dishwasher with load after load of cocktail glasses. She glanced over at the high top table where Danny sat with his friends. They were laughing and eating from a big bowl of popcorn she had brought from the back while they sipped their virgin tiki drinks. The smile on his face warmed her heart, and for a moment, she forgot about her interaction with Julia and the gossip hounds.

"Phew, I've made so many cocktails that my arms are sore!" Flo laughed, mopping sweat from her brow. She paused when she saw Sunny's serious face. "You okay? I thought you'd be happy that the Coconut is doing so well."

"I am happy about that, but when I brought Julia and her friends their drinks just a minute ago, I got the sense that they were only here to gossip about Jeb." Sunny picked up a clean dishrag and began to wipe down the bar.

"Maybe." Flo squinted and looked over at Julia's table.

"Has anyone asked you about… you know… …the–" She silently mouthed the word "death."

"A couple people," Flo admitted. "But I just told 'em that was nunnya', and that seemed to shut them up." She turned to take the order of a customer waiting at the bar. Another person walked up to get more drinks, and Sunny busied herself with their order. While she poured pineapple juice and spiced rum into a cocktail shaker, Sunny overheard two men talking in hushed tones.

"So they said that's where he died right over there." One pointed to the peacock chairs where Jeb had been sitting merely twenty-four hours before.

"You know I didn't want to come out tonight, but I was curious about it." The other shook his head. "Little risky drinking the same cocktails that killed Jeb," he grimaced.

"They taste pretty good though," the first man shrugged, tipping his glass back to drink it in one go. Sunny's heart sank. She thought everyone had come to the Cajun Coconut to support her new business, but instead, her bar was filled with people who wanted to snoop around and learn more about how a member of their town had died.

Chapter 21

"Y'all have a good one." Flo walked the last two tiki bar patrons out and turned the lock on the door. "Phew wee! Usually, if I want to get a good night's sleep these days, I've got to get out my melatonin gummies, my magnesium spray, my cooling pajamas...But I think I'm going to be dead to the world the minute my head hits the pillow tonight. What about you, Sunny?"

Sunny didn't respond. The only sound in the room was the clinking of cocktail glasses as she stacked them behind the bar.

"Cheer up." Flo lowered into one of the bar stools and yawned. "I'm sure not *everybody* who was here tonight came just to snoop around."

"But it seems like most people did." Sunny stopped stacking cups and moved around the bar to sit next to Flo. "I'm the town murderer! I'll never make any friends now." Tears welled up in her eyes.

"Come on, now." Flo patted her on the back. "You're just tired. Go home and get some rest. Things will look a lot better in the sunshine."

"I can't rest." Sunny wiped her eyes. "Every time I fall asleep, I see Jeb lying on the floor over there."

"How about a vacation?" Flo asked. Sunny eyed her suspiciously but didn't say anything. "Yeah, a vacation! You and Danny go somewhere for a week or maybe even two. Get out of this town. Lay low. By the time you get back, everyone will have forgotten about all of this mess."

"I don't know," Sunny said. "I've spent quite a lot of cash fixing up the house and building the bar. I don't really have vacation money right now."

After Flo had gone home, Sunny lingered in the bar. Sure, she had a few odd jobs to do here and there, but she was mostly sticking around for one thing. She sat on a bar stool and waited. No rumbling came from the floor. No mysterious ocean breeze wafted through the room. She walked up to the tall tiki totem in the back corner of the bar, the one that she was darned sure had spoken to her a few nights ago. Staring directly into his friendly wooden eyes, she willed him to speak.

"Talk!" she commanded. Silence. Sunny hid her eyes with her hands. "I'm losing it. Really losing it. Alright, Sunflower. Time to go home."

In bed that night, Sunny tossed and turned.

"I told Flo that I wouldn't be able to sleep," she huffed and reached towards the nightstand for her phone. She ripped it off the charger and typed in the URL for the local real estate website, the screen flooding her face with blue light.

"I wonder what I could get for this house if I sold it right now?" She wondered aloud as she scrolled through the site to see what was on the market in LouLou. "I've put quite a lot of work into the place, so surely, I could make something extra on what I paid for it."

Sunny wondered if moving to LouLou had been a mistake, if she should sell her house and move away, never to see or think about this town or any of its inhabitants ever again. She was heartened by the comparables in her area. Homes on the shore of Lake Pontchartrain seemed to be selling well these days. She put down her phone and stared up at the ceiling. Was she serious? Would she really sell and move? Maybe...

Chapter 22

Sunny woke up the next morning, sure of one thing. She needed out of LouLou, Louisiana. According to the real estate website, her house would sell quickly for a decent chunk of change. She could leave the Cajun Coconut for Flo to run. *Flo,* she thought with a pang of sadness. She would miss Flo. Even though Sunny had only lived in LouLou for a little over two months, it had felt like she and Flo had been friends forever. Still, she and Danny would find somewhere else to be their forever home, because this place wasn't working. Her mind was made up. She would tell Danny over breakfast.

When she walked into the kitchen, Danny was already eating a bowl of granola. Sunny blinked with surprise. Was her son already dressed and ready for school? *That's a first.* She decided to keep these thoughts to herself for fear of jinxing how well the morning seemed to be going.

"Mornin, Sunny's Little Sunshine," she smiled and made her own bowl of granola before sitting down at the table next to him. "Hey listen, I've got something I need to talk about." She cleared her throat nervously.

"Thanks for letting me and my friends hang at the Coconut last night." Danny interrupted.

"Did they have a good time?" Sunny pressed a smile on her face.

"Yeah, they did." Danny smiled too, but his grin was genuine. "I've got to get to school early because Mr. Spakes, the chemistry teacher, is letting me and two other kids do this extra credit lab experiment because we're the top grades in the class. It's going to be really cool." He stood and slung his backpack over one shoulder. "What did you need to tell me?"

Sunny looked at her son. He was finally settling into life here in LouLou, finding friends and feeling at home. Was she about to rip him away and make him start over again somewhere else just like she had done again and again when she was a nurse?

"I'll tell you later." She motioned for him to go to school. "It can wait. Have a great day at school." She rose and hugged him before he raced out the door. It looked like, if Sunny wasn't going to stay here for herself, maybe she should consider staying here for her son. At least for now.

Chapter 23

Sunny gathered her yoga mat and a water bottle. It was time to get her mind right. She headed for the area in the woods behind her house that had become her special yoga spot. It was a clearing in a pocket of thickly-planted loblolly pines, their tall and skinny trunks stretching to the sky with plumes of green pine needles bursting from their upper branches. Sunny liked how, when the wind blew through them, the pines seemed to dance around her.

After unrolling her mat and stretching through a half-hour of poses, she lay on her back and stared up at the sky, which was blue today, with puffs of cotton clouds drifting past. Every once in a while, a blue heron would fly high over the trees, gliding on the gentle breeze that was so welcome in these dog days of summer. With her yoga routine completed and her mind feeling calmer, she went back home and jumped in the car. Today was the day she would finally whip her garden into shape.

The land surrounding her little cottage could hardly have been described as pretty, or even tidy, but a patch of weeds on one side of the house could be made into a lovely vegetable garden if blessed with a bit of elbow grease. A little googling had told her that August in South Louisiana was the perfect time to plant cucumbers, bell peppers, and collard greens. She decided to start with those.

At Betty's Plant Place, a few minutes drive out of town, Sunny practically skipped down the aisles of flowers, herbs, shrubs, and veggies. In all her time traveling the world for work, there was one thing she couldn't have that she had terribly wanted–a real garden. Sure, she grew a few herbs in tiny pots that would fit on her apartment window sills that she carried from one place to another whenever she moved, but for this California farm girl, that never satisfied her itch to dig in the dirt and watch things grow. It was hard not to fill an entire shopping cart with plants, but she restrained herself, limiting her selection to a few pepper plants, cucumber vines, collard plants, and one impulse buy–a lemon tree. She had seen so many front yards with citrus trees growing, and the fruit seemed to thrive in the deep southern humidity and heat. She loaded her tiny car and carried her new plant babies home, the lemon tree sticking out of the passenger seat window.

Back at the cottage, Sunny realized that she had to contend with the angry knot of weeds that had taken over the ground before she could get down to the fun work of nestling the plants in freshly tilled garden soil.

"I can feel my future backache already," Sunny groaned, slipping on gardening gloves and stooping to get to business. Several hours of pulling weeds later, she was covered in a thick layer of sweat and dirt from her head to her toes. She heard her phone ringing from the front porch and welcomed the chance to sit in the shade.

"Tony, um, I mean, Police Chief Perez," Sunny stuttered. "Is everything okay?"

"Everything is fine," His voice was gentle and friendly. "And it's Tony."

"Tony," Sunny nodded, glad he couldn't see her cheeks flush over the phone.

"I was calling to let you know that the autopsy report came back." He said. "Usually, I only share this kind of info with the victim's family, but since you are connected to all of this, I wanted to let you know what they found. I think it will make you feel better."

"Okay, what did they find?" Sunny asked, a hint of shakiness in her voice.

"The lab found large amounts of grapefruit in his stomach. Jeb was on statins for his heart. Everybody knows you can't have certain foods when on that kind of medication. Grapefruit stops the statins from working. His heart attack had nothing to do with you or the bar. It was probably just the grapefruit juice in his cocktail that did it."

"I feel terrible that my drink might have killed someone."

"Your drink didn't kill him," Tony insisted. "His own decisions did. It's not your fault. You didn't even know he was on medication."

"That does make me feel better, I guess," Sunny bobbed her head sadly. "Thanks for the call, Tony."

She hung up the phone and stepped off the porch to return to the task at hand.

"Why did I think this god-forsaken devil's dirt patch could be a good garden spot?" she whined, her hands wrapped around a particularly stubborn clump of yellow nutsedge, pulling with all her might. When the roots finally gave way, Sunny lost her footing and tumbled onto her backside.

"Ow! Jeez Louise." She sat on the ground, brushing dirt from her palms. "Wait a minute." She sat up a little straighter, her eyes wide with the sudden flash of an idea. "Did Tony say that Jeb died from drinking grapefruit? Jeb and his mysterious female friend had mai tais, and my recipe doesn't have grapefruit juice. Rum, orange liqueur, lime juice, and orgeat. No grapefruit." *Strange.* Her thoughts were interrupted by a phone notification chiming from the porch. It was the sound of her calendar app. She rose from the ground and brushed the dirt from her knees. She opened her calendar and groaned.

"Book club."

Sunny had thought about skipping her activities for the day, or maybe even quitting them all entirely, but she had decided that if she was serious about staying in town and making LouLou work, she couldn't hide in her house forever. She wasn't going to be bullied out of living her life. "Guess I need to clean up." She frowned and went inside to shower.

She stood in front of her closet, chewing off her fingernails one by one. *What to wear?* For a brief moment, she placed a hand on her favorite linen sundress that her mother had sewn for her years ago, but she shook her head and reached for the new pink sheath dress she had purchased at the boutique. She struggled to zip up the back, the dress feeling a little too tight in places, and marched out the door.

The ladies' book club rotated the meeting location so that one person didn't have the burden of hosting every month. This month's meeting was at the library. Sunny parked her car in the first spot she saw on the square and hurriedly scurried into the library just as the meeting was kicking off.

The LouLou Library had three levels. The top floor, fitted into what was the old Victorian house's attic, was furnished with comfortable armchairs for reading, several computers for the community to have access to the internet, and a perpetually brewing coffee pot that gave the space an always-present aroma of praline pecan dark roast. The second floor was where the bulk of books were kept, with as many shelves as possible shoved in every available space, the ancient wooden floorboards groaning under the massive weight of literature. The first floor was at once open and airy yet cozy and inviting. There were shelves of books here, too, and a librarian's desk as well, but most of the space was kept open to accommodate the many community groups that used the library as their meeting place.

When Sunny walked in, the first floor was packed with book club members, and she suddenly felt shy. What if no one wanted her here? What if she saw Barbara, Jeb's wife? She forced herself to lift her chin. She would hold her head high. She had done nothing wrong.

She spotted the woman she wished to avoid on one side of the room. Barbara was dressed in mourning black, her pale, makeup-free face accentuating the dark circles under her eyes. She dabbed at her tears daintily with a monogrammed handkerchief while Suzy and Mary Kay cooed words of comfort and patted her shoulders. On the other end of the room, set under a pair of gothic Victorian windows, a long table was laid out with enough pimento cheese, spicy cheese straws, mini pecan pies, pralines, and pitchers of sweet tea to feed an army. Rachel was standing at the table, loading a paper plate with food.

"I might be walking into the lion's den, but at least it's got good snacks," Sunny muttered. It was easy for her to decide which side of the room she would walk towards.

"Rachel, hi!" she smiled, grabbing a plate.

"Sunny, how are you?" Rachel put her plate down and swept Sunny up in a big hug. "I'm so sorry about what happened at the Coconut. I can't believe it." She shook her head slowly.

"It's been awful, but I'm doing my best to move past it." Sunny tried to smile, but her eyes filled with tears. She swallowed the sob that was rising in her throat and turned her focus to the table. "What an amazing spread!"

"Marian is not only the best librarian, but she can cook too!" Rachel picked her plate back up from where she had set it down and resumed filling it until the paper began to buckle under the weight. "Aren't we lucky?"

"Welcome, ladies, to this month's book club meeting." Marian stood on a desk chair and clinked a writing pen against her sweet tea glass to quiet the room. "I'm so glad to see everyone's smiling faces." The women in the room applauded politely. Sunny and Rachel took their plates to the rows of chairs set up for the meeting and claimed two empty seats in the back row. As the meeting went on and Marian led the discussion on this month's book–a bodice ripper set in New Orleans called Pectorals, Parades, and Pralines, Sunny's heart began to lighten. Maybe it was the good food or the cozy library with its dark wood paneling and full bookshelves, but she was starting to enjoy herself. That was until she glanced over at the spot where Barbara still stood.

Like puppets with their heads tied to the same string, Barbara and her posse turned their heads in unison to glare at Sunny.

Sunny's face grew hot, and she squirmed in her seat. *Time to go home*. She gingerly rose from her chair, waved a silent goodbye to Rachel, and navigated through the crowded room, doing her best to make it to the library's front door undetected. She was almost there, three steps more, two steps more, one step more, her hand was on the glass door knob ...

"And where do you think you're going?" Barbara's voice sliced through her like icy wind through a worn cardigan. She slowly turned around to face them.

"Barbara, hi," her voice squeaked. "I just want to tell you how sorry I am about..."

"How sorry you are to have killed her husband, you mean?" Suzy sneered, a sparkle in her eye. *She's taking a lot of pleasure in this.* Sunny thought.

"I'm very sorry that your husband died." Sunny tried to ignore Suzy and Mary Kay's smirks and focus on

Barbara's face. "Truly I am, but I didn't kill him. We all know that."

"Oh, do we?" Mary Kay quipped.

"How dare you come to this book club after you... after you...after you KILLED MY HUSBAND!" Barbara began to weep loudly, burying her face in the sleeve of her designer cashmere sweater. At this point, the whole room had turned towards them, real life being much more entertaining than the fiction they had been discussing before.

"I think it's best if y'all get Barbara home." Marian patted Suzy on the back, and the wailing widow was escorted to her car. "And I also think it's best if we say this meeting is adjourned," Marian announced, and the book club members began to file out the front door.

"Murderer." A woman Sunny recognized as Charlene, the cashier down at the Hop, spat the word at her as she walked past and out the door.

"You don't belong here, you cocktail killer freak," another woman Sunny had never seen before hissed as she walked past.

"Mrs. Therriot, really!" Marian gasped. "I'm sorry, Sunny. Are you okay?"

"I'm fine." Sunny gritted her teeth as tears streamed down her cheeks. "I think I should go."

"Please don't worry about any of this. They're just upset. We all know you didn't kill Jeb."

Sunny didn't know what to say next, so she simply left the library without another word.

Chapter 24

"You okay?" Flo leaned on the bartop and studied Sunny. "Awfully quiet tonight."

Sunny had spoken very little in the last few hours. The Cajun Coconut wasn't as packed as the night before, but business was pleasantly steady. The stools that sidled up to the bar were occupied with happy patrons sipping fruity drinks. Other customers sat at the bamboo tables that stood around the room. Laughter and the soft lilt of tropical music filled the air. To Sunny's surprise and delight, Danny had brought the two friends from the night before along with two new friends. They all requested virgin Jungle Birds, and Sunny was happy to oblige.

She kept herself busy mixing drinks and doing odd jobs around the bar so she wouldn't have to tell Flo about what had happened at the library. She would tell her eventually, but it was all too raw right now.

"Me?" Sunny gave an innocent shrug. "I'm fine. Just tired, I guess." She plastered a grin on her face and got out the cutting board and paring knife to slice more lemons and limes.

"Uh-huh." Flo squinted suspiciously, not convinced. "I almost forgot that I made a pan of mac and cheese. It's in the truck. Be right back." Flo walked back inside a few minutes later, holding a foil-covered casserole dish.

"Is that Miss Flo's mac and cheese I smell?" Danny made a beeline for the bar, his friends following him.

"Sure is." Flo lifted the tin foil and reached under the bar where they kept the plates and silverware. "Y'all eat as much as you want."

The mac and cheese didn't last long with five hungry teenagers around, but Sunny didn't care. Her afternoon outing at the library had turned her stomach, and it was not just the abuse that had been hurled at her by the good women of LouLou that bothered her. There was something else niggling at her brain, too. It was the way Barbara had acted at the book club meeting. The black clothing, the lack of makeup on her gaunt face, the loud crying–it was almost as if she was playing a part in a theater production, and the book club attendees were the intended audience.

"Alright, first you give me the silent treatment, and now, you don't even eat any mac and cheese? What's up? Are you mad at me for something?" Flo crossed her arms.

"Not at all." Sunny stopped slicing limes and turned to face her friend. "I'm just distracted right now."

"By what?"

"Grapefruit." Sunny resumed her slicing, with extra rigor this time.

"Those are limes in your hand, sweetie," Flo laughed. "I know menopause can make us girls a little foggy-headed, but you're going to need to explain that one a little further."

"Tony, I mean, Police Chief Perez, called me this morning to let me know about Jeb's autopsy results." Sunny motioned for Flo to step closer to her so she could keep her voice low. "He told me that Jeb died from consuming grapefruit, probably found in his tiki drink that night. He was on statins for his heart, and grapefruit can have a bad interaction with that medication."

"Correct me if I'm wrong, but Jeb got a mai tai that night, and that drink doesn't have grapefruit in it," Flo frowned.

"Exactly!"

"So what are you saying?" Flo shifted uncomfortably on her feet. "That Jeb was murdered?"

"That's precisely what I'm saying."

Flo stood for a moment in silence, just staring at Sunny.

"I know it sounds far-fetched." Sunny could tell what Flo was thinking by her doubtful facial expressions. "But how else would he ingest grapefruit while in the bar? I've got a plan. Investigate his death. Solve the murder. Become the town hero, and everyone stops thinking I'm a killer."

"No one thinks you're a killer." Flo rolled her eyes. Sunny decided not to argue. The seashells on the front door clinked, signaling that someone had entered the bar. A large group of Tulane college students from across the lake in New Orleans stood at the bar, waiting to be served. They tabled the murder talk for the time being and got busy mixing drinks.

When the clock struck midnight and the last customers had gone, Sunny flicked off the neon “open” sign and turned the deadbolt on the door. She exhaled. It had been a good night for business. If things stayed like this, she could hope to start making a profit. She turned to Flo, who was mopping the floor, her mouth wide in a deep yawn.

“You’re exhausted,” Sunny said. “Let me finish cleaning up.”

“You sure?” Flo handed her the mop and took off the apron she had been wearing with a hula girl and the words “Tiki Time” printed on it. “I could use some shut-eye. I got up early this morning to get to the shrimp before the other boats.” She paused before she left and turned to Sunny. “Hey, listen. Don’t do anything rash with this idea you have about investigating what happened to Jeb. I’ll admit that it sounds fishy, but you could be walking into something dangerous. I don’t want you to get hurt, and I’m pretty sure Danny doesn’t either.”

“I hear you,” Sunny nodded, wringing the mop out and dipping it back into the bucket of hot water and vinegar. “I promise I won’t do anything stupid.”

“I’m going to hold you to that,” Flo said and went home.

Sunny finished mopping and began wiping down the tables and chairs. She cranked up the tiki music, and the cheerful tinkling of Martin Denny’s song, "Forbidden Island," energized her. She stood back to admire her work. Everything looked and smelled fresh and clean. *Time to go home.*

The slightest breeze hit her face, nearly imperceptible. She froze in place, a prickle of fear traveling up her spine. She convinced herself it was nothing and went to the cash register to count the night's earnings. Sunny twitched her nose and sniffed. Was that the smell of salt air? Coconut?

Of course I smell coconut. I work in a tiki bar. Half the drinks have coconut liqueur in them. She laughed at how easily she was sent into freak-out mode. She took the cash drawer out of the register and started counting out each stack of bills–first the ones, then the fives, then the tens. A blast of salty wind hit her in the face like an indoor hurricane.

She screamed and hid behind the bar.

Chapter 25

The wind howled as it filled the room, and from her hiding spot behind the bar, Sunny watched as the gales blew tiki mugs and glassware off the shelves, the sound of crashing glass assaulting her ears from the left and right. The bartop could buffer her from the worst of the winds, but it provided no protection once the rain started to fall. Water fell in sheets from the ceiling, pelting her with a force that took her breath away. She might have been able to convince herself that there was merely a leak in the building's roof if the rain had not been accompanied by loud claps of thunder and flashes of lightning that lit the whole room.

Sunny had to do something. She clawed her way to standing, holding onto the bar with a white-knuckled grip so the storm wouldn't blow her away. She made her way around the bar and crawled to the center of the room.

"What is happening?" she cried, looking up to the ceiling. Who was she asking? She didn't know. "Stop! Please!" she begged and fell to her knees. Like a flipped breaker on a fuse box, the storm stopped. The room was filled with the sweet scent of tropical flowers, and a gentle, warm breeze met her face where she knelt, her clothes and hair dripping wet and her heart racing.

"Sunflower!" A familiar, deep, and booming voice sounded through the room. It was the same voice Sunny had convinced herself didn't exist when she had heard it a few nights ago. Here it was again, and this time, there was no denying it was very real. "Sunflower, come to me."

Sunny turned in the direction of the voice and noticed Aunt Edna's large tiki totem looked different than it had a few moments ago. The tall statue's once wooden and lifeless eyes were now a swirling ocean blue–and were they blinking? She rubbed her own eyes, unable to believe what she was seeing. The mouth of the tiki totem opened, and Sunny thought she might faint on the spot.

"Come, Sunflower, it is time that we talk," the totem said, his mouth no longer stiff carved wood but instead a warm smile.

"How do you know my name?" Sunny stuttered. "And, wwwwwhy are you ..." She gulped, unable to finish the question.

"Talking?" The totem gave a low chuckle. "That is what we need to discuss, well, that and many other things. We are, quite honestly, a bit behind schedule."

"Behind schedule?" Sunny inched cautiously

towards the statue, unsure of what would happen next. Her whole body shivered in her soaked clothing, dripping in puddles on the floor.

"Yes, we surely are," the totem continued. "Edna had communed with our spirits for weeks before her tiki bar had even opened. You have been a tough one to reach."

"Did you say spirits? Like with an 's'?" Sunny whipped her head around the room, half expecting something to jump out at her from behind one of the fake palms. She didn't like the thought of there being more than one weird talking tiki thing. "So there's more than just you?" she half whispered.

"Okay, everyone," the totem called out. It is time!" The room filled with a cacophony of voices, bird squawks, cresting ocean waves' crashes, and more, rushing forth in a chaotic din that made Sunny cover her ears.

"Enough," the totem's voice boomed, making the floor tremble under Sunny's feet. The noise stopped.

"Hi, sweetie." One of the tiki masks on the wall, the small circular one painted with a green and white striped face, spoke in a warm, friendly female voice. "I'm Pearl, dear. I'm so glad to meet one of Edna's kin. She was such a good woman."

"Nice to meet you," Sunny nodded, unsure of what was considered polite when meeting a talking tiki mask for the first time. It wasn't like she could shake its hand or anything.

"And I'm Cora." The other tiki mask on the wall, a long oval-shaped one carved from driftwood, spoke next in calm tones that seemed to flow out like a tranquil river stream.

"Nice to meet you, Cora." Sunny dipped her head.

"Don't ye be forgettin' about the likes of us." Sunny jumped at the voices overhead. She looked up to see that the two taxidermied parrots hanging from the ceiling on bamboo perches were speaking now.

"Name's Barbossa," the red parrot said. "But you can call me Barry."

"Aye. And I'm Vincenzo, but my maties always called me Vin," the stuffed blue macaw said next. "You wouldn't mind troublin' yourself for a small samplin' of rum for old Vin, would you? Just a small samplin', mind."

Sunny stared at the bird, its once lifeless wings now fluttering like a real live bird, and its tiny beak moving up and down like one of those robots at Disneyland. She let out a sound that was mainly a laugh and partly a panicked cry.

"This is a joke, right?" She looked around. "I mean, come on. Who's doing this? Danny? Flo?" She called out and turned, expecting someone to pop out from the back storage room and yell, "Gotcha!" The room was silent.

"This isn't a joke, dear." The tiki mask, now known as Pearl, spoke up.

"Like, totally for sure not a joke, brah." From the velvet painting of surfers hanging ten on a tropical beach, the tiny surfer dude spoke to Sunny. She felt like she was going to throw up.

"Sunflower, please, sit down," the tiki totem said. "We have so much to tell you."

Sunny didn't know why, but she decided to do as she was told. She lowered into one of the peacock chairs and crossed her arms.

"I haven't introduced myself. I am Cook, and I was the first magical tiki item your aunt ever collected. Well, she didn't know I was magical at the time. She only knew that she was inexplicably drawn to me. Once she acquired me from an antique store in Bermuda, it wasn't long before more magical tikis found us, and as we grew in number, we also grew in power. When Edna built her tiki bar, we were all able to feed off each other's spirits and speak to humans for the first time. Of course, we only speak to a select few."

"Humans can be so annoying sometimes," Cora quipped.

"Oh, but not our dear Edna," Pearl cooed. "She was wonderful."

For the first time, it dawned on Sunny that she had finally found people or spirits or whatever they were that could tell her about her mysterious aunt.

"I imagine you have questions," Cook said, his voice kind and serious.

"That's an understatement," Sunny laughed. "Why are you magical? What kind of magic can you do? Was Aunt Edna magical? What was she like?" Her mind began to spiral.

"Let me start with your first question for now," Cook interrupted. "Over our time together, our powers to reach you will grow, but for now, the hour is late. Our ability to cross the realms and speak to you wanes." He took a deep sigh. "Some of us are spirits that have existed throughout time. Some of us began life as humans. Long ago, I was an explorer who navigated my ship to distant lands. Some would say that I wasn't always the most ethical of men. I colonized lands that were already inhabited, stealing people's homes and cultures, and making them sick with my foreign fevers. It was a grave mistake. I know that now. When I met a sticky end trying to flee an attack from natives off the coast of the Marquesas, my soul was cursed, doomed to spend eternity trapped in this tiki totem."

Sunny's mouth hung open. This morning, her only worries had been proving to the town that she wasn't a cold-blooded killer. From where she sat now, listening to a three-hundred-year-old spirit talk to her through a tiki statue, the morning felt like simpler times.

"The same happened to us, unfortunately," the red parrot–*what was his name? Barry?* Sunny wondered–spoke now.

"We're just two good old pirates, minding our own business," the blue parrot, Vin, said. "And now look at us, cursed for all eternity to live in these bird-brained dust collectors."

"You were two of the most vicious pirates on the high seas," Cora commented.

"So says who?" Barry asked.

"So says I," Cora's silvery voice was confident. "For three thousand years, I have been a spirit of the water. I have seen pirates like you two tearing up the ocean, leaving nothing but destruction in your wake."

"Hearsay, at best," Vin said casually.

"Water spirit?" Sunny asked. "Like a fairy or something?"

"Nature is full of spirits, sweet one," Pearl answered before Cora could. "I am an Earth spirit. I lived inside a giant fir tree in the wilds of Alaska for hundreds of years until, one day, my tree fell in a winter blizzard. Edna's husband used my tree's wood to carve this tiki mask, and now, here I am," she giggled sweetly.

"The power wanes. We must go," Cook boomed. "But before we leave you, you must know this. Evil lurks in this town. There is more to the death of the man than you know."

Sunny gasped in shock. How did they know about Jeb?

"To right these wrongs, you will need our help, and we will help you because, Sunflower, we live to serve you now."

"Wait, where are you going?" Sunny rose from her seat. "Will you come back?"

But it was too late. The spirits were gone. Gone for now? Gone for forever? Sunny didn't know.

Chapter 26

Sunny looked around at the mess the night's hurricane-force winds had created. Glass covered the floor. Potted plants were overturned, dirt spilling from cracked planters. The floor was wet and sticky. She closed her eyes and took a deep breath. There was no way she had the energy to clean up tonight.

"I'll come in early in the morning and take care of this," she muttered and grabbed her purse. On the drive home, her mind wandered, racing in loop-de-loops like a rollercoaster, from the tiki spirits to the murder and back to the tikis again. Did having spirit friends make things easier or harder? How was she going to explain all of this to Flo? *Was* she going to explain any of this to Flo? It would be weird to keep this from the woman who was becoming her best friend, but could she imagine sitting Flo down over a cup of tea and telling her that her tiki bar has magical powers?

"Flo, did you know my tiki masks can talk to me when no one is looking?" Sunny cackled at the thought. "I'd be sent to the hospital for an evaluation if I told her that." No, the tikis would have to remain a secret, at least for now.

The following day, Sunny got up extra early and rushed out the door, leaving a note for Danny that she would see him after school. She hurried to the bar with cleaning supplies in her car's trunk. Sunny wanted to get there and take care of the mess because she wasn't sure how she could explain away the state of the bar if Flo got there first.

To Sunny's astonishment, when she opened the door to the Cajun Coconut, the bar inside was completely clean. She stood frozen in the doorway and stared. The floor was mopped and smelled of lemons. The glassware was intact and back on the shelves behind the bar. The plants were upright. The tables and chairs were neatly in their places. Had she hallucinated the whole tiki spirits thing, or had Flo gotten her first and cleaned up the mess?

"Flo?" Sunny called out as she stepped inside and closed the door behind her. "Are you here?" There was no answer. "Well, if you spirits cleaned this place up, thank you, I guess." With nothing to clean, Sunny slung her purse back over her shoulder. She had other things on her agenda for the day, not least of which was solving a murder. *How does one actually solve a murder?* Sunny pondered, not for the first time in the last twenty-four hours. It was still early, though, and Sunny decided she had earned a little treat.

When she pushed open the pastel pink French

doors of Bunny's Boulangerie, the smells of butter and sugar gave her an instant dopamine rush.

"Well, hey there, Sunny," Bunny brushed her flour-covered hands on her lavender apron and waved. "Long time, no see."

"I know. I thought I would be coming by here more once the Coconut opened, but things have been, um, busy." She blushed. She wasn't trying to make a man's death be all about her, but frankly, murder could be, well, *embarrassing*.

"I get it." Bunny nodded and grabbed a plastic tray from a stack behind the counter. "What can I getcha today? The pecan praline croissants are just out of the oven."

"That must be what I smell!" Sunny fluttered her eyelashes at the sheer pleasure of scent that filled the bakery. "I'll take one, please. Oh, and a cafe au lait."

The day was unseasonably cool, one of the first since Sunny had moved to LouLou when the air wasn't a soupy mess of unrelenting heat. She decided to eat her treat on the bakery's outdoor patio. A table near the front door had several days' editions of the local newspaper, The Daily Trawl, piled in a messy stack. Sunny grabbed the morning's paper and headed outside.

"Here we are." Bunny set down a small china plate with the croissant and a large mug of coffee. "Enjoy." She smiled and walked away.

"Hey, Bunny," Sunny stopped her before she stepped through the doorway. "You wouldn't be interested in hanging out sometime? Like for a cup of tea or something?"

"Hanging out?" Bunny smiled politely. "Sure, I

guess. Sure." She nodded and shrugged.

"Great!" Sunny beamed. "What about tonight?"

"Oh, shoot. I'm busy tonight." Bunny started to walk away again. "But some other time for sure."

"Well, what about tomorrow afternoon?"

"Busy."

"Tomorrow evening?"

"Busy again." Bunny bit her lip. "I'm sure we'll figure it out. Enjoy that coffee before it gets cold, now." She turned and scurried inside.

Sunny shook her head. What was it that made her a local social pariah? She was polite. She was warm. She engaged people in conversation, and yet, they never wanted to move from acquaintance to friend. It was a mystery she was determined to solve. After she had solved the murder mystery first, of course. She took a sip from her coffee mug and spread open the newspaper.

A small town like LouLou didn't have much in the way of actual news to report. That was, until she had shown up. Little things like newborn babies, church potlucks, and who caught the biggest fish that week were big enough news to make the front page of The Daily Trawl. Sunny took a big bite of her croissant, and her eyes rolled into the back of her head. Holding a grudge against Bunny was hard when she could bake like a goddess. Something in the paper caught her eye. She stopped chewing and leaned in, squinting to read the small print.

"Funeral For Jeb Landry Today." Her mouth moved silently as she read the words. Jeb's funeral–she hadn't even thought about his funeral until now. Should she go? *Of course, I should.* She thought. *Right?* Doubt immediately started to set in, but she stopped her thoughts from spiraling out of control. If she didn't go to his funeral, her absence would practically convict her of the crime everyone in town was convinced she had committed. Not showing up would be the same as admitting guilt. Whether the townsfolk of LouLou liked it or not, she was going to that funeral.

Chapter 27

As her tiny Miata bumped down Moonlight Lane towards her cottage, a UPS truck almost side-swiped her driver's seat door as it zoomed in the opposite direction.

"Looks like I might have a delivery!" She clapped her hands in glee as she put the car in park in her driveway. . On her front porch stood a mountain of brown boxes waiting to be opened.

"It feels like Christmas!" She squealed, hoisting the boxes into her living room one by one.

Fortunately for Sunny (and maybe unfortunately for her credit card balance), she had been spending her sleepless nights online shopping. She had decided that to make this town her home, she might have to take her mission to fit in with the locals to the next level. It was time to press the "activate" button on Sunny 2.0.

She had never shopped in places like J.Crew or The Gap before now, so she blinked in disbelief as she stood in front of her full-length bedroom mirror wearing a sleek black sheath dress and black patent leather heels that made her wobble when she attempted to walk in them.

"This will work for a funeral." She turned to the left and right to examine her new look. Before she could talk herself out of anything–the dress or the funeral–she grabbed her car keys and headed to Saint Boudreaux's Catholic Church on the other side of town.

The funeral bells rang loudly at the top of the building's tall brick tower when Sunny pulled her car into the church's parking lot. A thick crowd of people all in black chatted in low murmurs as they filed inside the nave. Sunny walked through the church's front lawn lined with spiky green palmetto plants and white azaleas, scanning the crowd for at least one familiar and friendly face.

"Sunny, suga, how nice to see you." Julia Donahue approached her in the most exquisitely tailored black pantsuit she had ever seen. The Southern belle wore her requisite jewelry, and her layers of diamonds sparkled in the afternoon sun. She gave Sunny a polite side hug and leaned into her ear. "Pretty brave of you to come if you ask me." She chuckled and gave Sunny an exaggerated wink.

"I have every right to come." Sunny pulled back and stiffened. "I'm here to pay my respects just like everyone else. I may not have known Jeb very well, but I was with him during his… …during his… …well, you know, and I want to be here with him now. It's only right."

"Oh, I'm just kidding. You're taking my little jokey

out of proportion, dear." Julia gave a gaslighting laugh. She leaned in and spoke out of the side of her mouth. "Just steer clear of Barbara and Suzy, ya hear? It might not end well." She straightened up again and adjusted the jacket of her ensemble. "Nice dress, by the way. I've never seen you look so good." She waved and smiled at someone over Sunny's shoulder and walked away.

As Sunny stood there wondering if she had just been insulted or complimented, the church organ began to play, signaling the start of the service, and Sunny scurried inside to find a seat.

Saint Boudreaux's Catholic Church was larger and grander than a person might expect for such a small town like LouLou. Everything in the nave–the pews, the floors, the altar, even the walls–was built with warm, brown cypress wood polished to a glossy finish. It gave the impression that they were sitting inside a honey pot. The walls were lined with towering stained glass windows, and the vaulted ceiling was painted in traditional Cajun colors and motifs with red, white, and blue panels decorated with gold fleur-de-lis. Sunny quickly took a seat on the last pew.

From her seat in the back of the packed church, she could barely see Barbara sitting up at the front in a seat of honor. Even from such an obscured view, the newly widowed woman was hard to miss. Barbara wore a skin-tight black bandage mini dress, the kind that had a chokehold on every celebrity in the early 2000s, and it clung to every curve of her body. She completed the look with long, satin black gloves that stretched past her elbows, black stiletto heels, a black flowered hat with a brim the size of an alien flying saucer, and a gargantuan silver cross necklace that was perfectly nestled in her visible cleavage. *Was Barbara going for grieving widow or black widow?* Sunny smirked to herself.

As the funeral mass dragged on, Sunny found her thoughts turning more and more to her task at hand–solving the murder. Sure, she had come to the service to pay her respects to Jeb, but now that she was here, she might as well try her hand at investigating. She studied the faces of the people in the pews. *Who looks guilty?* She wondered. *Would the killer come to the funeral? Probably. If they didn't, it would make them look suspicious.* What motive did anyone have for killing the man? It occurred to her that she barely knew anything about Jeb. If she didn't know who Jeb really was, how was she supposed to understand why someone would want him dead? She had research to do.

From the front of the church, Barbara wailed loudly, dabbing her wet eyes with a monogrammed handkerchief. Sunny didn't know why, but she got the gut feeling she was watching yet another performance from the newly widowed woman.

Between Barbara's theatrics and the repeated dirty looks from fellow mourners in the pews, Sunny was glad to walk out into the sunlight on the church's front steps once the service concluded. She had done her duty. Now, she could go home and continue working on her garden with a clear conscience.

"Sunny, hi!" Marian from the library shouted from behind her. "So good to see you!"

Sunny smiled. *Finally, a friendly face!* she exhaled.

"Marian, hello." Sunny wrapped one arm around the librarian's shoulders and squeezed. "It's good to see you too. I was just headed home."

"Oh, you're not going to the reception at

Barbara's?" Unlike Sunny's interaction with Julia Donahue, Marian's question was genuine and without the slicing cattiness most Southern belles seemed to master so well.

"I don't think I would be welcome there." Sunny wrinkled her nose.

"Nonsense." Marian swatted the air with one hand. "You're a part of this town now, so you are just as welcome as anyone."

Twenty minutes later, as Sunny parked on the street in front of Barbara's towering Greek revival mansion, she hoped Marian was right.

Chapter 28

It took everything Sunny had to force herself to walk up the concrete path that cut through Barbara's manicured front lawn and into the house. Each step towards the door was painful, mostly because she was terrified of how the people inside would treat her, but also because the newly acquired Spanx she had worn to complete her ensemble was really starting to cut off circulation.

"The house will be so full of people that Barbara and Suzy won't even notice me," she muttered to herself as she opened the front door.

"Dear lord, look who it is." Suzy stood in the home's cathedral-like entryway and gasped. Barbara stood behind her, a shocked hand brought to her bosom. Sunny froze, her eyes wide. *Now what?* She wondered.

Should I just turn around and run?

"Barbara," Sunny began, trying to project a calm she didn't feel. "I wanted to come by and tell you again how sorry I am for your husband's passing."

Suzy pushed an indignant sound through her botoxed lips, but Sunny ignored her.

"I feel like we've gotten off on the wrong foot," Sunny continued. "And if there is anything I can do to right that path, please let me know."

Barbara glared at her with a glacial stare, and Sunny felt like her insides were turning to ice cubes. Suzy opened her mouth to give Sunny a good old-fashioned telling-off, but Barbara put a hand on her friend's shoulder.

"Let's go," she commanded, and Suzy did as she was told, following Barbara into the depths of the mansion, disappearing into the crowd of people that filled the home. Sunny exhaled, feeling a sense of reprieve, and decided it was safe to step inside the entryway with its vaulted ceiling that must have been two stories tall. She craned her neck to look all the way up, admiring the ornate staircase that unfurled from the second floor down to where she stood. She walked through to the large main living room where the reception guests mingled, drinking glasses of wine and chatting in muted tones. A harpist playing in one corner filled the room with subdued tunes. She leaned in to smell one of the many all-white floral arrangements, inhaling scents of lily and rose.

"These must have cost a fortune," she whispered.

"You made it!" Marian walked over with Rachel.

"Barely," Sunny muttered, primarily to herself.

"What?" Rachel asked, leaning closer to Sunny.

"Nothing," Sunny smiled. "It's good to see you, Rachel. How are the kids?"

"Fine," she said shyly. "Flo is watching them for me. What would I do without her?"

"Tell me about it," Sunny nodded.

Whenever Sunny felt socially awkward—which is to say, every time she entered a party or gathering—she would immediately seek the comfort of the snack table. Unlike the book club meeting's potluck-style smorgasbord of homemade cookies and treats, the food at Jeb's funeral reception was a catered affair served in sterling silver chafing dishes by tuxedoed wait staff. A blank-faced waiter offered Sunny a little something wrapped in puff pastry from a serving tray.

"Is there meat in this?" she asked before taking one.

"Don't know." The waiter gave a bored shrug. "I'm not sure what these are."

"I'll pass, but thank you," Sunny said. She looked around the room.

The clinks of a fork hitting the side of a wine glass sounded through the room, and everyone turned to see Mayor Roger Middleton standing on the seat of a chair.

"If I could have everyone's attention, please," Mayor Middleton addressed the room. He wore a blue linen sports jacket, and his lavender pocket square perfectly matched his purple paisley neck tie. "As mayor of our fine town, I wanted to say a word or two about our good friend, Jeb Landry."

He was about to launch into his speech when the sound of someone clearing their throat loudly interrupted. The mayor looked down from his perch on the chair to see his wife pulling on his jacket sleeve.

"Darling, I think as head of the ladies' committee at Saint Boudreaux's, I should be the one to address our friends here today," she smiled sweetly, but the way she pulled him down from the chair and stepped up to replace him was down right aggressive. "I want to take it upon myself to start this reception with a prayer," she bowed her head, and everyone in the room did the same.

"Dear Lord and Father, please be with the Landry family today as they say goodbye to one of their beloved members. We pray for the repose of Jeb's soul. May he finally find peace in the light of your righteousness. Amen."

The mingling and music resumed. Sunny scratched her head. Why did Mary Kay's prayer sound like a judgment on poor Jeb's life? She rolled her eyes, deciding that everything that woman did sounded judgy. She tapped one of the waitstaff on the shoulder.

"You wouldn't happen to know where the restroom is, would you?"

The waiter pointed to a hallway that led out of the living room. Sunny thanked him. A group of women were waiting in a line outside a closed door, and Sunny made an educated guess that she had found the restroom.

"Bathroom?" She asked and pointed at the door. Everyone standing in the hallway nodded, so she got in line. Sunny didn't recognize the three women in front of her, but she could tell from the way each of them slurred their words that they had already dipped into the reception's chardonnay supply.

"Well, you know, they never did have kids," the woman dressed in a bubblegum pink caftan trimmed at the sleeves with marabou feathers–a rather bold choice for mourning attire, Sunny thought–said in hushed tones.

"I always did wonder about that." Another woman, her brunette hair teased to high heaven and lipstick on her teeth, waggled her eyebrows to imply some sort of scandal.

"Back in the day, she told him she was pregnant, and that's why he had to marry her," the third woman, dressed in a somber black sundress and sensible black heels, retorted. "Come to find out, she lied. She wasn't pregnant at all, and she didn't come clean until after the wedding."

The pink lady gasped. The brunette shook her head in disgust.

"I love Barbara, so I'm not trying to talk bad about her, especially when she's in her bereavement." The black dress woman put a hand to her pearl necklace, an innocent look on her face.

"Never." The pink lady shook her head. "We love her, bless her heart."

"But she trapped Jeb," the woman in black continued. "And everybody knows it."

"Sure do," the brunette nodded. "May he rest in peace." She made the sign of the cross over her chest and did her best to look solemn.

The person holding the restroom hostage finally opened the door and walked out, and for some reason unbeknownst to Sunny, all three women went in together. She stood in the hallway alone, thinking about what she had just heard. *Barbara and Jeb's marriage was built on a lie. What else was there to know about the couple's relationship?*

Once she could finally have the restroom to herself, she used the facilities and returned to the living room, looking to find out more about Jeb and Barbara. In a corner of the room, Earl Hebert, Jeb's best friend, sat alone, a full glass of whiskey in one hand. Sunny moved towards him. If anyone could tell her more about Jeb, it was Earl. As she walked his way, Sunny noticed how sad he looked. His shoulders slumped, making the cheap black suit that he wore wrinkle in odd places, his gaze fixed on the ice in his cut crystal glass.

"Earl?" Sunny asked gently. "I'm Sunny. I just moved to town. Do you mind?" She motioned at the empty chair next to his.

"Go ahead," he nodded without looking up from his drink, and Sunny took the empty seat.

"I don't believe we've met, but I wanted to come tell you how sorry I am for your loss." Sunny looked at him with sympathetic eyes. "I moved into a little house on the lakefront, so I've seen you and Jeb out there fishing most mornings. You must have been good friends."

"Best friends." Earl looked up at her for the first time, and Sunny could see the searing pain that pierced the man's sorrowful green eyes. "Sunny? Are you the lady that opened the bar where Jeb... ..." His words trailed off. "Where it happened."

"I am." Sunny braced herself for his reaction, ready for another onslaught of hateful words to be flung in her direction. Instead, Earl's eyes grew wet.

"I'm just glad he didn't die alone." He looked down to hide his tears. "He didn't say anything before he died, did he? Did he mention anyone? I don't know. Maybe me?"

Sunny shook her head.

"I'm afraid not. He did go peacefully, though, so there's that," she said. "Tell me about Jeb. I didn't know him."

For the next twenty minutes, he told Sunny about his best friend. Earl became a different person as he told her about their childhood growing up together in such a small town, playing football at LouLou High before heading off together to Tulane for college. The despondent man who sat drinking his whiskey alone morphed into someone funny and lively. The more Sunny heard about Jeb, the more her heart ached. Sure, it was sad for her and the Cajun Coconut to be mixed up in someone's death, but it was much more of a tragedy that a man had died. Talking to Earl, Sunny felt that Jeb wasn't just some unknown guy with a heart problem. He was a beloved friend. She must find his killer, not only for her and the tiki bar's sake, but for his friends'. Sunny thanked Earl for talking to her and excused herself to get something to eat and drink.

"Is there anything else to drink besides wine?" Sunny asked the bartender at the open bar, wanting to keep her mind sharp while she looked around the reception for possible clues.

"We've got punch over there." The bartender motioned towards a large silver punch bowl filled with a fluorescent green liquid with clumps of an unidentified substance floating on the surface.

"Um...what is that...stuff...on top?" Sunny tried to hide her disgust.

"It's lime sherbet. It's a Southern tradition," the bartender shrugged. "Don't ask me. I don't drink it. It's an old lady thing."

Sunny eyed the bartender cautiously, wondering if he considered her an *old lady.* She decided not to ask because he definitely did.

"I'll just have some water, then," she nodded.

"Don't got any water." He shook his head. "The kitchen is back that way, though. I'm sure you could get some water over there."

Sunny thanked him–*for nothing,* she thought–and made her way to the back of the house. Passing the crowd in the main living room and through a hallway, she pushed open a set of swinging French doors to find the most glamorous kitchen she had ever seen in person.

"This is like something Martha Stewart would have," she muttered as she traced her fingers along the pristine marble countertops. She stood still for a moment, admiring the dark wood cabinets and the enormous white farm sink. *You know you're in a fancy kitchen when you can't tell where anything is,* Sunny thought. The unsightly functional bits of the kitchen that mere peasants, like herself, were forced to keep in plain sight–the trash can, the refrigerator, the microwave– were hidden away in rich people's kitchens, all neatly concealed behind perfectly placed shaker cabinet doors. She began to open cabinets, looking for a water glass. When she opened the first cabinet door, she stopped, and her heart began to race. Inside, sitting on the shelves, amber-glass bottles of essential oils stood in neat rows. In the center row was a large bottle of grapefruit oil. Sunny picked it up and turned it in her hand. She tilted it from side to side, letting the liquid contents slosh back and forth. The bottle was half empty.

"Excuse me, but can I help you?" The last voice Sunny would ever want to hear in this situation called behind her.

"Barbara," Sunny jumped. "I was just looking for a glass...to um...get some water." She suddenly became acutely aware of the essential oil bottle in her hand and the way Barbara was staring at it. "Oh, this? I was just admiring your essential oils collection." She quickly placed the bottle back in its space on the shelf. "I like to use natural stuff, too. I make all my cleaning supplies. That's something we have in common." She gave a nervous smile.

"That junk?" Barbara rolled her eyes. "I bought those at a party a friend was having. She was selling the stuff, and I felt too guilty to leave without buying anything." She reached into another cabinet and pulled out a drinking glass. "For your water." She narrowed her eyes as she handed it to Sunny, watching her with a hawk-like expression until the water glass was filled and Sunny had returned to the reception room.

Chapter 29

Sunny had never been happier to turn her car onto Moonlight Lane and head home. As she drove back to her cottage, the sunset on the lake had been a treat–ribbony layers of fiery reds and oranges. Now, the night had settled in, and she could see the lights from her home's windows shining like tiny yellow stars in the distance. With the Coconut closed out of respect for Jeb's funeral, all she wanted, for the next several hours at least, was to eat carbs and cheese, get into her pajamas, and watch trashy TV. *Hmmm...*Her face crinkled in thought. *I haven't been to the grocery store in a while. I wonder what I have left to eat...*

When she opened her front door and stepped inside, the spicy smell of peppers and sauteed onions welcomed her. A voice came from the kitchen, and Sunny followed it.

"Hey, Mom!" Danny called. I'm cooking dinner!" He stood at the stove, stirring sliced bell peppers and mushrooms in a sizzling pan, Sunny's pink *Kiss the Chef* apron tied around his waist. Flo stood beside him, grating a block of Monterey Jack cheese into a pile on the countertop.

"Smells amazing!" Sunny leaned towards the pan and took a big sniff. "Whatcha making?"

"Tempeh quesadillas." He smiled as he reached into the pantry for the pack of tortillas. "I told Flo she could come over and eat too, just so long as she brought dessert." He gave a teasing laugh.

"I've never had tempeh before, but there's a first time for everything," Flo nodded, placing the mountain of grated cheese onto a plate. "Luckily, I had just made a fresh coconut cake this afternoon." She dipped her head towards a three-layer cake on a cake stand on the kitchen table.

"Oh, goody, goody, goody!" Sunny clapped her hands in pure glee. "I don't have to cook dinner, *and* I get coconut cake? This day is looking up." She kicked off her shoes in the corner of the room and placed her purse on the floor next to them.

"Wait a minute..." Danny gave her an up-and-down examination with his eyes. A frown formed on his brow. "What are you wearing?" He cocked his head to one side.

"What do you mean?" Sunny looked down at her new dress and then at Danny's confused face. "My dress?" she shrugged.

"I'm not trying to be rude, mom." Danny slid one quesadilla into the hot pan to toast. "But in all my seventeen years, I don't think I've ever seen you dress like that. You look like something out of a J.Crew catalog. You look nice, just...*different*...I guess." He turned his attention to his cooking task.

"He's right." Flo tapped her chin thoughtfully. "And are those heels?" She raised one eyebrow.

"What, guys?" Sunny felt flustered. "It's just a dress, for Pete's sake. Am I not allowed to try new things?" She sat at the table and fidgeted with a hangnail on her pointer finger. The room was quiet. "Did I buy some new clothes in an attempt to fit in more around here? Yes. Is this dress out of the ordinary for me? Okay, yes. Do I feel the need to explain myself further? No." She crossed her arms.

"Hey, we didn't mean anything by it." Flo placed a plate with a golden brown quesadilla in front of her. "We just want to make sure you are doing what's best for you, that's all." Flo sat at the table, her plate in her hands. Not another word was said about Sunny's dress, shoes, polyester shapewear, or the fact that she was wearing lipstick from a drugstore and not her usual beeswax dyed with raspberry extract. Instead, they ate the crispy, cheesy goodness that Danny had prepared, only stopping every few bites to tell him how delicious his dinner was. When they were done, Sunny cleared their plates, and Flo stood to slice her cake.

"You know what?" Sunny put her hands on her hips and paused for thought. "I have a great coconut rum cocktail that would go really well with this cake. Care to imbibe?" She asked Flo.

"Sounds good to me." Flo placed three cake slices on three plates. Sunny gathered everything needed for her cocktail: coconut rum, melon liqueur, pineapple juice, and limes. She poured everything into a cocktail shaker and vigorously rattled it.

"Is it okay if I take my cake to my room?" Danny asked. "My friends are playing World of Witchcraft online in a few, and I wanted to join them."

"I'd say you earned it, kiddo." Sunny handed him a piece of cake and a fork, and he disappeared down the hall.

"Want to take this outside to the porch?" Sunny turned to Flo and held up two cocktail glasses. "I have something I need to talk to you about." She glanced down the hallway, making sure Danny was in his room and out of earshot. Truth be told, Sunny knew that once Danny put on his gaming headphones, she could march around the house playing the tuba, and he wouldn't be able to hear a thing. But she wanted to talk to Flo about Jeb Landry, and she surely didn't want Danny to know anything about that.

The night air was stiflingly hot. Sunny had never lived in such a humid place as Louisiana, and she still marveled at how heat was a constant presence in her life now. Day or night, sunny or cloudy, the humidity wrapped the summer heat around them like a thick, sweaty blanket. *At least the lake looks pretty,* she reasoned as she lowered into one of her rocking chairs and gazed at the moonlit water. Flo sat in the other rocker beside her and placed the cake slices between them on the side table.

"So," Flo took a sip of her cocktail and nodded in approval. "What's up?"

"I wanted to talk about Jeb's funeral." Sunny took a bite of her coconut cake, smiling when the buttery, sweet coconut frosting hit her lips. "Oh, my stars! Flo, this cake is fantastic!" She took another greedy bite.

"I swear your secret ingredient must be witchcraft. No mere mortal could bake like this."

"Psshhhh." Flo brushed off the compliment, but her small, satisfied grin said she enjoyed hearing it. She leaned forward in her chair. "Now, tell me about the funeral."

Sunny told Flo everything, doing her best to remember every detail–the conversation outside the bathroom with the ladies who said Barbara had trapped Jeb into marriage, the way Earl seemed to be the only person close to the deceased who was sad, and most suspicious of all, the grapefruit oil in Barbara's kitchen.

"She was not happy that I found that." Sunny shook her head, scraping the last cake crumbs from her plate with her fork. "You should have seen how she looked at me with that dagger stare of hers." Sunny shivered. "That lady has that if-looks-could-kill thing down to an art."

"You really think Barbara could have killed Jeb?" Flo gazed out at the lake, her eyes squinted in deep thought.

"I do," Sunny nodded vigorously. "Think about it. Who else would know that he couldn't have grapefruit? And it was right there in her kitchen!"

"Okay, but how did she get the grapefruit in his drink? You were at the bar the whole time. Did you see her?"

"Well, no, but..." Sunny's voice trailed off. She didn't have an answer.

"What we need to be asking ourselves is who knew about the fact that Jeb took statins for his heart, a medication that meant he couldn't have anything with grapefruit in it?" Flo drained the last of her cocktail glass.

"His wife, his doctor, his..." Sunny couldn't think of anyone else.

"His best friend?" Flo wondered.

"Earl?" Sunny gasped. "No way. You should have seen him. Jeb's passing completely tore him up."

"Was he faking it, possibly?"

"If he was, he sure fooled me," Sunny shrugged.

"We're forgetting one very obvious person." Flo began to rock her chair, leaning her head back.

"Barbara," Sunny answered immediately.

"Forget the wife for a sec." Flo continued to rock. Her eyes closed as if a secret map that could guide them to the killer was written on the inside of her eyelids. "Someone could have easily put that grapefruit in his drink, and she could have done it right in front of us without anyone knowing."

"Who?" Sunny asked impatiently.

"The mystery woman in the bar with Jeb that night." Flo opened her eyes and stopped rocking. "We don't even know who she is. Is she a girlfriend? Lover? Secret daughter? Heck, for all we know, she could be a trained assassin. We need to find her, and we need to find her soon."

Chapter 30

When Flo said goodnight and went back to the Sweet Pea, Sunny gathered the dirty cake plates and drink glasses and went back inside. She quickly washed the dishes and dried them on a dish towel on the kitchen counter before heading to the living room.

From her comfy armchair, she could hear the faint sound of Danny talking to his gamer friends as they fought monsters with magic...or were they the monsters, and they had the magic? She couldn't remember. Danny had tried to get her to play the game with him once, and while she loved her son dearly, video games would never be her thing. She reached for her book on the side table beside her chair and opened it to the next chapter. After a few minutes of reading, she shut the book. Her distracted mind wouldn't stop going over the details of Jeb's murder, the sadness in his best friend's eyes, and the anger Barbara had shown her when Sunny had found the essential oils in her kitchen cabinet. She rose from her seat and walked down the hall, dipping her head into Danny's room.

"Hey, love. I'm going out for a minute, but I'll be right back," she said. Danny gave her the thumbs up.

On the subject of Jeb Landry, Sunny had some questions that needed answers, and there were a few people she thought might be able to help. It was an unconventional investigation method, but she grabbed her keys and headed to the tiki bar anyway.

When Sunny put the key into the Coconut's front door, she paused before turning the lock. *What am I doing? Am I really going to walk in here and talk to some... what are they anyway? Ghosts? Spirits?...and ask them to help me solve a murder?* Sunny shook her head. She had clearly lost her ever-loving mind. Against her better judgment, she turned the key in the deadbolt and went inside.

The bar was dark and quiet. Sunny went around the room, flicking on the lava lamps and tiki lanterns, giving the room a rainbow glow in shades of red, green, and blue. She stood in the center of the room and put her hands on her hips. *How do I do this?* She wondered silently. She had never summoned tiki spirits before, and the only time she had spoken with her new enchanted friends, *they* had done the summoning, not her.

"Hello?" She called out, feeling very foolish in the empty room. "Um, guys? Hello?" She waited for a response. Nothing. "Cook? Cora? Pearl?" The room was still. Had she felt a whisper of a tropical breeze? She stood for several moments, anticipating. When nothing happened, she walked to the door, shoulders slumped.

"Well, I feel like an idiot," she sighed as she reached for the doorknob. As she twisted it in her hand and opened the door, a familiar breeze hit her on the back of the neck. The scent of salt air and sunscreen tickled her nose. She spun around.

"Sunflower, you need us! Come," Cook, his eyes once again two swirling oceans, his wooden features softened and lively, called to her. The room twittered with the chatter from the tiki spirits. Sunny smiled.

"You know, um, I actually prefer Sunny, but…" She waved a hand in the air. "You know what? Don't worry about it."

"You prefer Sunny over Sunflower?" Barry, the parrot pirate, asked from his ceiling perch. "I would stick with Sunflower if I were you."

"I agree completely," Vin squawked from his hanging bamboo perch, his blue feathered wings flapping excitedly. "It's got real pizzazz."

"Never mind," Sunny blushed. "That's not why I called on you guys." She pulled one of the peacock chairs closer to Cook.

"Your face looks troubled," Cook remarked.

"Oh, dear!" Pearl worried. "You aren't sick, are you? Or hurt? Or sad? What can we do to help you, sweetie?"

"It's not about me," Sunny began to explain. "Well, it is, but it isn't."

"Ugh, humans," If Cora had the ability to roll her driftwood eyes in annoyance, she would have. "They never make any sense. Spit it out already."

"Now, Cora, dear, that's not very nice." Pearl's words maintained their usual honey sweetness, but her tone had a touch of vinegar. "We are here to help our Sunny."

Cora gave a low, muted grumble but said nothing else.

"Sunflower–" Cook paused. "Sunny, please go on."

"It's about the man that died here at the bar." Sunny shifted uncomfortably in her seat. "What can you tell me about that night? I feel like there are clues that could help me solve his murder that are right here in front of my face, and I just don't know what those clues are." She rubbed the tension in her temples.

"We remember the night he died," Cook said sadly, the swirl of his eyes shifting from blue to green.

"Awful, it was," Vin squawked.

"Just terrible," Barry agreed.

"Sinful." Pearl's voice was weepy.

"Boring," Cora sighed.

"Cora, now really!" Pearl gasped.

"Well, it was," Cora quipped. "These humans live for such a short time. Compared to us nature spirits, they are the equivalent of mosquitos."

"Cora, you take that back!" Pearl yelled.

"Enough!" Cook boomed, and the room quieted. He turned his attention to Sunny. "We saw who murdered the man that night."

"You did?" Sunny sat upright in her chair. "This changes everything! Who was it?" Her heart began to race.

"We don't know," Pearl's voice said sadly.

"What do you mean?" Sunny's voice grew agitated. "What did they look like? Was it a man? A woman?"

"The night the man died, you went to the back

room to organize the rum. The man went out to the front patio to smoke a cigarette," Cook explained. "When you were out of the room, someone snuck through the bar's side entrance."

"The one that leads to the back alley?" Sunny puzzled.

"Yes," Cook said patiently. "Whoever they were, they were clever. They covered themselves from head to toe—black hat, black face mask, and a large black coat. With their disguise, not only could we not see their face, but we could not tell if they were a man or woman. The person slipped into the bar, sprinkled something into the man's drink, and slipped out again before you or the man returned."

"The grapefruit oil." Sunny sat back in her chair, her mind buzzing. "Someone snuck in and put the grapefruit oil in his drink." Up until now, Sunny had been working on blind faith in her assertion that Jeb was murdered. Not even the police chief believed her when she told him that Jeb's death was suspicious. Now, here it was–complete confirmation that she was dealing with a murder case. If only the word of a three-hundred-year-old tiki spirit would hold up in court.

"I have another question to ask you." Sunny snapped out of her swirling thoughts. "The woman that came in with the man–do you know anything about her? What were they fighting about? I couldn't hear anything they said from the bar across the room."

"Their conversation was very cryptic," Cora spoke in a cool, silvery tone. Sunny smirked. *Guess humans aren't as dull as you thought then, Miss Water Spirit.* Cora continued, unaware of Sunny's amusement. "She kept telling him that he had to come clean. He was living a lie, and it was time to tell the truth."

"Time to tell the truth...I wonder what that means," Sunny frowned. "Did they talk about anything else?"

The lights in the room flickered. The gentle tropical breeze strengthened several knots, pushing Sunny's chair back in one powerful gust.

"Our time wanes, Sunflower," Cook called to her, his voice growing distant and hollow. "We must leave you for now. Please remember what we have told you before: that danger lurks in this town. You are not safe..." His last words faded, and his face stiffened into a wood carving once more.

Chapter 31

The following day, Sunny sat at the foot of her bed, out of breath from the effort it took to pull her legs through her new shiny pink spandex leggings. She had a lot of competing thoughts running through her mind. She agreed with Flo that the mystery woman at the bar with Jeb that night needed to be questioned, and she had to admit that several people could have known about Jeb's medication. But despite all the evidence to the contrary, she couldn't stop thinking about Barbara. After talking to the tikis the night before, she decided not to give up on Zumba even though her dancing skills left much to be desired. Not only would taking the exercise class help her waistline and cholesterol levels and maybe even help her make a new friend or two, but going to Zumba would also give her access to Jeb's widow.

"Let's go over the agenda for the day," Sunny muttered to herself. "Go to class, make an idiot of myself as I attempt to keep up with the dance moves, and then casually ask a woman if she murdered her husband." She examined her fitness look, having paired the bright pink leggings with a neon green polo top made out of some slippery synthetic material that Sunny couldn't identify, and the overall effect was something to behold.

"What the heck are you wearing?" Sunny turned around to find Danny standing in her bedroom doorway, his mouth agog.

"We've been over this, *dear.*" She tried to keep her voice light, but it wasn't easy. "Just doing my part to blend in." Sunny turned towards her full-length mirror again and gave her outfit another glance.

"I'm sorry, mom. I love you, but I've got to be honest." Danny shook his head. "You look like a 1980s Workout Barbie!"

"I am choosing to take that as a compliment." Sunny raised her head high and walked past him to the living room. She laced up her sneakers and headed out the door.

Sunny pulled her Miata into the last empty parking space at the Community Center and ran up the front steps into the center's large main lobby.

"Late as usual," she mumbled as she hurried to the room where the class was held. Just as she reached the doorknob, she heard her name.

"Sunny?"

She turned around to see Police Chief Tony Perez standing in front of her, his face flushed from exercise and his lips smiling.

"Chief, hi," Sunny said, suddenly very self-conscious of her fitness ensemble.

"I told you. It's Tony," he said. Sunny almost couldn't hear him as she stared, in the grips of admiring how great he looked in his grey sweats. "What are you up to? Besides teaching Ken and Skipper how to do step aerobics." He chuckled.

"Hey!" Sunny swatted at him playfully. "I like my outfit, thank you very much. The 80s are in again."

"My bad." He laughed. "I'm not as down with the kids as you are." He gave her a wink. "Actually, I'm glad I ran into you. I wanted to ask you something."

"Is it about Jeb? Did you find some new information?" Sunny asked anxiously.

"What? Jeb? No." Tony's face registered mild surprise. "I wanted to ask if you wanted to go..." His phone rang, and he reached into his pocket. "Police Chief Perez?" His face grew serious as he listened to the caller on the other line. He put his hand over the receiver and whispered to Sunny, "I've got to take this. Can I call you later?"

She nodded, and he walked away.

The Zumba class went as expected. Sunny struggled to dip and bend at the correct times, and she always seemed to clap her hands thirty seconds later than everyone else. Even so, she had to admit that dancing was fun, and the upbeat music lifted her mood. When the class ended, she collapsed onto the floor, out of breath and completely exhausted. She chugged from her water bottle until it was almost empty. Mopping the sweat from her forehead, she needed to wait for the people in class to leave so that she could get Barbara alone. She piddled around to kill time–pretending to rummage through her gym bag for some item or another, drinking water, bending her legs into a stretch, checking her phone for any missed messages. When it was finally just her and Barbara in the room, Sunny saw her chance.

"Great class, Barbara!" Sunny said as she approached where the woman stood by the long row of mirrors that covered the length of one wall. "I really enjoyed it."

Barbara said nothing, responding to Sunny with only a quick nod and a forced smile. *Someone still blames me for what happened. Or does she?* Sunny had been up all night thinking about this. Barbara had blamed Sunny for Jeb's death from the word *go,* even when the Cajun Coconut was cleared of all wrongdoing. Sunny had taken this cold shoulder as the irrational actions of a grieving widow, but now she suspected that was what Barbara wanted her to think. With the anger and accountability placed solely on Sunny and her tiki drinks, Barbara kept anyone from suspecting her. Who would question the poor grieving wife whose husband was poisoned in a bar run by a new person in town that nobody knew or trusted? Sunny steeled her nerves.

"Um, Barbara? Wait a sec," Sunny called to her as Barbara made her way to the classroom door.

"Yes?" Barbara rolled her eyes in annoyance and turned to Sunny.

"I have some questions I need to ask you," Sunny stuttered, losing her confidence now that they were standing face to face. Barbara crossed her arms in front of her chest and waited. Sunny took that as permission to continue.

"Um," Sunny stammered. "Do you remember the opening night of my bar?"

"Are you asking if I remember the night my husband died?" Barbara looked incredulous. "What do you think?" She raised one perfectly plucked brow.

"Right, stupid question," Sunny blushed. "Well, do you remember what you were doing that night? Say from eight until about eleven or so?"

"What?" Barbara's usually bronzed complexion drained to white. "Why would you ask me that? And why would it be any of your business?" She turned to walk away without giving Sunny any answers.

"You heard me." Sunny summoned all of her remaining conviction. "Where were you the night Jeb was killed?" She put on her toughest-looking facial expression and glared.

"What do you mean *the night Jeb was killed*?" Barbara spat out the words breathlessly. "He wasn't killed. He died from drinking that cocktail you made him. The idiot knew he wasn't supposed to have grapefruit, and he still gulped whatever concoction you made down his gullet." Her neck began to flush in red blotches.

"I didn't put grapefruit in his drink. Someone else snuck in and tainted his cup with it, and I think that person was you." Sunny stood a little taller.

"Me?" Barbara put a hand to her chest like Sunny had just shot a bullet through her heart. "You think I snuck into your little bar and..." And then her face did something strange. All the anger, hurt, and hatred morphed into something else–cruel laughter exploded from her mouth and rang through the empty classroom.

"I'm serious." Sunny grew flustered. "I know you have grapefruit oil. I saw it in your kitchen. You killed your husband!" She was shouting now. Barbara's laughter stopped, and her face grew stony and serious.

"Prove it," she said cooly as she turned away and walked out of the room.

"I think I will," Sunny said out loud, her fists clenched. "I think I will." She gathered up her things and headed down the hallway. Halfway to the main lobby, the hall split in two directions–left to the main entrance and right to the staff break room. Sunny looked around her to see if anyone was watching before taking a right.

Standing in the doorway of the staff room, she scanned the space. There was a lumpy old floral sofa against one wall, a table against another with a coffee maker, random packets of coffee creamer and sweeteners, and a pile of various exercise equipment in one corner. The room was empty, so Sunny stepped inside. What was she looking for? She didn't know yet, but maybe something here would lead her closer to convicting Jeb's wife. She stopped, her eyes laser-focused on the wall opposite her.

Bingo. On the wall hung the staff calendar. Sunny moved quickly, unsure if someone would be walking into the room at any second. The calendar featured a spreadsheet for every day of the month, listing all classes taught and who was teaching them. She flipped the pages back to the date of Jeb's death and scanned the classes and names. Finally, she found what she had hoped to see - Zumba - 8:30 pm to 9:30 pm, teacher Josie, subbing for Barbara.

Old Barb was supposed to teach that night, but she had the night off. Her whereabouts are unaccounted for. Sunny's heart gave a leap. A real clue, or at least the start of one. She heard footsteps from down the hall and froze.

"What are you doing in here?" A man in yoga clothes gave her a suspicious look.

"Just looking for the, um, restroom." Sunny pushed past him quickly. "Took a wrong turn, I guess. Sorry!" She ran out and didn't stop until she reached her car.

Chapter 32

"So, you just walked up to Barbara and told her that you think she murdered her husband?" Flo's face was screwed up halfway between laughing and crying.

"Sort of," Sunny winced. "I didn't mean for it to go that way, but things sort of escalated." She shook the cocktail shaker high over her left shoulder for several seconds before straining her newest cocktail creation, The Pineapple Princess, into two tiki mugs and garnishing them with pineapple spears and fresh orchid flowers. She handed one glass to Flo and took a sip from the other. It had been a slow but steady night at the Cajun Coconut with a consistent flow of customers to serve. By midnight, Sunny was glad to unplug the electric sign in the front window and take a load off her tired feet.

"Honestly, I'm surprised you lived to tell the

tale." Flo shook her head. "That woman scares me."

"There's more." Sunny told Flo about the staff calendar and Barbara's absence from teaching Zumba that night. She took a deep sip from her drink and waited for Flo's response.

"Does that prove anything, though?" Flo decided to play devil's advocate for a moment. "Okay, she wasn't in class, but that doesn't mean she was off killing her husband instead." She shrugged. "Barbara could have been anywhere–shopping at the mall, at the movies. Heck, I don't know, maybe even having an affair. Who's to say?"

Sunny scrunched up her face and slumped back onto one of the barstools. She knew Flo was right. She would simply have to keep digging deeper before she struck sleuthing gold.

"Do me a favor. Let's put a pin in Barbara for a second," Flo suggested.

"Actually, I'd love to." Sunny gave a devilish smirk.

"I mean metaphorically." Flo cut her eyes at Sunny reproachfully. "Let's turn our focus towards the mystery woman at the bar that night. Any thoughts?"

Sunny paused. She did have news to share with Flo about the woman at the bar, but if she shared that information with her, would Flo want to know where she heard it from? How could she look her only friend in town in the eyes and say that the tiki decor on the walls around them was haunted by spirits that talked to her when no one was around, and those tiki spirits told her what the mystery woman said to Jeb?

"I don't know who that woman was, but I think she was here to urge Jeb to come clean about something he had been hiding, a secret he needed to be honest about." Sunny looked down into her drink and slurped on her straw.

"Really?" Flo cocked her head to one side. "How do you know that?"

"Just a hunch." Sunny jumped up and busied herself, wiping down the bartop with a clean rag, so she wouldn't have to make eye contact with Flo.

"That is a very specific hunch." Flo eyed her curiously.

"Anywho..." Sunny did her best to seem unbothered. "How are we going to find this lady? I've never seen her around town since that night. Have you?"

Flo shook her head in the negative.

"Oh!" Sunny stuck one index finger into the air. "I almost forgot." She reached under the bar and pulled out a square Tupperware container. "I packed the last two slices of the coconut cake you made yesterday as a little closing-time treat." She quickly grabbed two plates and two forks, divvying up the cake and passing one plate to Flo. "This cake is the best thing I've ever eaten!" She stuffed another heaping forkful in her mouth.

Flo gave a proud smile and shifted in her seat, always a little uncomfortable receiving a compliment.

"Seriously, you should make more cakes and sell them here at the bar." Sunny pressed a finger onto her plate's last cake crumbs and ate them before setting her dirty dish into the sink behind her.

"That's not a bad idea," Flo agreed. The next twenty minutes were spent closing down the bar, cleaning the tabletops and dishes, sweeping the floor, and dusting the tiki decor. While they worked, Flo and

Sunny chatted and shared stories about their lives–stories of the good times and also the bad ones. As Sunny watched Flo mop the floor, she realized what a good friend and kindred spirit she had met in this crazy little town in Louisiana that she moved to by chance. Whatever happened with the other people in town, whether they came to accept her as one of their own or continued to shun her and her weird West Coast ways, she knew that she could always count on Flo, and the thought warmed her heart.

The following day, Sunny rummaged through her kitchen pantry, and it registered in her mind that she hadn't been to the Hop for groceries in quite a while. Danny had eaten the last of her homemade granola before school, so her breakfast options were a dusty can of cannellini beans or a stale box of whole wheat crackers.

"Gary's Diner it is," she decided, and went to her room to get dressed. She threw her purple cotton nightgown over her bedside chair, and it landed atop her growing procrasti-pile–all of the clothing not dirty enough for the laundry hamper but not clean enough to hang back in her closet. She went to the corner of her room where a tall pile of boxes from online clothing stores was stacked and rummaged through them until she found what she was looking for—a new pair of jeans. After her hippie childhood, followed by living in medical scrubs for most of her adult years, jeans felt like an act of rebellion, and she practically cooed as she slipped her legs into the dark denim. She grunted a little as she pulled the pants up to her hips and had to lay back on the bed to get the fly to zip–*ugh, thanks, menopause*–but once the zipper was secured, she stood in front of the mirror and admired her reflection. She paired her new jeans with a pink polo shirt with a ruffled collar and a pearl necklace. Okay, it wasn't exactly her style, but she decided that preppy was a look she could pull off. She grabbed her car keys and headed to town.

Gary's Diner was one of only two restaurants in LouLou. This might feel boring or limited in any other small town, but given that the food mecca of New Orleans was just a quick forty-five-minute drive across Lake Pontchartrain, it didn't bother townspeople much. It helped that Gary's was some of the best eating anywhere–lots of butter, sugar, and salt served in heaping portions on heavy plates. Sunny could almost taste the sweet potato pancakes flecked with chopped pecans and drowned in Steen's–a Louisiana cane syrup that beat the pants off of the maple stuff any day.

When she swung open the diner's double glass doors, the smell of bacon and dark roast coffee welcomed her in. The place was hopping, and Debbie, Donna, and Claudine, the triplet sisters who owned and operated the restaurant, were rushing around the room, refilling coffee cups and chatting with their customers.

"Take a seat anywhere you like, hun," Donna shouted, and Sunny nodded before slipping into an empty booth in the front corner by the restaurant's large picture window that overlooked the square. She waited patiently until one of the sisters came over for her order–sweet potato pancakes and the largest coffee possible.

"Thanks, Claudine," Sunny smiled, handing the waitress her menu.

"It's Donna, sug." The waitress winked and patted her teased brunette bouffant hairdo.

"Sorry!" Sunny cringed. She had been to the diner several times and still couldn't tell the sisters apart. They each wore the same red t-shirts with Gary's Diner printed on the back in large blue letters, the same blue and white gingham ruffled aprons, the same white sneakers, and the identical brunette beehive hairstyles teased to the ceiling, seemingly defying the laws of gravity. While Sunny waited for her food to arrive, she walked over to the diner's bar–a 1950s-style lunch counter with a Formica table top edged in chrome.

"May I?" She asked a man sitting at the bar, pointing to the daily newspaper. He nodded, and she took the paper back to her seat. The week Jeb died had been an unprecedentedly eventful time to be a journalist in LouLou. Now that the news of his death was stale, it was back to business as usual for local reporters–writing stories about high school sports, local ladies sending in their famous shrimp remoulade recipe, or letters to the editor complaining about potholes in the town streets. The front page headline was about the high school football team's devastating loss in the big game the night before. Sunny scanned the story with disinterested eyes. She would never understand Southerners and their next-level obsession with that barbaric sport.

"Here we are, honey bun." One of the triplets set down a towering stack of fluffy pancakes, the weighty plate making a small thud as it hit the table. "Can I get you anything else?"

"That's all I need, Debbie. Thank you so much. This looks delicious." Sunny leaned forward to deeply inhale the cinnamon and sugar aromas.

"It's Claudine, dear," the waitress corrected her. "I see you're reading about the game last night." She shook her head in dismay. "It sure was awful. I've never seen the boys play that bad."

"Was the other team really good?" Sunny asked, not caring one bit about the game but wanting to seem friendly.

"No, not at all," Claudine chuffed. "Our team's been really off ever since Jeb died. The new guy isn't half the coach Jeb was."

"That's right." It dawned on Sunny that the triplets might be able to give her more insight into Jeb's life. "I forgot that he was the high school football coach."

"And basketball…and baseball…and soccer…" Claudine went on. "He's going to be missed at the high school, that's for sure."

"Is the school doing anything for him? Like maybe a memorial or something like that?" Sunny asked.

"The football team got together and collected money from their classmates to donate to his widow, Barbara. They presented it to her on one of those big cardboard checks at last night's game. You know, like the ones you see on TV when someone's won the lottery?" She blew air through her pursed lips and rolled her eyes. "Not like she deserves it."

"What do you mean?" Sunny's ears pricked up like little radars.

"I'm not trying to talk ugly about anybody." Claudine looked over her shoulder at the plates piling up at the kitchen window, ready to go out to waiting diners. She turned back to Sunny and talked quickly. "That was one couple that should have never married. She always pretended everything was perfect, but everybody knew that Jeb was having..." She looked around to see if anyone else was listening. "An *affair.*" She mouthed the last word silently.

"Claudine, where y'at?" Debbie yelled from across the room. "You gonna help serve breakfast or let me do all the work?"

"Hold your horses!" Claudine snapped back, giving Sunny a knowing look before heading back to work.

Sunny dug into her pancakes, her mind turning over what Claudine had said. If Jeb was having an affair, this changed everything. Infidelity meant there were new lines of inquiry to follow, new motives, and new suspects. Now, all she needed to discover was who Jeb was having an affair with–the mystery lady that was with him in the bar that awful nigh, perhaps? It takes two to tango, and whoever the lady was, she needed to be questioned ASAP.

A tapping sound came from the window, and Sunny looked up from her plate. Police Chief Tony Perez was standing on the sidewalk waving at her with a wide grin on his face. Sunny's heart skipped a beat, and she hated herself for it. As Tony rounded the corner and walked through the diner's front door, Sunny did her best to covertly wipe the cane syrup from the corners of her mouth and the pancake crumbs from the front of her shirt.

"Hey there!" Tony beamed. "This seat taken?" He pointed to the other side of Sunny's booth.

"Yep," Sunny nodded. "By you." She motioned for him to sit, and he happily slid onto the bench opposite her.

"Two times in a week. How'd I get so lucky?" He took a pair of reading glasses from his front pocket and put them on to read the menu. Sunny silently wondered if he looked cuter in his reading glasses or the sweats he had worn to the gym the other day, annoyed with herself for harboring a schoolgirl infatuation at her age. If someone had told twenty-year-old Sunny that she would still be crushing on guys at the age of fifty-five instead of being a sultry, sophisticated woman lucky in love, twenty-year-old Sunny would have been deeply disappointed. As it turned out, the world of romance hadn't always come easily to Sunny, and here she was, a little older than she wanted to be and still *on the market,* as her mother would say.

"The pancakes here are fantastic," Sunny said, shyly raising her eyes to meet his. "And the coffee... to die for!" She winced at her use of that unfortunate phrase. "Ugh, I'm sorry. That's probably an insensitive thing to say given the circumstances."

"What circumstances?" Tony looked confused.

"You know...Jeb," Sunny explained. "Most of my conversations with you have been about what happened at the Cajun Coconut that night, so I thought maybe what I said was a little tacky."

"You had nothing to do with Jeb's death." He

leaned forward and put his hand on hers. A shock of electricity zipped through her arm. "It was an accident. Plain and simple." He took a fork and stole a rogue pecan from her plate. She shot him a playful look of admonishment.

"About that," Sunny hated ruining what felt like the start of a nice moment, but she needed to talk seriously with the Police Chief, and she wasn't sure how he would take it. "I need to talk to you about something."

"Okay." His face changed from cheerful to more solemn. Just as Sunny began to speak again, Claudine came over and took Tony's order. When she walked away, Sunny cleared her throat.

"I think that Jeb was..." She cleared her throat again and restarted her sentence. "I *know* that Jeb was murdered." She braced herself for his response.

"And you know this...how?" He looked up as Claudine set down a mug of coffee and a small silver pitcher of cream. He picked up the pitcher and poured a splash into his coffee. The only sound between them was his spoon clinking on the ceramic mug as he stirred his cup. Sunny examined his face, unsure if he was angry, annoyed, amused...

"I know this because the drink I served him that night contained no grapefruit." She tried to sound confident. *And I know this because tiki ghosts told me about how he died.* "Someone snuck in and put grapefruit oil in his drink, knowing he couldn't have it because of his medication. I've been asking questions around town, and I know Jeb and Barbara's marriage wasn't happy. Did you know that he was probably having an affair?"

"Wait, what do you mean you've been asking questions around town?" Tony's jaw clenched slightly.

"Oh, just a few questions here and there. That's not the point. The point is…"

"The point is you are going to get yourself in trouble stirring things up around here," he interrupted. "Look, maybe Jeb was murdered. Maybe. If you really think the grapefruit couldn't come from the cocktail you made him, I will get my guys to look into it. But the investigation needs to come from *me* and not *you.*"

Sunny crossed her arms and sat back in the booth, deciding there was no point in arguing with him further. There wasn't a snowball's chance in Hell that she would stop her investigation, and she had accomplished what she needed for now–the police chief had agreed to look further into the circumstances around Jeb's death. She took a big bite of pancakes and hoped Tony would change the subject. Fortunately, he did.

"You planning on going to the Labor Day picnic next week?" he asked before taking a sip of coffee.

"I'm not sure," Sunny shrugged. "If I'm being honest, I had hoped that LouLou would feel more like home by now, and well…"

"It isn't?" His food had arrived, and Tony sliced a sausage link in half before eating it.

"No." Sunny's face drooped. "Don't get me wrong. I like it here. I like my house. I like the bar. I like that my kid is making friends and enjoying himself. But here it is, a few months since I've moved here, and other than Flo, I can't say that I feel like I fit in with people in town."

Tony ate silently for a moment, studying her as he shoveled scrambled eggs and a biscuit with sausage gravy into his mouth.

"You forget," He wiped his face with his napkin. "I'm an outsider too. It gets better. Promise." He looked at her with warm eyes. "Come to the picnic. It will be fun. Besides, you are wrong about one thing."

Sunny gave him a questioning look.

"You've got two friends." He held up two fingers. "Flo...and me."

"Thanks." Sunny's cheeks were hot.

"So tell me you'll come to the picnic. It's a town tradition," he insisted.

Sunny said she would think about it and motioned for one of the sisters...*Claudine? No, Debbie? Donna? Oh, shoot...*to bring her the check. After she had paid, she turned to Tony and smiled.

"This has been nice," she said, raising her purse strap over her shoulder.

"We should do it again sometime." Tony's eyes twinkled. "I'll call you."

Sunny nodded, her face grinning like the cat that got the cream. She practically skipped from the diner to her parked car. She drove home, giggling over the prospect of a date with the police chief in one breath, chastising herself for being silly in the other. Should she start dating again? Would she even remember how? Danny was hardly a little kid anymore, but was he ready to see her with a boyfriend? Was she ready to have a boyfriend? She had spent the last seventeen years single, and she liked the freedom she had to do what she wanted when she wanted. There was no denying the loneliness, though. She turned her car down Moonlight Lane and towards home.

Chapter 33

In the week that followed, Flo and Danny had not only convinced Sunny to attend the LouLou Labor Day Picnic but also persuaded her to show up as her genuine self–no preppy clothing, country-club-lady hair, thick makeup, pearls, or high heels.

The day of the picnic was sunny and hot, and Sunny stood nervously in front of her closet, fingering the flax linen dresses she had shoved to the back to make room for her new LouLou outfits. She selected a turquoise linen maxi dress with purple embroidered flowers and her trusty pair of Birkenstock sandals. She let her hair hang loose and wavy, dabbing a little patchouli oil on her neck and wrists. She had wanted to bring something safe to the potluck, like maybe a seven-layer bean dip and tortilla chips or some other dish the townspeople were familiar with. Still, Danny had reassured her that her famous tofu and taleggio cheese casserole would be a big hit. Once dressed, she went to the kitchen and wrapped the warm baking dish in a tea towel.

"Danny?" She stuck her head out from the kitchen doorway and called down the hall. "You ready?" She waited for her son to slip his feet into sneakers, and they were off to the picnic.

With Danny sitting in the passenger seat of her tiny Miata, the casserole dish sitting on his lap, and his long legs scrunched up to the dashboard...*I should think about getting a bigger car...*they headed first to the marina to pick up Flo.

"Are you sure I should bring this to the potluck?" She turned to face the backseat where Flo was sitting. "I don't think half the people in town even know what vegetarian food is."

"This is a big step," Flo said in support. "You are going to go out there and be yourself."

"Easy for you to say," Sunny sulked as she pulled the car onto the square. "When you be yourself, you show up with a caramel cake so good it would make Oprah cry. When I show up as myself, well..." She eyed the casserole dish doubtfully and let out a resigned sigh.

The LouLou Labor Day Picnic was held every year on the green lawn surrounding the library. Today, folding tables and chairs were scattered around the grass, and a long table was set to one side for the food. The library's front porch was converted into a makeshift stage, and a local Zydeco band was setting up to perform. Brightly colored balloons were strung up around the lawn, and an enormous "Welcome" banner hung from the library's second-story windows.

When Sunny first stepped from her car, a pleasant breeze caressed her face, carrying the sweet scent of the blooming jasmine vines that seemed to grow on every building in town in late summer. She took a deep breath, willing her nerves to calm down. She would walk over to the potluck table. She would place her dish next to the other casseroles, dips, and salads. She would smile and act natural, like she belonged here. *I can do this.* She murmured through gritted teeth.

"Coming?" Flo asked. Sunny nodded, and they all walked to the picnic together.

When they reached the town green, Flo and Danny dispersed, waving to people they knew and walking over to socialize, leaving Sunny standing awkwardly on the lawn, her casserole dish in hand.

"Let me help you with that," Marian patted Sunny on the shoulder, smiling warmly as she took the dish from Sunny's hands and placed it on the already-full food table. "Smells good. What is it?"

"My tofu and taleggio casserole," Sunny blushed. "I hope everyone likes it. It's probably not what people are used to."

"Can't wait to try it," Marian said, although Sunny noticed that when the librarian grabbed a plate and began to fill it up, she avoided the tofu. "I've been meaning to stop by your bar, but the girl that does the night shift at the library keeps calling in sick. I will get to you one of these days here soon." She continued to heap scoops of chicken and rice casserole, jambalaya, and boiled shrimp onto her plate. Sunny grabbed a plate and followed behind her, hoping Marian didn't notice her carefully inspecting the dishes before deciding what to eat. In Louisiana, most vegetable dishes were cooked with enough pork products that they almost could be considered more meat than veggie. She loved the smoky scent that a ham hock gave Flo's collard greens, but Sunny could never eat pork. She had raised a few pigs on her parents' farm as a kid, and they were the kindest, sweetest, smartest animals she ever knew.

"I would love for you to come to the Coconut," Sunny enthused. "Come any night you want, and I will make something special just for you."

"I definitely will." Marian walked over to one of the tables and sat down. Sunny accompanied her and sat in one of the folding chairs, its legs sinking into the thick, damp grass as she did.

"Marian?" A woman called, walking over to them with a clipboard in her hand and a harried expression on her face. "I told the face painters that they could set up in that corner over there, but they are setting up where the kid's craft table goes instead. Will you come talk to them?"

Marian nodded and rose from her seat, walking away with the stressed-out woman and leaving Sunny alone at the table. She liked the librarian a lot and thought they could be good friends if Marian ever slowed down enough to have a cup of coffee or a tiki drink, but she always seemed to be too busy to spend any time with Sunny. *Is she too busy, or does she simply not want to hang out with me?* Sunny wasn't sure. She pushed the insecure thoughts out of her mind because there were bigger crawfish to boil at the moment.

The night before, as she lay awake, staring at the bedroom ceiling and dreading today, it had occurred to her that the picnic was the perfect place to investigate. When else would the entire town be gathered together in one spot? She picked up her fork and scooped up a bite of a dish labeled *Hopping John*.

It looked vegetarian-friendly—black-eyed peas, rice, celery, onion, and spices. She put a forkful in her mouth. *Nope...* What she had assumed was red bell pepper was definitely sausage. She sighed and gave up on eating for the moment.

Instead, she turned her attention to the picnic-goers. The library's lawn was full of people eating and drinking, and kids running around laughing and playing. Sunny scanned the crowd. Who was she looking for? What was she hoping to see? She didn't have exact answers to those questions just yet, but what she did know was that Jeb Landry was having an affair. More than likely, his ex-lover was here at the picnic. How would she find them?

"Look who it is."

Sunny practically jumped out of her skin when a voice sounded behind her. She whipped around to see her rival bar owner, Buzz, standing there, his plate piled high with a rack of ribs, a smirk on his barbecue-sauce-stained mouth.

"Yes?" Sunny said snootily. There was no point in hiding her disdain for the man.

"Just thought I would come over and say hello," Buzz sneered. "Seems like your little tiki bar is doing alright. Not as good as my bar, but then again, my bar gives the customer what they actually want–cold beer, big TVs–not some namby-pamby fruity drinks." He bent one hand at the wrist the way *macho bros* did to make fun of all things feminine. Sunny rolled her eyes and turned back towards the table, focusing her attention on her plate. When Buzz laughed and walked away,

Sunny breathed a sigh of relief that he had taken the hint to get lost.

She rose from her seat and went looking for Flo. *Where had that lady gone off to?* She walked amongst the tables, spying Danny as he sat with the friends from school he had been hanging out with lately. She smiled to herself, glad things were going in a better direction for him.

"Well, hello there, Sunflower!" The honeyed drawl of Julia Donahue reached Sunny's ears, and through a parting in the crowd emerged the Southern belle herself. Julia stretched out her jewelry-clad arms to embrace Sunny in a hug. When she had Sunny close, she gave a small sniff. "What is that alluring perfume you are wearing, honey? It smells like...dirt or grass or something." Julia pulled away, her nose scrunched up in disgust.

"Oh, my patchouli oil," Sunny said. "You can take the girl out of California, but..." She shrugged.

"Interesting," Julia smiled and nodded. "Is that what we have going on here?" She waved one hand, motioning to Sunny's dress and shoes. "I always thought California was for surfer girls, not...*this.*" She smiled sweetly.

"What do you mean?" Sunny inwardly cringed.

"It's just that this is a very different look from what you've been wearing here lately," Julia explained coolly. "Very woman-of-the-woods, very earthy."

Sunny smiled. It was always hard to tell whether Julia Donahue loved or hated you. Her comments had a way of sounding like compliments but feeling like insults. When Sunny offered nothing by way of explanation, Julia changed the subject. "I heard about you looking into the *you know what.*" She whispered the last words, narrowing her eyes and tapping the side of her nose with one finger.

"How do you know about that?" Sunny panted, panic rising in her throat. The last person she wanted to know about her murder investigation was gossipy Julia Donahue.

"I hear things," Julia said casually. "But it's not me that you have to worry about, honey. It's Suzy." She turned her head and directed her gaze to where Suzy and Barabara were holding court, surrounded by all the women who were too cool to talk to Sunny at book club meetings. Sunny stared at them and their perfect golden bronzer, expertly-applied lipstick, their enviable ability to fit in. Julia's words shook her out of her thoughts.

"What do you mean I should be worried about Suzy?" Sunny cocked her head to the side. "It's Barbara that I've gone after. Not that I think anyone will believe me."

"You should most definitely be scared of Suzy, sweetie, because Suzy has spent the majority of her lifetime being utterly devoted to old Barb over there." Julia drew closer to Sunny and whispered. "Ever since our school days, Suzy has been Barbara's sidekick. When they were on the cheerleading squad, Barbara was captain. Suzy was co-captain. When Barbara was the lead in the school play, Suzy was her understudy. Barbara was valedictorian. Suzy was salutatorian. When Barbara was..." She stopped and put a hand on Sunny's arm. "Well, you get the picture."

"Wouldn't that make Suzy jealous? Always playing second fiddle?"

"If she was envious of Barbara, she never let it show on the surface," Julia shrugged. "From what I could see, it seems that Suzy has grown more devoted to the woman with each passing year. She would do anything for Barbara. Heck, she might even kill for her." Julia froze, suddenly very obviously self-conscious of what she let slip out. "I'm not saying that she has." Her eyes grew big.

"I'm sure you were just using a turn of phrase," Sunny said, backing away and turning her face one way and then the other to look for Flo. "You didn't really mean that Suzy would kill for her friend," Sunny reassured her, but inside, her sleuthing radar was pinging wildly. The band started playing, and a jazzy accordion tune kicked up in the air. Sunny felt a hand on her lower back.

"Sorry to interrupt, ladies," Tony leaned in and shouted to be heard over the music. "But, I'm going to have to steal Sunny for a dance."

Julia gave Sunny a flirty wink, and Tony led Sunny onto the space on the lawn cleared for dancing. He put one hand around her waist, the other hand clasping one of hers, and guided her gently into the rhythm of the two-step.

"You looked like you could use rescuing," he chuckled.

"You are my hero," Sunny laughed. "That Julia is something else."

Soon, other couples joined them on the dance floor, each dancing in time to the music, two-stepping the way their grandparents had done and their great-grandparents before that. Sunny was the only one who hadn't grown up dancing like this, her feet struggling at first to find the beat, but Tony was a good lead. Soon, he had her moving with confidence through one song and then another. When the second song ended, the lead musician playing the final notes on his fiddle, Sunny exhaled, a little out of breath.

"I have been meaning to ask you something," Tony said as the band began playing another song. "I wondered if you would ever want to…"

Sunny's attention turned away sharply. *Was that–? It couldn't have been.* She watched a woman move around the food table, her concentration so focused that she couldn't hear the words Tony was saying three inches from her face. The woman turned so that Sunny could see her face at a direct angle. *It was.*

"Tony," She said abruptly. "I'm so sorry, but I really have to speak to someone over there. Can we talk later?"

"Sure." Tony gave her a bewildered look. "Another time…" He called to Sunny's back as she ran away.

Chapter 34

"We need to talk." Sunny didn't feel the moment required a lengthy prologue. Things were too urgent. She needed to speak with the mystery woman from the bar now before she had a chance to disappear again.

"And you are?" The woman began to back away from the table, a suspicious look on her face.

"I'm Sunny. I own the tiki bar." She pointed towards the direction of the Cajun Coconut. The cloud of confusion seemed to clear in the mystery woman's eyes as she registered who Sunny was, and her unsure look was replaced with one of guarded tension. "I have a lot of questions for you, and I desperately need you to be willing to answer them."

"Fine," the woman relented and looked around the picnic with nervous glances. "But not here."

"Let's go to my bar," Sunny suggested. "I'll mix you

a drink, and you can tell me all about your connection to Jeb Landry."

The woman willingly followed her from the picnic and towards the Cajun Coconut. Sunny unlocked the front door and flicked on the overhead lights of the empty bar. She looked around and wondered if Cook and the other tiki spirits could see and hear her right now. Given the fact that she had just invited a potential murderer to be alone in the bar with her, she hoped they could do something to help if danger arose.

"Mai tai or zombie?" Sunny asked, slipping behind the bar, getting out the cocktail shaker and jigger.

"Zombie," the woman decided, taking a seat on a barstool.

"Good choice," Sunny said as she gathered the necessary ingredients and tools for her famous zombie recipe–rum, limes, grapefruit juice, grenadine, bitters... She paused, forgetting something...*That's right*...She grabbed the bottle of falernum, a heady syrup made from ginger, almonds, and allspice. They sat in silence as Sunny poured everything into the cocktail shaker and mixed. The only sound in the room was the ice hitting the sides of the shaker like a frosty maraca. Sunny poured the golden liquid into two tiki mugs and garnished the glasses with sprigs of mint. The mystery woman took a sip and braced herself for Sunny's questions.

"Just tell me this," Sunny decided it was time to get down to business. "Who are you?"

The woman took her time answering, seeming to Sunny like she was seemingly parsing out what she wanted Sunny to know from what she didn't.

"I'm a friend of Jeb's," she finally confessed. "Well,

sort of a friend. My name is Annie."

"A friend that comes into town, gets into a nasty fight, hears that her friend has died, and then doesn't go to the funeral?" Sunny wasn't buying it.

"I can see how that would look kind of suspicious." The woman squirmed in her seat, tracing a finger around the rim of her tiki mug in anxious circles.

"Have the police questioned you about Jeb's murder?" Sunny leaned forward onto the bartop, propping up on her elbows.

"What are you talking about?" The woman's pixie-like face grew pale. "Jeb wasn't murdered. He died of a heart attack." She shook her head and glared at Sunny.

"Someone put grapefruit oil in his drink," Sunny explained. "Jeb was on statins and couldn't have grapefruit. It caused him to have a heart attack. Did you do it?" She bore her eyes into the mystery woman's face.

"No!" The woman gasped. "I would never do that." She hurriedly slid from her perch on the barstool and stood, reaching down to the floor for her purse. "I'm out of here." She turned to storm out but then suddenly turned back, dropping her head and slumping her shoulders in resignation. "I'm a bartender in New Orleans. I got to know Jeb very well over the last two years when he would come into my bar with someone we will call a *special friend.* Their relationship had gotten serious, and Jeb refused to be honest with his wife and come clean about the whole thing. I met with him that night to beg him to see sense–leave his wife and be with his lover for good. You can probably tell by how our conversation went that night that I was unsuccessful. I didn't kill Jeb because I'm not a murderer. Here." She tossed a shiny red lacquered business card onto the bartop. “This is where I’ll be if you have more questions.” She gave Sunny a curt nod and left.

Sunny washed the tiki mugs, locked up the bar, and returned to the town green. The sunlight was waning now, but the day was still as hot as ever. Back at her last nursing gig in Minnesota, Labor Day marked the end of the summer’s heat, when it was usually time to get the boxes of sweaters down from the attic. In LouLou, Labor Day was simply one more summer celebration. By the time Sunny reached the picnic, most of the festivities were over. The band was still on the library’s front porch, but they had stopped playing and were packing up their instruments. The food table had been cleared. Only Sunny’s Pyrex baking dish remained. She walked over and noticed with dismay that most of her casserole was left uneaten. She groaned inwardly and carried it away.

“There you are!” Flo called to her. “I’ve been looking everywhere for you. Where’ve you been?” She held a cake stand in one hand, *an empty cake stand,* Sunny noted. *People had no trouble gobbling up Flo’s cooking.* Sunny tried to push away a pang of jealousy.

She was about to tell Flo all about her rendezvous with the mystery woman, who she now knew to be Annie Roche, a bartender at a place in New Orleans called The Corner Pocket. Just as she opened her mouth to do so, Danny ran over, his cheerful face flushed a rudy red from the heat and the fun of the day. Sunny decided to tell Flo about Annie later.

“Ready to go home, Mom?” Danny asked, taking the baking dish from her hands to carry it for her.

“Am I ever!” She sighed, and the three of them

headed to Sunny's car.

They rode home in companionable silence, Sunny's new favorite Martin Denny tiki music playlist lilting from the car speakers and filling the space between them with happy, relaxed vibes. After dropping off Flo in front of the Sweet Pea at the marina, they headed for Moonlight Lane. Once inside the house, Sunny winced. For the first time, she felt the sunburn that had turned her shoulders a deep red. The all-natural sunscreen she had mixed from zinc paste and coconut oil was no match for the intense Louisiana sun. She would need to go back to the drawing board with that recipe.

"I'm going to take a long bath," she announced and headed for the bathroom. She added a few scoops of lavender-infused Epsom salts and a little peppermint bubble bath before sliding into the warm water with a sigh. Leaning her head back onto the tub's edge, she tried her best to relax, without succeeding. There was just too much to process from the day–Julia's backhanded compliments, the awkward way the townspeople treated her when she showed up as plain old hippy Sunflower instead of preppy and neat Sunny, the way Tony had whirled her around the dancefloor with his hand on her lower back, and most of all, Annie...

She sat up in the tub and leaned over the edge, stretching towards her linen dress on the floor. She reached inside her dress pocket and took out Annie's business card. She grabbed her phone from the tub's edge and typed the name of Annie's place of employment, *The Corner Pocket,* into the search bar. A website for The Corner Pocket came up right away, and when Sunny clicked on the link, she gasped. The Corner Pocket was a gay bar.

"This whole time, we thought Jeb was having an affair with a woman!" Sunny said out loud. "We had it all wrong!" She jumped from the tub, bubbles and water splashing everywhere. Ignoring the soapy mess, she moved in a flash–drying herself, dressing in another linen dress from her closet, and grabbing her car keys.

"I'll be right back!" she called out to Danny. She had to talk to Cook and the others about this, and there was no time to lose.

Chapter 35

"Hey, guys!" Sunny burst into the bar and flicked on the tiki lighting. The room lit up in dim, colorful shades, and the bamboo lanterns that hung from the ceiling cast a warm golden glow on the walls and floor. "I need you to wake up. I have something really, really important that I need to talk about right this minute!" She panted with excitement, collapsing into a chair and resting her elbows on the table in front of her to catch her breath.

The faux palm trees in the room began to sway in an otherworldly breeze, and Sunny smiled as the ocean waves on the velvet painting began to crash to the landscape's sandy shore. The surfer girl and guy came alive, hanging ten on the end of their boards. Cook's face softened as he let out a cavernous yawn. The pirate parrots began to twitter from their perches overhead.

Cora and Pearl began to move, arguing, as if they had been summoned to life mid-conversation.

"Sunny, what's wrong?" Pearl stopped her quarrel with Cora mid sentence. "Are you okay? I can feel your excitement coming through very strongly."

"Let'er talk, matey," Vin shook his blue-feathered head and let out a loud, exasperated squawk.

"It's about Jeb." Sunny consciously tried to slow down and speak her words calmly and clearly. "I spoke to the mystery woman who came into the bar with him that night? Or maybe you already know that? Can you hear what goes on in here when you're... you know... quiet or whatever?" She stopped speaking and cocked her head to the side.

"Of course, we can hear what's happening in the bar when we are in our other realm," Cora chided.

"Well, then you already know," Sunny shot Cora an annoyed look. "The mystery woman from that night was a bartender from New Orleans, and apparently, Jeb made frequent trips there accompanied by a *special friend.*" She raised her hands to make air quotations. "But when I looked up the bar online, I found out that it was a gay bar. Jeb wasn't having an affair with a woman. His lover was a man." She got it all out in one breath and fell back into her chair, panting.

"It seems our victim led a second life full of secrets," Cook spoke for the first time, the swirls of his eyes picking up speed as his face formed a concerned frown. "This is worrisome."

"What do you mean?" Sunny sat up.

"It's possible that the killer hoped that when Jeb died, his secret would die with him," Cook explained. "Anyone who knows the secret keeps it alive and, therefore, might be the killer's next target."

"I guess I didn't think of that." Sunny bit her bottom lip.

"Oh, Cook!" Pearl quivered. "I'm worried for our Sunflower!"

"Don't worry about me," Sunny reassured her. "I'm perfectly safe."

"On the contrary," Cook corrected her. "You are in more danger than we thought."

Chapter 36

Early the next morning, Sunny could hear Danny's deep breathing as he slept soundly behind his bedroom door.

"Time to get up for school!" She called, knocking gently. She padded to the living room and reached for her yoga mat, which was rolled up in a corner. When she stepped outside, a light, cool breeze caressed her face, and she smiled, delighting that the worst of summer's heat might soon be over and that autumn could be arriving soon.

She stopped momentarily to admire Lake Pontchartrain as the first rays of the morning sun began to dance on the rippled water. Then, she turned toward the forest and headed to her yoga spot. Her phone rang as she unfurled her mat onto the cushy, pine-straw-covered ground.

"Who on earth is calling me this early?" Her heart skipped a beat, worrying in the several seconds that it took to pull her phone out of her pocket that the call was coming from her parents or, worse, Danny. She breathed a sigh of relief when the name at the top of the screen read *Police Chief Tony Perez.*

"Tony, hi," she stuttered. "Is everything okay?"

"Everything is fine. " His voice was warm, making Sunny feel a flip in her chest. "I called because I wanted you to hear it from me first instead of reading it in the paper or hearing what will undoubtedly be a tidal wave of local gossip." He paused, and Sunny could hear his muffled voice talking to another police officer. *He must be at work,* she concluded. *But why this early?*

"Sorry about that." Tony was back on the line. "After we spoke at the diner the other day, I had my people look into Jeb's death one more time to see if there was anything we missed."

"And?" Sunny asked anxiously.

"And, when we looked at the pathologist report in conjunction with the autopsy, the coroner concluded that the grapefruit Jeb consumed that night couldn't have come from a drink...unless you have a habit of using extremely concentrated essential oils in your cocktails."

"Which I don't," Sunny interjected.

"Right, meaning whoever put that grapefruit into Jeb's drink could have possibly done it to cause harm." He sighed. "We've reopened the case, and it's now being investigated as a homicide."

"What does that mean for me? For the Cajun Coconut?" Sunny winced. "Are we going to have to close again?"

"Nothing really," Tony reassured her. "We searched your bar. No grapefruit oil was found on the property, which is good news. The bad news is we're starting this search for the killer from square one, and no one on the LouLou police force has ever been in a murder investigation." He groaned. "I've seen my share of murder cases back in L.A., but I was just a low-ranking officer then, and my precinct had a lot of experienced detectives. I think I'm in over my head. I might need to call in reinforcements from New Orleans for this."

"No, you're not," Sunny insisted. "You've got me. We can find the murderer together."

"Sunny..." Tony's tired words trailed off. She heard a second distant voice on the line, another officer calling for Tony. "I've got to go," he said wearily. "Please don't do anything dangerous."

"Tony, wait! There's something I need to..." Sunny started to tell him about the oil in Barbara's kitchen cabinet, but with a click, he was gone.

Sunny sat on her mat, no longer interested in yoga. Her mind buzzed, and her thoughts felt like waves crashing onto a beach, a relentless barrage one after another. She rose from the ground, rolled up her mat, and placed it under one arm, hurrying home. This morning, sleuthing would be served with a helping of sweet potato pancakes.

When Sunny walked through the doors of Gary's Diner an hour later, the entire restaurant, once a buzzing hive of activity, stopped to turn and stare at her. She blushed and directed her gaze to the floor, quickly walking to an empty booth in the back corner of the room. *I'm guessing everyone in town has heard about Jeb's death being declared a murder.* She thought as she rummaged in her purse for her reading glasses before realizing she was wearing them on top of her head. Lowering them onto the bridge of her nose, she perused the breakfast menu even though she already knew exactly what she wanted to order.

"Would you look at that?" Claudine slapped the morning newspaper on Sunny's tabletop without saying hello. "What can I get you, hun? Sweet potato pancakes and a large coffee, right?" She reached into her apron pocket for her notebook and pen.

"Yes, please," Sunny nodded to confirm her order before reading today's headline.

JEB LANDRY DEATH SUSPECTED FOUL PLAY

"I'll be right back." Claudine wrote Sunny's order in her notebook and headed to the kitchen window to hand it to the cook. While she was gone, Sunny scanned the article, stopping on a crucial sentence.

When questioned about possible suspects, Police Chief Perez emphasized that for now, no one at the Cajun Coconut, the bar where Landry died, was under suspicion. The tiki bar had been thoroughly investigated and does not appear to be connected with the death.

Sunny sat back in the booth's bench seat and sighed with relief. She was sure that the town would be talking of nothing else for the next several days at minimum, but at least she wouldn't be seen as a murderer. Right? Still, thhe whole business made her feel uneasy.

"How'd you do it?" An older man walking with a cane made his way over to her table. Sunny had seen him once or twice around town–in the library or the Hop, but she didn't know his name. He narrowed his eyes and whispered the question again. "How did you manage to kill Jeb and get the cops off your back?"

"Excuse me?" Sunny choked. "I didn't...I would never...the article says it right here. I'm not the killer!" She didn't realize that she had screamed the last sentence, causing everyone in the room to turn and pay attention to her for the second time that morning.

"Mr. Clancy, you quit it." Claudine stood behind him, a plate stacked high with pancakes in one hand, a steaming coffee in another. "You leave Sunny alone. She said she didn't murder anybody, and Tony said she didn't murder anybody. Case closed." She set the plate and coffee mug on the table and placed her hands on her hips, giving the man a scolding glare. He relented and walked away.

"Thanks, Claudine," Sunny muttered gratefully. Claudine gently patted her on the back before rushing off to take another table's order. Sunny hoped that the majority of LouLou would think like Claudine, but from the murmurings and sideways glances in the diner, she worried that they did not.

That night, when the Cajun Coconut opened for business, Sunny hoped the suspicious whispers would have died down. Much to her disappointment, the bar patrons who came into the tiki bar that evening smiled to her face but eyed her with distrustful glances when they thought she wasn't looking. The bar was packed with people for the first time in weeks. Every bar stool was occupied. Every table was taken, and bar patrons stood shoulder-to-shoulder in all available space. Sunny noticed that while this crowd should have felt like the wildest party in town, instead, the bar had a strange, tense energy, like a balloon filled to the brim with air, moments away from popping. The people in the room sipped their tiki drinks slowly, whispering to each other in wary pairs and looking around the room, sizing up those around them.

Sunny and Flo hadn't been able to speak much. They were too busy mixing drinks, washing dishes and tabletops, and slicing fruit garnishes to chat.

"Here we go," Sunny smiled politely as she handed Julia Donahue a bamboo-shaped tiki mug filled with a Blue Hawaiian.

"Thank you, honey," Julia drawled. "I'm here to meet Mary Kay Middleton. You haven't seen her yet, have you? It's so crowded in here that I can't tell if she's here or not."

"I haven't seen her yet." Sunny winced. *And trust me, I would know if that you-know-what walked into my bar...*

"If you see her, tell her I'm in that back corner over there." Julia motioned with her tiki mug.

"Sure, I..." Sunny froze. Did she see the surfer dude moving in his painting? *Surely not.*

"Sunny? Sunny?" Julia's voice was calling. Sunny shook herself out of her thoughts. "You alright, darlin? You looked like you were having a spell or something."

"I'm fine." Sunny smiled. "I will tell Mary Kay you are here when I see her," she nodded. As Julia walked towards her spot in the bar's back corner, Sunny felt a breeze. It was slight, almost too soft to be perceptible, but she was sure she felt it. In the corner of her eye, she saw Cook's face–its regular wooden features showed a flicker of movement. She grabbed a cleaning rag and walked towards the tiki totem. Pretending to be busy wiping down an already clean table, she leaned towards him.

"Cook?" She whispered from the side of her mouth. "What is it?" She turned slowly in the most casual way possible, making sure no one was watching her seemingly talking to herself. The tiki totem remained silent. From the nearby wall, she saw Pearl's eyes give a brief twinkle.

"Someone's coming," Pearl whispered. "Someone's..." The door of the Cajun Coconut burst open and in walked Buzz.

Chapter 37

"Buzz, you aren't welcome here." Flo rounded the bartop and planted her feet defiantly in front of the leather-clad man. Everyone in the bar stood stock-still, wondering what would happen next, soft tropical music from the surrounding speakers filling the quiet, anticipating room.

"Relax, woman." Buzz pushed past her, bumping her shoulder intentionally as he went. "I come in peace." He sat down on the only empty barstool and grabbed a drink list from nearby, reading over it like his presence in the Coconut was the most ordinary thing in the world. "What's good?" He eyed Sunny over the top edge of his menu.

"Um, well, the, um, mai tai is pretty good," Sunny stuttered. "Pardon me, Buzz or Mr. Buzz or whatever you go by, but...what are you doing here? You haven't exactly been the biggest fan of my bar." The room remained silent, as if everyone in the bar was wondering the same thing.

"Can't a man change his mind?" Buzz gave his head an indignant shake. "Now, y'all nosey nellies, get on back to your cocktails!" He turned and yelled. The room came to life again, everyone returning to their own conversations. He leaned over the bar and whispered. "Forget that may tay or whatever it is you said. I'm a beer drinker. Look, I need to speak with you in private."

"Whatever you need to say to Sunny, you can say right now in front of everyone," Flo snapped.

"You sure are a feisty little thing, ain't ya?" Buzz fought back a grin.

"Flo, I've got this." Sunny motioned for Flo to stand down and led Buzz into the back storage room. She moved several boxes of cocktail napkins and cleaning supplies to make space for them to sit at the flimsy folding table and chairs that were the only furniture in the room. Sunny sat, clasping her hands on the tabletop and waiting for Buzz to begin.

"I know I haven't been the nicest fella in the world to you." Buzz shifted in his seat, partially from guilt and partially because the cheap chair began to buckle under his girth.

"You can say that again," Sunny sniped, halfway under her breath.

"I've lived here all my life, and I don't mind sayin' that I don't like change." He held up his hands as if in surrender. "But when I saw this, I knew I needed to show you." He took a small red flash drive from his leather vest pocket and put it on the table between them.

"What is this?" Sunny frowned with confusion.

"This is a short video–just a few minutes of footage from the security camera I keep in the alleyway between my bar and yours. When I read the news in the paper this mornin' about how Jeb's death was probably murder, I looked back at the security footage for that night. I don't know why I did it, but I thought there might be something there." He shrugged, and then his face brightened. "And there was."

He asked if Sunny had a computer in the bar, and she said she did. A few minutes later, they were plugging the flash drive into the side of her laptop, the security camera video lighting up the screen. Sunny sat silently, her mouth agog as she watched a car pull up in the alleyway and park. A person emerged from the car and headed inside the Coconut. They were dressed all in black, their body obscured by an oversized, puffy coat, *just as the tiki spirits had described,* Sunny thought to herself. Within thirty seconds or less, the figure had returned to the screen, jumped back into the car, and sped away. Sunny shook her head slowly, astounded at what she had just seen.

"And do you want to know the best part?" Buzz narrowed his eyes, a devilish grin on his face. "I know who that car belongs to."

Chapter 38

Sunny thanked Buzz, gripping the flash drive with one hand and excitedly shaking his with the other. The tiny piece of plastic in her palm contained the clue that could change everything. Sunny and Buzz stepped out of the bar's back room. Buzz walked out of the bar, tipping his head and placing two fingers to his temple in a salute as he passed Flo.

"What was that about?" Flo stopped drying freshly-washed tiki mugs and turned to Sunny with a bewildered look.

"Flo, you are never going to believe this!" Sunny smiled, her whole body shaking. She motioned for Flo to move away from the customers and join her in a side corner of the room. Leaning in to whisper and covering her mouth so that no one could read her lips, she told Flo about the flash drive and the footage of someone parking in the back alley, slipping into the Coconut, and hurrying away moments later. “And that’s not the best part!” Sunny practically squealed. “Buzz knew the owner of the car. It’s Suzy!”

“Suzy!?” Flo whispered, sucking in a shocked breath so rapidly that she almost choked. “You can’t be serious.” She crossed her arms. “You need to go to the police with this. I think you should call Chief Perez right now.”

“I plan to.” Sunny looked at the coconut shell clock on the wall. It was ten o’clock. “But it's late now. I’ll call him in the morning. Plus, I’ve got some things to look into before I show him this.” She slipped the flash drive into her dress pocket.

“Like what?” Flo asked.

“Oh, nothing much. Just this and that.” Sunny’s eyes cut over to the lifeless Cook.

“Would you mind closing up alone tonight? I need to go spend time with Boo. She’s due any day now, you know?” Flo rubbed her tired eyes. “Between here at the bar and my morning shrimping runs, I feel like I’ve been pulling double shifts. The cats have not been happy about that.”

“You know I love having you help out around here. In fact, I don’t know what I would do without you, but you don’t have to be here so much. I know it has to be exhausting.” Sunny frowned. “At least, let me pay you for your time here.”

“Nah,” Flo shook her head. “I like helping out here. It’s probably the best part of my day.” She grabbed her trusty fisherman’s hat and moved towards the door.

“Give the kitties extra treats for me,” Sunny smiled, thinking how nice it would be to come home to a feline friend of her own.

"Will do." Flo turned to Sunny before leaving. "I wouldn't tell anyone about the you-know-what." Her eyes moved to Sunny's pocket. "If the killer knows you have that, there's no telling what they will do to stop the police from getting it." She donned her hat and went home to her cats.

Sunny scanned the room, looking for bar customers that needed her assistance. She grabbed a serving tray from under the bartop and walked from table to table, gathering up empty tiki mugs and asking the patrons if they needed anything else to drink. Once everyone in the bar was happy and cared for and fresh tropical drinks were served, Sunny returned to her perch behind the bartop. The Coconut would close in less than two hours, so she decided she might as well start the nightly clean-up process, filling the large wash basin behind the bar with hot, soapy water. She dunked the dirty cocktail glasses one by one into the sink, scrubbing them clean before nestling them into a dish rack to dry. She was glad that the Coconut was crowded, grateful for the money she made from the drinks sold, and she didn't want to seem unwelcoming to the bar patrons that now filled the room. But she desperately wanted to talk to the tiki spirits, and she needed the bar to close to call them out.

"Sunny?"

A shy and familiar voice sounded from over her shoulder. Sunny turned around, her hands covered in soap suds.

"Marian!" She beamed and reached for a tea towel to dry her hands. "You came!"

"I told you I would." Marian slid onto a barstool

and placed her purse on the bar top. "The girl that does the night shift is thankfully back on duty, so here I am." She gave an unsure smile. "Truth be told, I'm not the bar-going type. I'm more of a read-a-book-at-home kind of person." She chuckled.

"I totally get it," Sunny laughed. "Usually, I am, too. What can I get you?"

"Let me see." Marian reached for the reading glasses that hung from a chain around her neck. "I don't usually drink alcohol," she blushed.

"That is no problem at all!" Sunny reassured her. "Let me whip you up one of my favorite mocktails! You're going to love it."

Several minutes and a quick dance with a cocktail shaker later, Sunny and Marian were happily chatting away while the librarian sipped on a mango-and-mint mocktail. Sunny learned that she and Marian had a lot in common. Like Sunny, Marian was single and had never been married, was a homebody at heart although she loved to travel, and had once been considered a LouLou *outsider* herself.

"When I left New Jersey and moved here ten years ago," Marian said between sips. "I thought I would never fit in! People around town would listen to my thick Jersey City accent for approximately ten seconds before they decided I was not one of them." She rolled her eyes.

Sunny was surprised to hear this. Marian seemed to be perfectly at home in LouLou, just as rooted as the jasmine vines that covered the library's columned front porch, and in all of their interactions, she hadn't once detected even a hint of an accent in Marian's voice. A decade in Louisiana had softened the librarian's speech into a rounded, almost Southern way of speaking.

Sunny wondered if that would happen to her stubborn California accent eventually. She groaned a little, not quite ready to start using phrases like *y'all* and *fixin' to.*

"And how did you finally feel like you, I don't know, *belonged* here?" Sunny leaned onto the bar and focused on Marian as the din of conversation in the crowded bar faded to white noise.

"You know, for so long, I never thought I would," Marian shrugged. "I think it just takes time. You'll see." She gave Sunny an understanding look. Sunny sighed. *Time.* She didn't want to wait ten years before she felt like she fit in. *Heck, I don't even want to wait ten months...* She sighed again. The two women chatted some more, and the next time Sunny looked at the clock, it was midnight.

"Closing shop, folks," she called to the few remaining people who sat in clumped groups around the bar. "I've really enjoyed spending time with you, Marian." She smiled at the librarian, meaning every word she said. Talking with Marian had made Sunny feel less alone and more optimistic. She knew she would fit in with the townspeople...eventually.

"I've enjoyed it too." Marian stood and gathered her things. "Maybe next time we can get together at my place?" She got out her wallet to pay for the mocktail, but Sunny refused her money. "I could make us dinner one night. You're welcome to bring Danny along, too," she added brightly. "Oh, and I almost forgot! We've got an event at the library tomorrow morning–Dan Thibodeaux, a local photographer, does lots of nature stuff around the swamps and bayous–anyway, he's presenting his latest book. It's going to be a lot of fun. Will you come?"

"Sounds interesting," Sunny nodded. "I will see you there."

When Marian left, Sunny had a spring in her step. *Three real friends.* She thought. *I've got three real friends–Flo, Rachel, and now Marian. Maybe four if I count Tony, but...do I count Tony as a friend or maybe something more?* It was the first time in a long time that Sunny could say such a thing, and she wouldn't take it for granted. Once the last customer had paid and left the bar, Sunny turned the deadbolt on the front door with a satisfied exhale. She quickly finished her closing work–sweeping and mopping the floor, pushing chairs and tables back to their spots, and refilling the napkin and straw dispensers.

After closing the cash register and locking the cash box, she hurried to one of the peacock chairs in the back corner of the room. Her forehead glistened with sweat from her rushed work, and her heart raced with excitement.

"Guys!" She called out. "Cook? Pearl? Vin? Barry?"

The familiar tropical breeze, this time laced with the spicy scent of Hawaiian ginger, pushed her hair away from her forehead and shoulders. She smiled. *Correction.* She thought. *I actually have more than three friends now...as long as three-hundred-year-old pirates and ancient nature spirits count.*

She waited as the tiki spirits came to life, groaning and stretching, stiff from their long rest.

"I notice you didn't call my name," Cora quipped, her long, oval face contorted into a frown.

"And why would she? Rude as you always are." Pearl's usually sweet tone had a bite to it.

"Oh, stop it, you two." Barry shook his body

from head to tail, his red feathers ruffling. "Stop your squawking."

"Aye," Vin nodded his tiny, pirate-hat-topped head. "Don't you know that's our job? We're the parrots, after all." He and Barry erupted into a fit of clucking laughter. Cora and Pearl began to quarrel in earnest.

"Settle down, everyone," Cook's voice boomed, and the room went quiet.

"I wanted to talk to you guys because I have important evidence that might help us find Jeb's killer." She held up the flash drive, wondering if ancient spirits would know what a flash drive even was. "This contains a video of a car that belongs to Barbara Landry's friend, Suzy. It was taken on the night of the murder." She explained further about the car and the suspicious behavior of the person in it. "And the frustrating part is the person in the video is exactly how you described–so concealed by layers of clothing that you can't tell who it is. Heck, I can't even tell if it's a man or a woman." She gave an exasperated sigh. "But it has to be Suzy or Barbara. I mean, I have Suzy's car caught on video. Who else could it be?"

"There's one thing you aren't asking, Sunflower." Cook's swirling blue eyes glowed brighter. "If Suzy killed Jeb, was she doing it for Barbara?"

"Right," Sunny nodded. "The question isn't, was it Suzy or Barbara? The question is...Was it Suzy *and* Barbara?" She grew excited. "That makes so much sense. I've already been told that Suzy has devoted her whole life to her friend. Of course, she would help her murder her husband!"

"Oh, be careful, sweet one," Pearl's voice quivered. "You could be stepping into a wasp's nest if Suzy is devoted to Barbara as much as you say."

"She's right, lass," Vin nodded. "I've known pirates who would cut your throat for accusing them of less."

"Suzy's not a pirate," Sunny brushed off the parrot's concern. "I'm sure she was a mean girl in high school, but she's middle-aged now. Surely, we fifty-somethings are all older and wiser than we used to be. Would she cut my throat? Doubt it." Her confidence began to diminish the moment the words left her lips. Did the tiny flash drive in her dress pocket put her in danger? She reasoned to herself that she would turn it in to the police first thing tomorrow morning and be done with it. No drive, no danger. She crossed her arms, satisfied with her decision. "I have another question."

"Yes?"

"Where do you guys…*go*…when you aren't here?" Sunny cocked her head to one side. It was a quandary she had been pondering for a long while.

"I can't say I know what the place is called," Cora answered. Her voice always sounded so silvery and cool, like it was spoken from a great distance away, even though Cora was right there, her driftwood face hanging on the wall.

"It's a between place," Pearl interrupted. "Somewhere in the middle of the mortal and the spirit realms."

"For me and the pirates," Cook's gaze lifted toward Barry and Vin. "We've been banished for our bad deeds. Not allowed to ascend to the spirit world, not allowed to be free in the mortal realm."

"So just stuck in between, somewhere," Vin added.

"It doesn't sound like a happy place," Sunny frowned. "Can I help you be free?"

"The middle place isn't happy or sad," Pearl explained. "It just is..." She added quickly, "But we get our greatest joy from connecting with you, dear. You give us purpose again."

Sunny nodded, her head spinning with exhaustion. She told the tiki spirits good night and left the Coconut, locking the door behind her.

On the way home, she drove her car in silence–no music, podcast, or audiobook. She recapped the evening in her mind–the flash drive, Suzy's car, her budding friendship with Marian, and the tiki spirits. Should she find a way to set them free?

Sunny stood in front of her bedroom closet, a clothes hanger in her right hand and another in her left. On one hanger, she held her favorite sky-blue linen dress with a white batik pattern embroidered along the neckline and skirt. On the other hanger, she had a pastel pink sheath dress from J.Crew with little pearl buttons down the middle. She sighed and put the pink-and-pearls dress back in the closet, deciding that the people of LouLou would simply have to take her for who she was. After all, she did have three friends in town. THREE. And they liked her just fine. *And once I solve this murder, I will have more friends in town that I will be able to shake a stick at,* she reassured herself, slipping her feet into a pair of red hiking sandals and heading to town and the photography event at the library. She slipped the flash drive in her pocket and planned to make a stop at the police station after the library.

She swung her car into the last parking spot on the square, wincing a little at the tight squeeze, even for her tiny Miata. *Why are things so busy here today?* she wondered as she stepped onto the sidewalk in front of Pinky's Nail Salon. She did a double take when she saw who was sitting in one of the pedicure chairs by the salon's front window. *Suzy.* Sunny looked over at the library, where a line of event-goers stood before the heavy Victorian doors. She looked back at the salon and bit her lower lip. Now was her chance to question Suzy, but that would mean being a no-show for her new friend–one of only three friends in town, she added thoughtfully. But Suzy...She gave a resigned sigh and walked through the glass double doors of Pinky's.

"Good morning, ma'am. What can I do for you today?" The teenager staffing the salon's front desk asked her in a bored voice before blowing a large pink bubble with her chewing gum and letting it deflate on her lips.

"I'd like one of those, oh what's it called? Pedicures." Sunny crossed her arms over her chest self-consciously. She'd never gotten her nails done before, and she wasn't exactly sure how it all worked. What she did know was that the smell in the place was awful. She tried not to wrinkle her nose at the strong nail polish fumes that lay thick in the air. *So many chemicals,* she sighed, but if getting her toenails shellacked with the toxic junk known as nail polish helped her find out who killed Jeb, she would just have to suck it up and do it. A nail tech wearing a pink apron walked to where she stood at the front of the salon to greet her.

"Right this way." She smiled politely as she led Sunny to the sturdy pedicure chair directly next to Suzy.

"Suzy, what a surprise!" Sunny exclaimed as she sat down and settled her feet into the chair's jacuzzi foot bath that swirled with warm, eucalyptus-scented water. "Good to see you."

"What are you doing here, and why the heck are you talking to me?" Suzy scowled. The nail techs kneeling at both women's feet shot each other surprised looks. Sunny felt embarrassed. Was this a mistake? Her nail tech was already busy at work scrubbing her feet with a lavender exfoliating treatment, so she decided to press on.

"Just here to get my nails done," Sunny replied casually. Having never had a pedicure before, Sunny flinched as her feet were wrapped in a hot towel. Once the awkward spa treatments were done, Sunny sighed with relief as the nail polish was painted on, and she was left alone to let her nails dry. When Suzy's nails were also drying, and the two women sat in their chairs, feet propped up and unable to move, Sunny saw her chance.

"I've got something very important to ask you."

Sunny turned to Suzy with a serious face. "Why did you sneak in and out of my bar on the night Jeb died?"

Suzy's face drained of its color. *Hard to do with all of that self-tanner,* Sunny thought cattily. Suzy said nothing, just glowered at Sunny with wide eyes.

"You might wonder how I know you snuck into the bar that night," Sunny continued without waiting for Suzy's response. "I've got your car on security camera footage. There's no mistaking it's your car, and once my pretty pink toenails are dry, I'm marching right over to the police department and handing them the footage."

"I...I...I have no idea why my car would be anywhere near your bar that night." Suzy seemed to be genuinely caught off guard. "I was at home all evening the night Jeb died. Earl and I were watching TV."

"Can Earl vouch for that?"

"Well, sort of. He fell asleep on the sofa beside me for most of the night." Suzy's face was lined with worry. "Look, I didn't even have access to my car that night. My son, Beaux, was home for the weekend from LSU, and I let him borrow the car."

"So why did he drive it to the Coconut, and sneak in and out only moments before a man died?" Sunny whispered as more salon customers came in and sat in the chairs next to them.

"Why would my son want to kill Jeb?" Suzy hissed. "Jeb was like an uncle to the boy. He was devastated when he heard what happened."

"I don't know. Maybe the police can figure it out when I give them the video." Sunny narrowed her eyes. She knew Suzy had more information to give.

"That won't be necessary," Suzy pleaded. "My son's

pre-med, for goodness sake. He doesn't need anything like this on his record. I'll make you a deal. You don't tell the police that he had the car that night, and I'll tell you everything you want to know about Barbara. I know you've been snooping around asking questions about her. Well, what do you want to know?"

Sunny hesitated. She knew she should give the flash drive to the police, but the longer that security footage stayed in her possession, the more information she could squeeze out of Suzy.

"Where was Barbara on the night her husband died?" Sunny asked. "I know she was supposed to teach a Zumba class at the community center, but she got a sub to do it instead."

"What you need to know about Barbara is..." Suzy looked around, hoping the sound of their conversation wouldn't carry. "It's not just Zumba and good genes keeping her slim."

"What do you mean?" Sunny was getting impatient.

"She takes...*Ozempic.*" Suzy spoke the last word in a hushed tone, the word seemingly too shameful to say out loud.

"What's Ozempic?" Sunny frowned. "And what does this have to do with Barbara's alibi?"

"You really are one of those all-natural woo-woo types, aren't you?" Suzy shook her head in amazement. "I can't believe you've never heard of Ozempic!" She gave a tight chuckle. "It's a weight loss drug, honey. You have to see a doctor to get a prescription for it, and because Barbara doesn't want anyone to know that she takes it, she drives to New Orleans in secret and gets it from a doctor over there."

"A doctor that meets with patients at eleven o'clock at night?" Sunny raised a skeptical eyebrow.

"The doctor she gets her prescription from stays open late a couple times a week to accommodate patients who work office hours. At least, that's what I've been told. I myself would never need a doctor like that." She raised a hand to her hair and patted a bleach-blonde strand back into place. "She told me that after her appointment, she stayed in the city for dinner," Suzy explained.

"What's the doctor's name? What restaurant did she go to for dinner?"

"Dr. Oliphant on Bienville." Suzy leaned forward to inspect her newly polished toes. "Then she had dinner at La Petit Grocery on Magazine. My toes are dry. Can I go now?"

"Fine," Sunny relented. "But if I have any other questions, and I will, I'll ask you for answers. Don't think I'm going to keep evidence from the police for nothing."

Suzy gave her a curt nod and walked to the front desk to pay the salon, shuffling awkwardly in the foam flip-flops the nail tech had slipped on her feet. Sunny sat back in her chair, chewing her bottom lip in deep thought. Barbara might have a concrete alibi for the night of Jeb's murder, but how could Sunny verify that she actually went to her appointment like she told Suzy that she had? It's not like the doctor's office would break privacy laws to tell her about a patient's information, but...Maybe a little trip across the lake would be a good idea.

Chapter 39

"I still think you should have taken that flash drive straight to Tony." Flo shook her head as she drove her pick up across the Lake Pontchartrain Causeway Bridge with Sunny in the passenger seat.

"I know, I know." Sunny put her feet up on the dashboard and leaned back, taking in the view of the lake surrounding them as they sped towards New Orleans. "And I will just as soon as I get all the information out of Suzy that I can. There's something that woman is hiding, and if she knows I gave the flash drive to Tony, she won't trust me anymore."

The day was cloudy, but the summer's heat had returned, and the air outside was muggy and hot. Even though the trip promised to be a serious one, and maybe even a little dangerous, Sunny was excited to spend some time in the Big Easy.

When Sunny moved to LouLou, she had expected to travel over the bridge to New Orleans all of the time, wandering the streets of the French Quarter and exploring all of its little antique shops and restaurants. But, with all of the work that had to go into fixing up her house, building the Coconut, and then the murder, she had yet to visit New Orleans once. The Causeway Bridge was one of the longest in the world, and it took cars nearly twenty-five minutes to cross one way. The truck's gentle bumping up and down as they drove almost put Sunny to sleep. She rubbed her eyes to stay awake, watching the pelicans dip in and out of the water below them, looking for their fish breakfast.

When they finally reached the bridge's end, Sunny looked at her phone to read the directions to Bienville Street, their first stop of the day. Flo eased her old truck onto the expressway overpass that led into the city, wincing with unease at driving in the chaotic traffic. The road system of New Orleans was a knotted, confusing mess, looking to all the world like it was designed to resemble a bowl of spaghetti that had been spilled on the floor. After several wrong turns and a few swear words, they eventually pulled to a stop in a parking lot in front of the red brick office of Dr. James Oliphant.

"So, what's the plan here?" Flo paused, her hand poised to open her car door. Did Sunny think they would waltz in and ask the doctor for private information about a patient? And then what? The doctor would simply tell them everything they wanted to know?

"I've got us covered," Sunny nodded, reaching to the floorboard for her purse. "I made an appointment with the doctor. I will pose as a patient and possibly get him talking about other people he knows from LouLou, like Barbara. While I'm in with the doc, you will go through the computer to see if Barb had an appointment when she said she did." She opened her door and slid off the truck bench seat.

"Are you crazy?" Flo gasped. "You think I'm going to break into the computer like I'm some super spy? I barely know how to work my computer at home." She stepped out of her door and slammed it shut.

"I know this might not work, but we've got to try." Sunny insisted. "It's one of the only leads we have."

"What about the receptionist?" Flo followed Sunny up the ramped walkway to the office door. "Won't there be a receptionist guarding the computer the whole time? How do I get them away long enough for me to snoop?"

"I've taken care of that too." Sunny gave a satisfied smile. "I noticed that Dr. Oliphant's website had a post about hiring new office staff, and when I called to make the appointment, the doctor himself answered the phone saying something about being short-staffed and having to do his own office work. I'm almost positive you will have the lobby to yourself once I get the doctor in the examination room."

"You're a natural at this." Flo stared at her in amazement. "It's almost a little scary."

"Thanks!" Sunny smiled with glee. "Finally, all those nights on the sofa with a pint of Ben and Jerry's and old episodes of *Matlock* are paying off!" She swung open the office front door and went inside.

The lobby was decorated in a trendy minimalist style with two boxy white sofas, a coffee table shaped like a curvy modern art sculpture, and several uncomfortable-looking chrome chairs. The stark white walls were bare except for a large canvas with a black and white photograph featuring a close-up of an alligator's mouth, its craggy jaws lined with sharp teeth. They stood in the lobby for a moment, wondering if anyone else was there, when a tall, smiling man in a crisp, white lab coat walked in from a door at the back corner of the room.

"Mornin'. I'm Doctor Oliphant, but everybody calls me Jimmy." He extended a hand to Sunny. "How can I help you ladies today?" The contrast of his blindingly bleached teeth with his deeply tanned face made the doctor seem slightly unreal, and his obsessively neat appearance, coupled with the all-white room, made Sunny feel like she was floating in an unsettling dream. She shook herself back to reality.

"My name is Sunny Beach, and I have an appointment at 9." She smiled politely. "This is Flo. She's just here for moral support."

Flo nodded wordlessly.

"Great." The doctor stepped behind the white lacquered desk in the middle of the room and fired up his computer. He leaned closer and squinted into the screen. "There you are." He found her name in the appointment log, typing something before looking up at her again, teeth gleaming as he smiled. "Right this way, Sunny." He motioned for her to follow him into the examining room. Sunny walked behind him, turning to Flo before she left the lobby and giving her a covert thumbs up.

The luxury minimalist theme continued into the examining room, where Sunny perched on a cold, chrome armchair while Doctor Oliphant did the same opposite her.

"What brings you in today?" The doctor asked, reaching for an iPad on a square end table and poising his fingers to start typing notes. Sunny had done her research. She knew Doctor Oliphant's practice was not the kind you came to when you had the sniffles or a sprained ankle. His clinic specialized in what trendy circles called *wellness.* When Sunny was growing up on her parents' farm, wellness meant organic food, lots of fresh air, and long hikes in the California hills, but Doctor Oliphant's definition of the word was quite different. The walls of the examining room were plastered with advertisements for every kind of cosmetic procedure imaginable, all aimed at women of Sunny's age. She crossed her arms, suddenly feeling about a thousand years old.

"I wanted to come to your clinic because I heard from a lot of my friends that you're the doctor to see if you want to lose a few pounds," she lied. "A lot of women I know are on that Ozempic, so I thought I would give it a try."

"Well, we can certainly get you fixed up there." He typed some notes into the iPad.

"You've helped one of my dear friends, Barbara Landry," Sunny cooed. "She speaks so highly of you."

"Barbara's a great lady." The doctor nodded, his eyes still focused on the screen in front of him. "Let's get some bloodwork done, and then I'll send this prescription to the pharmacy."

"That sounds great, um, speaking of Barbara," Sunny shifted uncomfortably in her hard, metal seat. "Have you seen her lately?"

Doctor Oliphant raised his eyes and gave her a

puzzled look.

"What do you mean?" he asked, his congenial Southern gentleman persona dropping for the moment.

"Has she been in to see you recently? Just wondering."

"I can't share that kind of information, but Barbara is a patient of mine." He quickly stood. "Let's get you to the lab for that bloodwork." He opened the examining room door and moved to the side for her to exit.

In the lobby, Flo gave her a wild-eyed look.

"I got it," She whispered to Sunny. "Let's get out of here!"

"On second thought," Sunny called to Doctor Oliphant halfway down the hall and towards the lab. "I'm going to think about it for a little while longer. Thanks anyway!" She turned to Flo, and they scurried out of the office

Chapter 40

Twenty minutes later, Sunny and Flo were walking through the French Market, a long, covered outdoor pavilion where New Orleanians had been shopping for well over two hundred years. As they passed stalls selling everything from vegetables to alligator foot keychains to used books to brightly colored African sarongs, they talked rapidly, excited about what they had discovered from their espionage at the doctor's office.

"So, you looked at the doctor's calendar, and you saw that Barbara had an appointment for the night of Jeb's death." Sunny went over what Flo had told her again. Flo nodded, pausing to examine a stall selling hand-made candles. Sunny continued. "But next to Barbara's appointment entry in the calendar, the doctor had marked it as a no-show."

"Yep," Flo said, holding a pair of purple beeswax taper candles. "How much?" she asked the candlemaker. When told the price, Flo handed over a ten-dollar bill and slipped the candles into the tote bag she carried on one shoulder.

"This is huge news!" Sunny's whole body was trembling. This was the biggest break so far in her investigation. "Barbara told Suzy and possibly even the police that she was in New Orleans at that appointment, which was a lie. She never showed up!"

"Should we tell Tony?" Flo gave Sunny a sideways glance.

"Not sure." Sunny bit her lower lip and frowned. "The last time I tried to give him information, he got pretty upset that I had snooped around. I get where he's coming from, and I appreciate his concern. But he's not the one the whole town is calling a killer, now is he?" She turned her attention to a stall selling custom-made LEGO figures. "I remember when I couldn't walk through my house without stepping on a million of these things." She chuckled and then grew a little sad. Her son had outgrown playing with LEGOs, and she felt her time with him was going too fast.

"Hungry?" Flo asked, breaking Sunny out of her motherly reminiscing. "There's a po' boy stand over there. I could really go for a shrimp po' boy right about now."

Sunny was delighted to discover that King's Krewe Po' Boys featured a menu with several vegetarian options. Within minutes, she was sidled up to the service counter, sitting on a bar stool, and enjoying the yummiest creation she had eaten in a while.

"I've never had a fried okra po' boy before," she

said through a mouth full of food, "but it's fantastic!"

After they finished lunch, Sunny and Flo walked a winding path through the French Quarter, navigating the short distance from the French Market to their next destination–The Corner Pocket. When they arrived at the bar, they were stopped in their tracks by something hanging on the front door.

"This has me worried," Flo said, staring at the black floral mourning wreath before them.

"There's only one way to find out what's going on."

When Sunny opened the door, loud rap music blasted them in the face. The Corner Pocket was full of people talking, laughing, and drinking. Sunny walked up to the large, square bar in the center of the long, brick-lined room.

"Hi," She yelled over the music. "We wanted to talk with Annie. Is she here?"

The bartender, a man in his early twenties, wearing a hipster beanie and plaid flannel shirt unbuttoned to the navel, looked at her with sad eyes.

"How do you know Annie?" he said, his voice breaking.

"We live over in LouLou," Flo explained. "She's friends with a friend of ours."

"I'm sorry to have to tell you this." The bartender leaned in so that they could hear him more clearly. "But Annie has died." His mouth quivered, and a few tears escaped from his eyes.

"What?" Sunny gasped. "How? When?" She couldn't believe the young woman she had spoken with only days before was gone.

"A house fire." The bartender shook his head.

"Annie lives..." He swallowed hard. "*Lived* in one of those old houses in the Bywater neighborhood. The police said it must have been faulty wiring or something. The whole thing burned to the ground, and Annie didn't get out in time." He was having a hard time keeping his composure. "Excuse me." He pushed past them and ran outside. Flo and Sunny exchanged worried looks.

When they walked out, the bartender was sitting on the sidewalk curb, smoking a cigarette with a shaking hand.

"I'm terribly sorry to hear about Annie." Sunny stooped down and put a hand on the man's shoulder. "She seemed like a lovely person." She stood and began to walk away but stopped. "This might sound weird, but would it be possible to give you a call sometime?"

"I'm sorry, dear, but..." He gave her a sympathetic look. "I'm not interested in women."

"Oh, nothing like that," Sunny reassured him nervously. "Just in case I have any questions...about Annie...or I don't know," she shrugged.

"What kind of questions?" His eyes narrowed, and he stubbed out his cigarette on the pavement.

"I'm not sure yet." Sunny suddenly felt ridiculous. "You know what? Forget it. Come on, Flo."

"Wait." The bartender stood, taking a scrap of paper from his pocket and the pen behind his ear. "Here." He wrote down his number and handed it to Sunny.

"Thanks. I'm Sunny. This is Flo." She smiled, putting it in her purse.

"Johnny," the bartender nodded, wiping a tear from the corner of his eye. Sunny smiled at him one last time, hoping to channel as much kindness and sympathy to the man as she could, and they walked away.

Sunny felt torn. On the one hand, she wanted to linger in the French Quarter and wander its charming streets, sipping on one of those Hand Grenade cocktails all the tourists were drinking as a saxophone's jazzy riff floated through the air. On the other hand, with the information they had gleaned from their trip across the lake, it was time to get down to the business of solving this murder.

"Do you think Annie's death could be linked to Jeb's?" Flo asked, once again driving her truck across the Lake Pontchartrain Causeway Bridge.

"I have no doubt in my mind that the two are linked." Sunny slapped the truck's dashboard for emphasis. "Think about it–the woman comes to LouLou with the sole mission of getting Jeb to come out of the closet and leave his wife. Then Jeb is killed, and then she dies too." Sunny shook her head. "That's too coincidental not to be connected."

"And if the police don't know about Jeb's little secret, how would they ever know to connect the two deaths?" Flo squinted into the distance. They rode in silence over the bridge, neither knowing the answer to Flo's question. When they turned onto Moonlight Lane, Sunny's face was grim.

"It's possible that Annie's death was simply an accident," she said slowly. "But there's also the very real possibility that two people have died to keep Jeb's other life a secret."

"I think you could be right," Flo nodded gravely. "But how on earth are we going to prove it?"

Chapter 41

Late that night, Sunny sat up in bed, unable to sleep yet again. It had been a busy night at the Cajun Coconut. Her back was aching from all of the hours she spent serving up tons of tropical drinks, but the annoying pain wasn't what kept her from finding sleep. It was Annie.

Sunny couldn't stop thinking about that poor woman, and she was worried that the bartender's death so soon after Jeb's murder was more than just a tragic coincidence. She reached for her phone, charging on the nightstand, and checked the time. It was one in the morning. *Too late to call?* She wondered. Her finger hovered over the number the bartender at the Corner Pocket had given her that afternoon. She pressed the call button.

"Hello?" The voice of Johnny, the bartender,

came on the line, pulsing club music blasting in the background. "Who is this?" he yelled into the receiver.

"Hi, this is Sunny!" she shouted to be heard, wincing, worrying that she might wake Danny, who was sleeping across the hallway. "The lady you gave your number to this afternoon."

"Oh, Sunny, hold on," He seemed to step outside the party zone because suddenly, the loud music stopped, and he began to talk in a level tone. "Can you hear me better now?" he asked.

"Much better," Sunny sighed, thankful that her clubbing days were behind her. "I hope it's okay to call you this late, but I have a few questions about Annie, and you might be the only person I know who can answer them."

"It's okay. I'm still at work, so you didn't wake me," he answered politely. "What is it you need to know? I'll answer what I can, but I'm not sure how much help I'll be."

"My main question is this–did Annie seem particularly worried or jumpy in the few weeks leading up to the house fire? Was there anyone that she said was harassing her or making her feel nervous? Like any of the bar's customers or maybe an ex-boyfriend?"

"Hmmmm," Johnny thought. "I'm not sure... wait a minute. Now that you ask, I remember she started making a habit of asking me to walk her out to her car every night. She blamed it on the uptick in crime in the city lately, but when I walked with her, she looked around like she expected someone to jump out and get her. I thought it was a little over the top at the time." He paused, the realization of Sunny's question sinking in. "But why are you asking me this?"

"I'm not sure yet, Johnny, but I think that Annie's death might not have been an accident." Sunny's voice was grave. "Can you think of anyone who might have frightened her? Who did she think would be waiting at her car after her shifts?"

"I have no idea. All of our regulars are good people who just want to chill and have a drink. Except for that one time…" His voice trailed off.

"Yes?" Sunny prompted anxiously.

"Well, I've only been working here for a little less than a month, so I wasn't here when this happened." He explained. "We get a lot of religious nut jobs in the French Quarter that go around telling anyone who likes to party that they're going to Hell. You can imagine what those people think of The Corner Pocket." He gave a bitter chuckle.

"I'm sorry you have to go through that. It's not right," Sunny lamented.

"It's okay. I'm used to it by now." He cleared a lump in his throat. "But one night a few months ago, before I started working here, one of those religious crazies stood outside the bar, yelling and losing her mind about how homosexuality was sinful, and we're all going to burn, and yatta yatta yatta. Annie had to go out and tell this woman that if she didn't leave, she would call the cops. Turns out, the crazy lady knew a couple of regulars, and she kept yelling into the bar that they were cheating on their wives and God would smite them down." He clicked his tongue in disgust.

Sunny had a thought flash into her mind. Did Johnny know Jeb from his visits to New Orleans? If Johnny knew Jeb, could he identify Jeb's lover? She explained to Johnny how Annie had come to LouLou to convince Jeb to come out of the closet, how Jeb had been murdered, and now Annie was dead too.

"I wish I could give you more information," Johnny's voice began to sound impatient. "But Annie told me that when that crazy lady made her big scene in front of the bar, the couple never came back. Luckily, the nut job never came back, either. If she even tries that junk again, we have the police on speed dial. I'm sorry, but I've got to get back to work. My manager is giving me the stink eye."

"That's okay," Sunny reassured him. "You've been a huge help."

"If you think Annie was killed, I will do whatever it takes to find out who did this," his voice quavered.

"I know you need to go, but one more thing." Sunny looked down at her phone and pulled up her photos. Scrolling through her pictures, she came to one of Barbara and Suzy taken at the last book club meeting. She texted the picture to Johnny, "I just sent you a picture. I know you weren't there the night the woman made a scene, but any chance you recognize either of these two?" She crossed her fingers, hoping for a match.

"No, sorry. Gotta go," Johnny said quickly and hung up the phone.

Chapter 42

The next day was sunny and pleasant, and the humidity that seemed never to leave Louisiana had given way to a light, cool breeze. Sunny sat on the top deck of the Sweet Pea, helping Flo repair her fishing nets. Once a month, Flo spread her large trawler nets from one end of the deck to the other and sewed the many rips and tears the nets incurred from a month's worth of shrimping. Usually, she was forced to do this tedious task alone, and it took her hours of back-breaking work. Now, with Sunny by her side, the work zipped along, fueled by strong cups of coffee and good conversation. Sunny was surprised to learn that she was a natural at net repair. All those years watching her mother sew the family's clothes meant the needle and thread used to repair the trawler net holes felt natural in her hands, her fingers nimbly stitching as she chatted with Flo.

"So, you showed Johnny the picture of Barbara and Suzy, and he didn't recognize either of them?" Flo asked, lowering her corner of the net into her lap and reaching for her coffee mug. "That's disappointing."

"I know," Sunny said, concentrating on a rather tricky repair. "It would have made connecting the two deaths so much easier if Barbara or Suzy had been harassing Jeb and his partner." She held up the net to examine her work. Flo's black cat, Boo, rose from her spot, curled up at Flo's feet, and walked over to Sunny.

"Look at you, little lady." Sunny cooed, bending down to pat Boo's pregnant belly. "How much longer until we have those kittens?"

Boo gave a loud meow as if to say *not soon enough.* She rubbed her sides on Sunny's legs before settling down again in a cozy sun ray.

"From what you told me, I think we can start to make a case that Jeb's killer also murdered Annie." Flo stood, scooped up her calico, Oyster, and cradled him like a baby, kissing the top of his head. "Johnny said that a woman connected with Jeb made a scene at the bar, and then after that, Annie acted nervous at work." She bent over double and gently placed Oyster on the deck. "That can't be a fluke."

"If only we could figure out who the woman was." Sunny stopped stitching and stared out at the water. Little waves lapped against the marina pilings, splashing the cypress trees that lined the shore, their roots–or *knees* as they were called–pushing through the shallow water like tiny mountain ranges. *Find that woman, and we find the connection between Annie and Jeb's deaths.*

Sunny's phone rang.

"Tony, hi," Sunny's voice went an octave higher, and she blushed.

"I was calling to see if you want to come by my house tonight." Tony's voice was warm with a hint of nervousness. "I know it's last minute, but I'm having some of my friends from work over for a shrimp boil, and I wanted you to come."

"I would love that." Sunny ignored the fact that she didn't eat shrimp for the moment. "Thanks for the invite." She got his address and hung up the phone.

"Well, well," Flo laughed. "Someone is going on a date." She slapped her knee, her eyes gleaming.

"It's not a date." Sunny rolled her eyes. *It wasn't a date…right?* She started to feel nauseated. "Dates are for one-on-one time. He's invited a bunch of people, therefore, not a date."

"You are going to do fine." Flo gave her a reassuring pat on the shoulder.

"I know. It's just a get-together at his house… with all his work friends…who will meet me for the first time…in his house…" A look of terror washed over Sunny's face. She wasn't ready for this and decided to call Tony back and tell him so. "I'm going to cancel." She reached for her phone, but Flo put up a hand to stop her.

"Hold on a sec." Flo disappeared inside the boat cabin and returned a few minutes later carrying a small bottle of pink liquid. "Take this." She handed the bottle to Sunny.

"And this is for?" Sunny raised one eyebrow.

"It's for confidence," Flo nodded. "Dab a little bit of this behind your ears and on your wrists, and everything will work out just fine." She returned to her seat and resumed her repair work as if she hadn't just handed Sunny a love potion.

"Okay." Sunny decided not to ask any more questions as she slipped the tiny bottle into her pocket, following Flo's lead and sitting down again to sew. "If it is a date, which it's not, I'm not sure how good it will go, considering I need to tell Tony about that security camera footage. He won't be happy when he hears we're still investigating."

"Tony's a reasonable man," Flo shrugged. "He'll understand."

The two women worked in companionable silence for the next hour until the holes in Flo's shrimping nets were closed and secure.

"Thanks for all of the help." Flo stood and began folding the nets into neat squares. "This went so much faster with you working with me."

Sunny's eyes grew wide. The most enormous pelican she had ever seen had landed on the boat railing behind Flo and was inching its way closer to her unassuming friend.

"Flo!" Sunny hissed. "Turn around! There's a...a... giant bird!" She pointed a shaking hand at the boat railing at Flo's back.

"Oh, that's just Milton!" Flo turned to face the pelican, putting a hand on its large head to ruffle its faded brown feathers. "He comes for a visit most afternoons," she explained to Sunny and turned back to talk to the bird. "I don't have any shrimp today, old boy, but I do have some leftover redfish in the fridge. Be right back." She walked inside the cabin.

"Don't leave me out here with that...that pterodactyl!" Sunny shrieked. Milton had to be twice the size of the pelicans she had seen around the lake, his bucket-like beak looking ominously powerful.

"Milton won't do you any harm." Flo returned, a small fillet of raw redfish in her hand. She held it over the pelican's head, and he readily gobbled it up. "See you later, boy." She gave his head another quick pat, and he flew away. Sunny shook her head, a look of amazement on her astonished face. Flo simply shrugged.

On the walk back to her parked car, Sunny bumped into Earl Herbert. He was carrying his fishing rod and a bucket of live bait.

"Going fishing?" Sunny asked cheerfully. "It's the perfect day for it."

"That was the idea." Earl dipped his head and stared at the bait bucket in his hand. "But now, I don't know." His eyes welled with tears.

"How are you doing, Earl?" Sunny asked sympathetically.

"I thought a day of fishing out on the lake would make me feel better," he nodded sadly. "But now that I'm here, all I can think about is how Jeb is gone. I think it's best if I just go home."

"I'm so sorry, Earl." Sunny reached out and touched his shoulder. "If I can do anything or you need to talk, please let me know."

He thanked her and went on his way.

I have a not-a-date in exactly four hours. Sunny winced as she shifted her car into drive. *What on earth am I going to wear?*

Chapter 43

Several hours later, Sunny sat in her car, frozen with fear. She looked at Tony's house across the street from where her Miata was parked, and her heart dropped to the floorboard. *It's not a date. It's not a date. Just go in there, act natural, and be yourself.* She muttered every confidence-building cliche she could think of, but nothing seemed to help. Suddenly, she remembered…

She took Flo's bottle of mystery liquid out of her dress pocket and examined it in the fading afternoon sunlight. The strawberry-hued syrup sloshed thickly back and forth as she tilted the bottle this way and that.

"Might as well try it," she shrugged and screwed open the top. The scent of roses filled the car. Sunny did as Flo instructed and dabbed a little on her wrists. She waited for something to happen. *Nope, still freaking out.* She sighed, angling the rearview mirror downwards to take one last look at her hair. "Can't sit in this car forever, Sunny." Resigned to her fate, she stepped out and walked up to Tony's front door.

Tony's house was in a small cul-de-sac neighborhood near St. Boudreaux's Church, and as Sunny stood on the doorstep, she could hear the tower bells ringing out the six o'clock hour. She pressed the doorbell and waited. The house was small but charming, with light blue siding, white trim, and a black front door. The front yard was neatly landscaped with several large birds-of-paradise, their beak-like orange and purple flowers giving the yard cheerful pops of color. Finally, the door opened.

"Sunny!" Tony stood in the doorway wearing a red and white Hawaiian shirt, a bottle of Abita beer in one hand. "I'm so glad you could make it." He hugged her quickly and led her through the house and to the backyard.

"Glad to be here." She gave a timid smile and looked around. Three people stood around a large, silver pot bubbling away over a portable gas stove.

"Hey, guys!" Tony called to them. "This is Sunny. She's new in town, so be nice." He gave her a wink. " Sam, Jerry, and Laura are friends from work." He motioned to the others who each gave a polite wave. "Can I get you a beer? Wine?"

"Beer would be great." Sunny stood awkwardly on the back lawn for a moment while Tony disappeared into the house to get her beer from his kitchen fridge. Thankfully, his friends walked over.

"Sunny, it's so nice to meet you," Laura was tall with cafe-au-lait skin, short twisted braids, and kind eyes. "Tony's been talking about you non-stop," she laughed.

"Really?" Sunny blushed, deciding to change the subject as quickly as possible. "I've never been to a shrimp boil before." She still hadn't worked out the issue of her being vegetarian and most definitely not eating shrimp.

"It's easy." Sam, a young guy in his twenties, motioned for her to walk over and look into the pot. "You always do your boil outside in a pot like this. You've got your shrimp, some potatoes, some corn, and a good amount of seasoning." He grabbed what looked like a wooden oar used to paddle a boat and stirred the pot.

When Sunny forgot that little creatures were bubbling away in the pot, she had to admit that the smell rising in the air was divine. Tony came back and pressed a cold beer bottle into her hand. She thanked him and took a long sip, hoping for some liquid courage. The group stood around the yard, making happy, chatty small talk and waiting for the shrimp to cook. When the food was done, Tony put on a pair of oven mitts and, gripping the pot's interior steamer basket, lifted the strainer pot into the air before dumping the shrimp, potatoes, and corn onto a newspaper-lined table on the other side of the yard.

"Let's eat, y'all," Tony smiled, handing out paper plates.

"Tony," Sunny spoke in an almost-whisper. "Can I talk to you for a sec?" She waved her hand for him to come closer. She looked at him with sheepish eyes when they were over in a corner away from the others. "The food looks amazing, and I'm loving getting to know your friends, but I'm actually a vegetarian. Don't worry, though!" She quickly reassured him. "I'm totally fine just hanging out and eating something when I get home."

"I've got you covered," he grinned and took her hand, leading her inside to his kitchen. He reached inside the refrigerator and pulled out the loveliest, fresh garden salad Sunny had ever seen. "Made it this morning from my garden. I grew everything in here except for the lettuce." He beamed with pride.

"I'm impressed." Sunny had to admit that she was crushing hard on Tony Perez. Now, what did she plan on doing with those feelings? She wasn't sure yet.

The evening turned out to be one of the most enjoyable in Sunny's recent memory. Tony was charming and funny, regaling the group with hilarious stories from his days working as a cop in L.A. Tony's friends were kind and welcoming, and Sunny felt completely comfortable talking with them. When the evening began to wind down, the group moved inside, walking through the house and towards the front door as they said their goodbyes.

"Guess we better get going," Laura yawned. "Lots of work to do tomorrow now that the Jeb Landry case is open again."

"Right, especially since with the possibility of a second murder." The minute the words left her lips, Sunny knew she had made a mistake.

"A second murder?" Laura's eyes grew sharp. "What do you mean?"

"Oh, nothing. Just a little theory I have, but it's nothing, really. Nothing." Sunny fiddled with her purse strap and looked down at her shoes.

"Right." Laura stood a little straighter,

examining Sunny with scrutinizing eyes. "Good night, y'all."

Sam and Jerry said their goodbyes, leaving Sunny and Tony alone on the front steps.

"Did you have to do that?" Tony looked annoyed.

"What?"

"The possibility of a second murder?" He fumed. "I've been humoring you and turning a blind eye to your snooping around town, but if my work colleagues find out you are putting yourself in harm's way, I'm in big trouble." He crossed his arms over his chest and squared his jaw.

"I'm sorry. Don't be mad at me." Sunny gave him a pleading look.

"I'm not so much mad as I am concerned." His stony features softened. "You aren't a police officer or a detective. If you keep sticking your nose where it doesn't belong, you will get hurt."

"I need to tell you something, and I might as well do it now while you are already angry with me." She pulled Buzz's flash drive from her purse and placed it in his hand. "This is security footage showing Suzy Herbert's car parked in the back alley by the Cajun Coconut the night Jeb died. I think it's significant to the case."

"You think it's significant to the case?" Tony's eyes were wide. "How long have you been holding this back?"

"Not long." Sunny shifted her guilty eyes. "I know you don't want to hear this, but I think you need to bring Suzy and Barbara in for questioning."

Tony blew air through pursed lips in protest, but Sunny kept going.

"No, really," she insisted, placing her hands on his shoulders. "I know for a fact that neither of them have a real alibi. They are as guilty as sin. You have to believe me."

"I know Suzy's alibi is shaky, but how do you know that Barbara's alibi isn't solid?" He eyed her suspiciously.

"Not important." She pulled back and turned to leave. "Promise me you will bring them in for questioning."

"I can't make any promises." Tony followed after her. "Sunny, wait!"

Sunny kept walking to her car. She had to get out of there before she confessed to posing as a patient to break into Doctor Oliphant's files, a fact that she was pretty sure could land her some jail time. There was something about Tony and his warm brown eyes that acted like a truth serum. She was powerless to keep a secret from the man. "Gotta go!" she called over her shoulder.

"Not yet."

When Sunny reached her car, she turned to see Tony standing in the street behind her. He walked towards her and put an arm around her waist.

"Sunflower Beach, you are an infuriating woman," he whispered, inches from her mouth. He leaned in and kissed her. "Stay out of trouble, please." He turned and walked back home.

Chapter 44

"Wastin' away again in Margaritaville..." Sunny shook her booty to the beat and sang along with Jimmy Buffett while she poured a Pearl Diver cocktail into a tiki mug shaped like a dolphin. She handed it to the waiting customer with a smile. "Here you go."

"Someone's in a good mood." Flo suppressed a grin. "I'm guessing the date went well last night." She hung her purple fishing jacket on a hook behind the bar and got to work serving the long line of customers forming around the bartop.

"It wasn't a date, but..." Sunny let out a small giggle.

"He kissed you!" Flo gasped, grinning so wide her cheeks hurt.

"How did you know that?" Sunny stopped mixing a Mai Tai and turned to Flo, her hands on her hips.

"You used the stuff I gave you, huh?" Flo took a ten-dollar bill from a customer and brought it to the cash register to make change.

"Yes," Sunny said sheepishly, returning to her work. Flo said nothing, only gave a happy, knowing nod.

"I brought a little something with me tonight." Flo turned to the tote bag she had brought into the Coconut earlier. "Thought we could sell it by the slice like you suggested." She lifted a large Tupperware cake carrier from her bag and placed it on the counter.

"Is that your famous coconut cake?" Sunny was practically drooling. "I might have a tough time selling it to people because I plan to eat it all first."

Flo laughed and returned to her bag for a white ceramic cake stand. She slid the cake onto the stand and set it out for customers to see.

"What do you think?" Sunny got a notecard and a pen. "Three dollars a slice?" She wrote the price on the card and stuck it in front of the cake. "I'm going to owe you three dollars because I'm eating a piece right now." She got a long knife and sliced into the fluffy, white, three-tier cake.

Julia Donahue burst through the front door from where she had been sitting on the Coconut's front patio, drinking with a few friends. "Y'all are never gonna believe this! Get out here! Everybody!" She ran back outside.

Everyone in the bar ran out the door and stood on the patio, wondering what the woman had been so excited about. They didn't have to wonder for long. A police car drove slowly down the street past the Cajun Coconut and turned toward the police department.

That wasn't anything unusual, Sunny shrugged, but then she saw who was riding in the squad car's back seat–Barbara and Suzy.

Chapter 45

The gossip in LouLou the next day was so electric that the air practically crackled. As Sunny pushed her buggy through the aisles of the Hop for her weekly grocery shopping, she heard whispers all around her, her fellow shoppers bubbling over with the news around town. For a moment, Sunny almost felt bad for Barbara. The gossipers took a practically gleeful delight in recounting her very public ride to the station for interrogation.

Sunny's stomach rumbled. She had skipped breakfast, something she never, ever did, and after loading the last bag of groceries into the trunk of her car, she decided she was now too tired and hungry to cook lunch. After dropping her grocery haul back at home, she headed to the diner instead.

Like the Hop, Gary's diner was buzzing with the news of Barbara and Suzy's ride in the back of the squad car. She sat at an empty booth and waited for one of the triplets to take her order. Without looking up from her menu, she could feel the weight of a pair of eyes on her. She lifted her gaze to see the same older man she had seen on her last visit to the diner, the one that spat accusations of murder at her before hobbling away. This time, he didn't speak, but from the look on his face, it was clear he wanted to start a conversation.

"May I help you?" Sunny didn't want to be rude, but she wasn't in the mood for more of his nastiness.

"I just wanted to say that I'm sorry," he said with a tremble in his voice. "I accused you of killing poor Jeb, and it looks like you didn't do it, so...Sorry." He returned his attention to his scrambled eggs and grits. Sunny sat up a little straighter in the booth. Barbara and Suzy hadn't been convicted yet, but she was sure that once Tony questioned them thoroughly, he would see she was right to accuse them of the crime. They would be charged and sent to jail, releasing Sunny and her tiki bar of any suspected wrongdoing. When Donna brought over a large coffee with extra creamer and a plate of sweet potato pancakes without taking Sunny's order first, Sunny sighed with satisfaction. It was all coming together. She had solved the murder. The police had the bad guys. People in LouLou would move past their misconceptions of her, and she would be accepted as one of them. Heck, she might even be on her way to having a boyfriend! She took a big, triumphant bite of her pancakes.

Back home, she put away her groceries and sat on the living room sofa. Danny was at school, and the house was quiet. She drummed her hands on her lap, wondering what to do next. Without a murder investigation to eat up her time, she didn't know quite what to do with herself. She grabbed her book from the coffee table and opened it to her bookmarked page. She began to read. The sleuth in her mystery novel had accused someone of being the murderer but had made a mistake, moving the case back to an unfortunate square one. She slapped the book shut. Maybe she should drive to the marina and see what Flo was up to. Or maybe go to the library? She knew that Flo was out working in the gulf, and she had already been to the library twice that week.

"I know what I'll do." She stood and went to the storage cupboard, where she kept the extra cleaning supplies. The tiki bar desperately needed a deep cleaning, and when she had been hunting down a killer, she never found the time for scrubbing. She loaded up her cleaning supplies and headed to the Cajun Coconut.

Once in the tiki bar, she donned her rubber cleaning gloves, mixed a batch of hot, soapy water, and began wiping down all the tables and chairs. Next, she got on her hands and knees, scrubbing the walls and baseboards. She stood, stretched her stiff back, and did a double take. *What is going on with the surfer dude?* She moved closer to the velvet painting of the surfers on the beach and cocked her head to one side, confused. Instead of the painting's usual sunny landscape and happy surfer couple hitting the waves, the picture's sky was stormy and grey, the waves choppy and rough, and the surfers…They were gone. Sunny felt a chill down her back. Something wasn't right. She opened her mouth to call out to the tiki spirits and ask what was the matter, but just as she did, the bar's front door opened.

"I was hoping I would find you here." Tony walked in, his face grim. Sunny's blood ran cold when she saw his expression, her heart sinking. *He regrets kissing me. He hates me. He never wants to see me again.*

"Why so glum, chum?" Sunny forced a laugh. "Can I get you something to drink?" She put down her wash rag and moved towards the bar.

"Not right now." He put up a hand to stop her. "I need to talk to you about Barbara and Suzy."

"Okay," Sunny said, relieved that he hadn't come to break up with her–not that they were even actually together. Even so, something in his tone made her worry about what he would say next.

"I've had to release them," he said.

"What?" Sunny choked. "Why? How? Huh?"

"When you gave me that security footage, it raised reasonable doubts about Suzy's alibi, and after doing some digging, I confirmed your suspicions about Barbara's alibi. She wasn't at the doctor in New Orleans as she originally told us. It was enough to bring them in for questioning. I felt we were close to making an arrest until Barbara's lawyer came in, and I had to let them go." He exhaled deeply and rubbed his tired eyes.

"Had to let them go?" Sunny stood and pinched the bridge of her nose in frustration. "What possible reason could you have for letting them go?"

"Their lawyer presented new evidence in the case, and Barbara came clean about her real alibi. We had no choice but to let her and Suzy go."

"New evidence? What new evidence? And what was her alibi?" Sunny's questions rushed out of her mouth.

"Look, I can't tell you any of that, and even if I could, I wouldn't want to." His cheeks flushed pink. "Can't you see that you've embarrassed me here? I followed your advice, and now, I've ticked off some of the town's richest, most powerful people. I'll be lucky not to be fired."

"Well," Sunny's voice began to quiver, her eyes threatening tears. "I'm sorry I've caused you such trouble. Maybe you should go."

"You're right. I should." Tony turned and walked out of the bar.

Sunny sank into one of the peacock chairs and wept. For one brief morning, she felt as if everything was going her way, and now, it had all come crashing down.

Chapter 46

Sunny was in no mood for tiki lights, luau music, and tropical drinks. Instead, she wanted to eat chocolate and hide in a nest of blankets on her sofa with the Hallmark channel playing on the TV. But, the Cajun Coconut was supposed to be open for business; if she didn't open the bar, no one else would. Flo's cat, Boo, was due with her kittens any day, and though Flo usually came into the Coconut to help run the place, she had asked for a few nights off to look after her very pregnant kitty.

Sunny flicked on the colorful lights around the room and unenthusiastically pressed play on the beachy music. The weather outside had turned stormy, with thunder rumbling and sheets of rain pouring down, so she didn't expect many customers. Every now and again, her eyes turned towards the velvet painting. Nothing had changed since she saw it that afternoon. The surfers were missing, and the waves remained roiled in a stormy sea. Sunny's stomach formed a worried knot.

Several hours later, only a few customers sat at tables, and Sunny did her best to occupy her hands and mind by taking inventory of what she needed to order from her liquor and wine supplier. She knelt behind the bar, counting rum and tequila bottles, but stood when she heard the clacking of the seashells on the front door.

"Flo!" She said with surprise. "I thought you were taking care of Boo."

"I was, but she seemed to be doing fine, and, well..." Her face was lined with worry as she hung up a dripping wet raincoat on the corner coat rack. "I just got the feeling that you needed me here."

Sunny looked around the half-empty bar. She didn't need any help serving customers, but she was relieved to see her friend all the same.

"I'm glad you're here. It's been a rough day." She told Flo in hushed tones about her visit from the police chief, tears escaping her eyes by the end of her story.

"That's not good news." Flo wrung her anxious hands. "And he never said what her real alibi was?"

Sunny shook her head in the negative.

"Whatever new evidence was brought forth must be pretty damning to have it sway the case as much as it has," Flo wondered.

"If only he would have told me what it was." Sunny's slammed a fist on the bar top.

The front door opened again, and in walked Suzy and Barbara.

Chapter 47

"I'll take your finest bottle of champagne with two glasses." Barbara's searing blue eyes danced as she doffed her dripping wet raincoat and hung it on the back of a chair. She sat down at a table, and Suzy joined her.

"Barbara? What are you doing here?" Sunny stood near their table, her face stricken, her body shaking.

"What do you mean *what am I doing here*?" Barbara sniped, her mouth formed a sweet smile, but her words were sharp. "If you must know, Suzy and I are celebrating." She gave a satisfied nod to her friend.

"Celebrating what?" Sunny's heart was beating wildly.

"You'll see." Suzy cooed. "Now get us that champagne."

"This is a tiki bar. We don't serve champagne," Sunny informed them.

"Well, get us two of whatever killed Jeb then." Barbara rolled her eyes. "Now, shoo." She waved Sunny away.

Sunny turned stiffly and made her way to the bar to mix two mai tais, briefly catching Flo's worried eyes.

"I'm worried." Flo moved closer to Sunny and spoke from the side of her mouth. "This isn't going to be good."

Sunny made the two cocktails with shaking hands and brought them to Barbara and Suzy's table.

"It's no Veuve Clicquot–" Barbara took a tentative sip from her tiki mug. "But I guess it will have to do." She rose from her seat and held her cocktail glass high. The room went quiet. "To Sunny, who tried to get me convicted of murder but will soon learn who's in charge in this town." She clinked mugs with Suzy and took a long swig. A flash of lightning lit up the bar windows, and a clap of thunder rumbled Sunny's body deep to her bones. The front door of the Coconut opened, and a rain-soaked Tony stood in the doorway. Sunny could tell by his stone-cold expression that he wasn't there for a cocktail.

"Flo Charboneaux, I am arresting you for the murder of Jeb Landry." He walked behind the bar and grabbed Flo by the hands, pulling them behind her back and clamping a pair of handcuffs around her wrists. Flo's face was as white as the sky over the lake on a foggy day.

"What?!" Sunny screamed. "What do you mean? What's happening? Flo?? She couldn't possibly..." She panted in a horror. From the corner of her eye, she saw Suzy and Barbara clink their mugs in another celebratory cheers.

Tony went silent, guiding Flo out the front door without making eye contact with Sunny.

"Answer me!" Sunny ran outside after them, the rain coming down in sheets, soaking her linen dress and loose wavy hair. "What evidence do you have on Flo? What motive could she possibly have for killing him?" Her wild eyes darted from Tony to Flo, lowering her head to slide into the squad car's back seat.

"It's going to be okay, Sunny." Flo's face was calm, but her voice was shaking. "Just find out who did this. It's up to you now."

Tony slammed the back car door shut and walked to the driver's seat.

"Tony!" Sunny ran to him, pleading. "Talk to me. What on earth is going on?"

He shut the door, put the key into the ignition, and drove away. Sunny, her tears now mixing with the downpour that pelted her face, stood watching the tail lights of the squad car as they faded into the darkness.

Chapter 48

She wasn't sure how long she had stood on the rainy sidewalk staring at the spot where the squad car had taken Flo away, but by the time Sunny went back inside the Coconut, Barbara and Suzy had gone.

Nice, Sunny fumed to herself. Not only had the women gotten her best friend arrested for a crime she didn't commit, but they had also stiffed her on their bill. *That's the least of my problems now, but still...*

She looked around the room at the remaining customers. A young couple, clearly on a date, sat in one corner, sipping Jungle Birds. Two men in business suits sat at the bar drinking piña coladas. Sunny began to shiver, noticing for the first time the puddle forming on the floor underneath her, her dress and hair soaked to the bone.

"I'm sorry to do this, folks," Sunny cut the

tropical music and made an announcement. "But I've got to close up shop early. Family emergency." She collected their mugs, promising not to charge them for anything they owed. With the customers gone, Sunny quickly shut down the tiki lights and locked the door. She told herself she could clean up later. There wasn't a moment to lose. She ran to her car and sped down the street.

The LouLou police station stood a mile or two outside the town center. It was a small, brick one-story building down a red dirt road surrounded by thick patches of pine trees. Sunny parked her car and raced inside.

"I need to see Flo!" She shouted at the front desk officer on duty. "Where is she?"

The desk officer eyed her warily, putting down his oyster po' boy and wiping a spot of mayonnaise from the corner of his mouth.

"And you are?" he asked slowly. His eyes flicked up and down Sunny's body, and it dawned on her that with her wet hair and clothes, she probably looked like Swamp Thing's insane cousin.

"Sunny Beach. I'm Flo's friend, and I have to see her," she pleaded.

"Florence Charboneaux is in a holding cell being questioned by Police Chief Perez." He took a toothpick from his desktop and began digging in his teeth. "She's not currently approved for visitation."

"Well then, let me speak to Tony. I mean, Chief Perez." She crossed her arms, shivering from the cold blast of air conditioning that began to blow from a window unit in the corner of the room.

"You think you can just stroll on in here and talk

to the chief?" He eyed her incredulously and gave an indignant chuckle. "Don't you know the chief is busy? Why, he don't have time for...What did you say your name was?"

But as she opened her mouth to answer, she heard a voice from over her shoulder.

"Sunny Beach." Tony stood behind her, his face as solemn as when he had come to the Cajun Coconut and taken Flo away. Sunny turned to face him, but before she could launch into the speech she had been practicing in the car, one where she verbally tore him several new holes in his body, he put up his hands to stop her from speaking. "Come this way, Ms. Beach." He motioned for her to follow him through a door that led past the front desk.

They walked down a long, white-walled hallway lit by fluorescent overhead bulbs, which made the space feel sterile and the faces that passed her look jaundiced. Midway down, he stopped at a grey door and held it open for her to go through. Flo sat in a plastic folding chair at a metal table in the center of the room, looking dejected.

"Flo!" Sunny leaped forward and wrapped her damp arms around her friend. A guard in the corner moved to stop her, but Tony held up a hand to allow it. "What is going on? Tony, what are you doing?" She searched his face for the kind man she had known before that twirled her around the dance floor to a Cajun waltz, his hand on her lower back and his eyes sparkling and warm. Where was that man? There was no trace of him now as they sat in the cold, bare room, unable to leave or, at the very least, find answers to why they were there.

"The police have told me they have evidence against me." Flo wrung her hands in her lap as she stared at Tony. He didn't return her gaze.

"But that's crazy!" Sunny shook her head in disbelief. "What evidence?"

"On further inspection of the victim's home, a suspicious bottle was found under the victim's pillow in his bed." Tony took a plastic evidence bag from his pocket. He placed it on the table between them. Sunny squinted at the bag. It held a tiny bottle with some sort of bits inside suspended in a clear, yellow liquid.

"This clears up nothing. What the heck is this?" Sunny was growing more frustrated by the minute.

"I've told Tony and every other officer that has questioned me that I gave this to Jeb because he was having trouble sleeping. Said he had a lot on his mind." Flo crossed her arms over her chest and sat back in her chair. "He was supposed to put it under his pillow, which he obviously did because that's where you found it." She gave an exasperated huff.

"You are conveniently leaving out the most incriminating part." Tony rolled his eyes. "This bottle?" He grasped the edge of the plastic bag and held it up. "It's full of grapefruit oil." He put the bag back on the table, rose from his seat, and began to pace the small room.

"But, Tony, why would Flo want to kill Jeb? It doesn't make any sense." Sunny followed him with her eyes as he walked back and forth. "Plus, Flo has been helping me find out who killed Jeb. Why would she do that if she was the one that did it? That would make her some sort of criminal mastermind. In all the years that you've known Flo, is that the impression she gives off? A cold-hearted murderer?" Sunny couldn't believe for one minute that Flo was guilty. Sure, she had only known the woman for a few months, but she trusted Flo with every atom in her body. Her friend was innocent, and as she sat in that holding cell, Sunny slowly realized it would be on her to prove it. "Right." She stood, gathering all of her remaining strength. "If you don't plan on finding out who the *real* killer is, I guess it will be up to me." She turned to Flo. "What can I bring you? I will get you out of here, but it might take a minute."

Flo needed nothing but was worried about her cat, Boo. Sunny promised to take Boo back to her house. She and Danny could pamper the momma-to-be and help keep the kittens healthy once they were born. She shot Tony a glare and left the room. Tony followed.

"Do you think I like this?" He asked her retreating back. "Do you think this is how I wanted any of this to go?" Sunny stopped and turned to face him. His eyes were filled with pain; his mouth turned in a downward arch.

"You didn't have to go and arrest an innocent woman," she hissed.

"You didn't have to go and convince me to tick off some of the most prominent people in town," he quipped in return.

"So, you've arrested Flo to, what?... Get back at me or something?" She narrowed her eyes.

"Of course not." He exhaled in frustration. "I arrested Flo because there was solid evidence against her, and if I keep showing you and your friends preferential treatment, I'm going to lose my job."

Sunny had nothing more to say to him. She turned and walked away, shaking her head and wondering what she had ever seen in Tony Perez.

Chapter 49

Sunny blinked her tired eyes as she left the police station and drove down to the marina. It was one in the morning, well past her bed time, and she swung a tired leg onto the top deck of the Sweet Pea with protesting muscles.

"Flo!" Tabasco squawked as Sunny opened the boat cabin door. "Where's Flo?"

Sunny moved closer to the bird's perch and gently stroked his feathers.

"Flo is going to be away for a few days," she told him. "She will be back soon." *Am I really talking to a bird? Can he even understand me?* She wasn't sure, but she watched as the bird nodded his green head as she spoke, as if in understanding. Sunny looked around the room, calling for Boo. Oyster emerged from under the sofa, meowing loudly.

"I know you're probably worried about Flo, too." She bent to pet his orange and black sides. "Don't worry. Everything is going to be okay." She straightened and looked once more for the little black cat. "Where is Boo?" A small meow sounded from the boat's tiny bathroom, and Sunny went to investigate. She peered inside to find Boo curled up in a cat bed layered with a fleece blanket. "There you are, little miss," Sunny smiled, scooping the kitty and the blanket into her arms. She grabbed the cat bed, a few cans of cat food, and a paper bag filled with kitty litter. Before leaving, she fed Oyster his dinner, making a mental note to return to feed him breakfast in the morning, and set out a fresh bowl of birdseed for Tabasco. "I'll see you boys in the morning," she called to them as she closed the door and left.

At home, she carried Boo and the cat's necessities inside. She placed the cat bed in a cozy corner of the kitchen and dumped the contents of one of the cat food cans into a small bowl. Rummaging around the hallway closet, she found a box that was the perfect size for a litter box and filled it with the kitty litter.

"There we go," she cooed as she petted Boo's round belly. "You get comfortable and don't worry about a thing. Danny and I have it all under control." She had never helped a cat give birth before, but how hard could it be? She was a nurse, after all. She had attended many human births. This was going to be a piece of cake. Her stomach growled. *Cake.* She would sell her left arm for a slice of Flo's coconut cake. She stood and opened the fridge door to rummage around for anything to eat. Alas, there was no coconut cake. She settled for hummus and a handful of pretzels, taking them into her room.

She changed into her nightgown and climbed into bed. *There's no way I will fall asleep after everything that has happened tonight,* Sunny sighed, placing her snack on her lap and reaching for her book on the nightstand. Within minutes, she was snoring in a deep, exhausted sleep.

"Um, Mom?" Danny's voice called from the hallway. Sunny woke with a jolt, sending pretzels flying from her lap, her book hitting the floor with a thud. She wiped the drool from the corner of her mouth and blinked in the morning sunlight. *I guess I could fall asleep after all,* she shrugged, swinging her legs over the side of the bed and sliding her feet into her slippers.

"Yes, Danny?" She stepped into the hallway. "What is it, dear?"

"Why do we have a cat in the kitchen?" His face was excited. "Did you get us a cat as a surprise? You know I've wanted one since forever!"

"Aw, I hate to disappoint you, Sunny's Little Sunshine," she gave him a sympathetic look, "but that's not our cat. Boo is Flo's kitty. We're just petsitting because Boo's about to have kittens, and Flo can't take care of her right now."

They walked into the kitchen to see Boo happily curled up in her bed, the gentle sound of her purr filling the room.

"Oh." Danny's shoulders slumped. He frowned. "Wait, why is Flo not able to take care of her? Is Flo sick or something?" Sunny's heart sank. She knew she would have to tell Danny the truth, but she also knew that the truth would be hard for her son to take.

"Well, I don't want you to worry." She took one of his hands and clasped it in between her warm palms. "Everything is going to be okay, but you know how that man died in the Coconut? The police have taken Flo to the station for questioning about his death." She studied his face to see how he would react.

"Questioning? The station?" Danny's anxiety rose in his voice. "Do you mean like *jail?"*

"I am doing everything I can to get her out." Sunny reached for a bowl and the cereal box and poured Danny some breakfast. "We both know Flo is innocent, and they can't keep an innocent woman in jail for long." She slid the bowl and a spoon across the kitchen counter in his direction. "Don't worry."

"Don't worry!?" Danny panicked. "How am I not supposed to worry? What can I do? I need to help Flo."

"There is something you can do to help." Sunny poured her own bowl of cereal. "I need to be out in town, doing research and trying to get the police to release Flo, which means I won't be here at home looking after Boo." She reached for one of the cat food cans and shook it into Boo's bowl. "I need you to stay here and take care of Boo and her kittens."

Danny nodded and finished his breakfast.

Sunny quickly showered, dressed, and drove over to the tiki bar. Weaving around the square at a too-fast speed, she had to remind herself to take her lead foot off the gas. She slowed the Miata to the speed limit and took a deep breath. Since Flo had been carted off to jail the night before, Sunny felt like a time bomb had been activated. It's loud ticking rang in her ears. Its weight pressed like an anvil on her chest. She had to find the killer. It wasn't just about her and the Cajun Coconut anymore. It wasn't even about her near obsession with being accepted by people in town anymore. Now, if she didn't find who murdered Jeb, and probably Annie, Flo's life could be ruined. She took another deep breath, anxiety tightening in her throat.

She burst through the front door of the Coconut.

"Cook! Pearl! Help me, please!" Tears welled in her eyes as she fell to her knees before the tall tiki totem.

"Sunflower, we have been waiting for you to come." Cook awoke, his eyes glowing like sapphires.

"We've been so worried ever since last night when your dear friend got taken away." Pearl's voice trembled. "Is she okay?"

"No, she's not," Sunny cried. "And she's not going to be okay until I find out who is committing these murders. But I feel like I'm nowhere near as close to finding the killer as I should be by now." She held up her desperate hands. "What should I do?"

"Calm yourself, lass." Barry's voice sounded from over her head. "Why don't you go take a wee dram of whisky? It will make ye' feel better."

"Typical of a pirate to think alcohol is the solution." Cora's tone was full of condescension. Even the sight of Sunny's heartbroken face couldn't put a dent in the water spirit's cool demeanor.

"If a spot of the good stuff ain't helpful, I ask you what is?" Vin defended his fellow feathery friend.

"How about actual information from a direct source about the crime?" Cora replied.

"What?" Sunny raised her head from her hands and sat up straight. "What do you mean?"

"Well, dear," Cora continued. "You forget that last night while you were outside freaking out and putting on a scene worthy of a soap opera, we were in here listening to every word those two trouble-making women said."

"You mean Barbara and Suzy?" Sunny's ears pricked up. "Well, go on then. What did they say that's so important?" she snapped, impatient.

"I heard them, too," Pearl announced. "They were not very nice indeed. Terrible," Pearl's voice shuddered.

"Get on with ye!" Barry demanded with a squawk. "You're going to give poor Sunflower a heart attack with all the waiting."

"Like I was saying," Cora hissed. "The two women said that they don't know who killed Jeb, but…"

"So that must mean that they're innocent," Pearl interrupted. "I know that will be hard for you to accept, dear one."

Sunny nodded, a grimace on her face.

"May I continue?" Cora whined. "They said they didn't know who killed Jeb but that it was probably one of his *special friends*, the ones that he took over to New Orleans when he thought no one was noticing."

"Did they say who his special friend was?" Sunny asked, and the tiki spirits all said no.

"So Barbara and Suzy think Jeb's lover did this," Sunny whispered halfway to herself. "How do I find out who his lover was? I mean, if his own wife couldn't find out who his lover was, how am I supposed to do it?

Sunny told the tiki spirits goodbye and left. She squinted as she stepped out of the dimly-lit tiki bar and into the bright morning sunshine. Opening her car door, she started to slide into the driver's seat but stopped. Something, or rather *someone,* caught her eye from across the square. Walking into Bunny's Boulangerie was Beaux Herbert, Suzy and Earl's son. Until then, the college student hadn't been the focus of her investigation, but maybe that had been a mistake. She slammed her car door shut and hurried across the square.

By the time she reached him, Beaux was leaning against the bakery counter, ordering a cafe au lait and an almond croissant the size of a football.

"Let me pay for that for you," Sunny pushed her way to the register before he could take out his credit card.

"And who are you?" He looked taken aback.

"A friend of your mom's," Sunny lied. "I just need to talk to you for a sec." She handed over a clump of wadded-up dollar bills and told the girl at the register to keep the change. They walked to a table in the crowded dining area and settled at one of the slim, blue bistro tables.

"Okay?" Beaux gave her a questioning glance.

"Right," Sunny nodded. "I own the tiki bar that just opened up a while back. Have you heard of it? The

Cajun Coconut?" She hoped the smile on her face was friendly.

"Yeah, actually, a couple of my fraternity brothers have been talking about that place," he nodded before taking a sip from his coffee mug.

"So, *you've* never been to the bar? Just your school friends?"

"Yeah, why?" He narrowed his eyes. "Look, my frat bros can be pretty wild sometimes, and I'm not responsible if they damaged anything in your bar or whatever. You need to take that up with them."

"I guess it's time for me to stop beating around the bush," Sunny sighed. "If you don't already know, Jeb Landry died in my bar." Sunny noticed a flicker of fear show in the boy's eyes. "The night he died, your mom's car showed up on security footage. The car pulled up to the alley behind my bar. Someone unrecognizable went in and came out again very quickly, only to speed off into the night. Your mother tells me that she didn't have the car that night. You did."

"So you're saying I snuck over to your bar, killed the man I considered a second father, and then ran away." Red splotches traveled up his neck, reaching his round cheeks.

"If that's not the case, please enlighten me." Sunny leaned forward, her hands clasped on the table between them.

"First of all, Jeb was part of my family. I loved him. We all did." His tone was grave. "And second of all, I didn't even have the car that night. Did Mom say I could use it? Yes. But a buddy of mine was having a party in the French Quarter, and I knew I was going to drink, so I got an Uber there and back. If Mom's car left the garage, it wasn't me driving." He held up his innocent hands.

"If you weren't driving the car, what about your dad? What was he doing that night?" Sunny remembered that Suzy and Earl's alibis could only be confirmed by each other. Married couples lie for each other all of the time. Earl and Suzy were supposedly watching TV all night, but one of them could have easily snuck away for a short time.

"Are you accusing my dad of killing his best friend?" Beaux's anger was building, his voice growing louder. People in the bakery were starting to stare. "My dad loved Jeb like a brother. He would never. Jeb meant the world to him." He pushed away from the table. "I've got to go." He left his uneaten breakfast on the table and stormed out of the bakery. Sunny wrapped the croissant in a napkin and slipped it into her purse. *Waste not, want not.* She had paid for the delicious pastry, after all.

She was satisfied to knock Beaux off her suspect list, but the puzzle of who was driving Suzy's car that night remained. If it wasn't Beaux, could it have been Suzy? Maybe...

Sunny was in a world all her own as she walked back to her car, chewing over every bit of evidence she had in her mind. She stopped walking, her feet frozen and her heart thumping loudly in her ears. A realization formed in her mind, a feeling akin to finding the last, perfect ingredient to add to a cocktail recipe. She knew who Jeb's lover was! It was the man who loved him more than anyone, the man who wept real tears at his funeral, the man who couldn't even bear to look at a fishing rod without him–Earl Herbert.

Sunny jumped in her car and raced to Earl and Suzy's house. With any luck, he would be home, and she could confront him directly. Within minutes, she pulled into the front circle drive of the Herberts' blue and white three-story Queen Anne house. She ran to the door and pressed the doorbell. She could hear the chimes ringing inside. She waited, but no one came to answer. She pressed the doorbell again, this time with a bit more force. Still no answer. She looked around the left side of the house. A long driveway led to the gated back garden where a large three-car garage stood. Wondering for a moment if she should risk being caught wandering around private property, she decided that she needed to speak with Earl now and made her way around the house to the back gate.

"Anyone home?" she called into the back garden. There was no answer, only the sound of the light summer breeze blowing through the thick bamboo plants that lined the backyard fence. Sunny pushed the gate open with a loud creaking of its metal hinges. She wrinkled her nose. *What was that smell?*

The garage door was only three-fourths of the way closed, and Sunny gripped the edge of the door and pulled it up and open. A thick cloud of car exhaust hit her in the face, and she coughed hard, waving her hands to fan away the fumes. Why was Suzy's car running in the garage? She gasped.

Inside the vehicle was Earl, and from where she stood, it looked like he was dead.

Chapter 50

"Earl!" Sunny raised the neck of her dress to cover her nose and mouth and ran into the garage. She wrenched open the driver's side door, reaching over Earl's body to take the key from the ignition. Once the car was off, she unhooked the seatbelt from across his chest and began to drag him out of the vehicle and to the fresh air.

"Come on, Earl," Sunny wheezed, pulling with all her might. "If you are alive and can hear me, I could use a little help on your part." Earl gave no response. Sunny managed to lug him out of the garage and lay him on the backyard's green lawn. She felt his neck for a pulse. A tiny thumping met her fingertips. He was still alive...barely. She reached for her phone and dialed for the ambulance. With help on the way, Sunny knelt in the grass over Earl and began performing CPR. With the sounds of the ambulance sirens growing louder over her shoulder, Sunny kept pumping his chest. After what felt like an eternity, Earl inhaled a ragged breath. Sunny collapsed onto the grass next to him as the wailing ambulance slowed to a stop in the driveway.

After explaining the situation to the EMTs and watching them load a now semi-conscious Earl onto a stretcher, an oxygen mask on his face, Sunny stood in the Herbert driveway for a moment, shock paralyzing her body. If she hadn't decided to come here and confront Earl, he would be dead right now. She shivered. Where was Suzy? Was she inside the house, possibly unaware of what was transpiring in her garage? She looked around the backyard but saw no signs of Earl's wife or anyone else. Before she left, she went back to Earl's car. Her eyes had registered something on the car's dashboard, but she hadn't stopped to look at it in her rush to save him. She quickly leaned over the steering wheel to snatch the piece of crumpled notebook paper and began to read its scrawled cursive.

"Dear Suzy, Beaux, and anyone else who might read this,
I want you to know that my ending my life has nothing to do with you and isn't your fault. I love you all very much, but I can't go on knowing the hurt and shame I have caused by my actions. I knew that having an affair with a man was not only wrong, but unnatural in the eyes of God. In this town, we are Christians, and it should stay that way. So, I am doing what I need to do. Love, Earl"

Sunny shook her head, her heart sinking. How sad that Earl couldn't live with the fact that he was gay.

Had he killed Jeb, and maybe Annie too, because of the shame? Or had he done it because he was angry with Jeb for not living out in the open with him? She took out her phone and snapped a picture of the note before replacing it on the dashboard, knowing that the police would probably be filing a report about the incident. She was a complete amateur at this whole murder investigation thing, but she knew enough not to get caught tampering with evidence.

She almost drove to the hospital, but turned her car towards home instead. She needed to talk to Earl, but she knew she could not get anywhere near him with the hospital staff standing in her way. After all, she wasn't family, and with all her years as a nurse, she knew they didn't let just anyone in to see patients. She needed a plan.

When she got home, Sunny found Danny lying on the living room sofa with a happy, purring Boo curled up on his chest.

"Someone looks happy," Sunny beamed, not sure who was more in blissful heaven with the situation–Danny or Boo. The cozy sight of them lifted her mood, like the sun melting morning frost. She patted Boo's head and ruffled Danny's hair before heading to her room. On her hands and knees, she rummaged through a box of her old work clothes stuffed in the back of her closet. She found an old pair of her nursing scrubs and one of the work badges she had carried at Minneapolis General. Stuffing them in a tote bag, she blew Danny and Boo kisses and went out to her car.

In the parking lot of LouLou Parish Hospital, Sunny was thankful for all of her time spent doing yoga as she twisted and contorted her body this way and that while changing into her scrubs in the cramped back seat of her car. Top and pants on, she stepped out of the car and exhaled. She stuffed the old work badge into her pocket and entered the hospital's glass doors.

Once inside, she did her best to look authoritative as she walked past the security desk and towards the hallway marked ICU.

Shoot. She started to get flustered. *The hallway is locked. I need to scan a badge. What am I going to do?* Her cheeks began to heat. She turned and noticed the guard at the security desk watching her.

"Hi," She tried to sound normal. "I'm new here. First day on the job!" She chuckled. "They gave me this badge," She quickly flashed her old badge from Minnesota, stashing it back in her pocket before the guard could get a good look. "But it isn't working right. Would you mind?" She gave him a questioning look. "I'd go down to the main office to get it fixed, but I'm already running late."

The guard thought for a moment before giving a shrug and a nod. Rising from his chair, he scanned his badge to unlock the door.

"Thank you so much," Sunny smiled and hurried away. She walked down the hall until she came to a central circular desk. Noticing that no one was around, she dipped behind the desk and found a clipboard with a list of patients staying on the floor. She scanned the names with her index finger. *Bingo. Room eighteen.*

Outside room eighteen, Sunny paused, hearing a familiar voice inside. The voice moved towards the door, and Sunny hurried around the corner to hide.

"I'll be back in a bit, darling," Suzy called as she walked out of room eighteen. Sunny craned her neck from her hiding place and watched Suzy walk down the hall and towards the main lobby. Now was her chance. Ducking into Earl's room before she could be seen and stopped, she closed the door behind her and paused at the foot of his bed. The lighting in the room was dimmed, and Earl lay in bed, his head propped up on several pillows and his eyes closed. Sunny was surprised to see how frail he looked, and a pang of guilt knotted in her stomach. Should she be bothering him right now?

"Earl?" She took a step closer and whispered, unsure if he was asleep. "Earl, are you asleep?" She gently touched his arm.

"Ah!" Earl jolted awake, his eyes wide. "Who are you? What are you doing here?" He blinked in the dark room until his eyes registered Sunny's face. "Oh, it's you." He visibly relaxed. "Sunny, right?"

Sunny nodded and sat in the metal chair beside his bed.

"I didn't know you were a nurse." He attempted to sit up but was too weak to pull his body upright.

"Well, I used to be a nurse," Sunny explained. "But I don't exactly work at this hospital."

Earl opened his mouth to question her, but she stopped him short.

"Earl, I don't have much time," Sunny spoke urgently. "I know this will be painful, but I need to know. Did you attempt suicide because of what you did to Jeb?"

Earl's whole demeanor seemed to crumble before Sunny's eyes, and he sank further into his pillows, his eyes blinking back painful tears.

"I would never kill Jeb," he whispered in a weak voice. "I loved him more than I ever loved anyone. I could never…" His voice trailed off.

"Even if he refused to live out in the open with you and leave his wife?" Sunny pressed.

"How did you know about that?" Earl's eyes lit up with surprise. "Who told you that?"

"Annie," Sunny said. "And now she's dead. I think the same person that killed Jeb also killed Annie. And as much as I want to be wrong, I think that person could be you."

Earl wordlessly shook his head.

"Then why would you try to kill yourself? Did you mean what you wrote in that note? That you felt ashamed about how you've sinned before God?" She shook her head.

"What note?" Earl narrowed his eyes. "I didn't write a note. I didn't try to kill myself either. Is that what the doctor is saying?" He grew agitated and tried to sit up again.

"What do you mean *what note*?" Sunny gasped. "The one on the dashboard of your car. The one that explained why you were…you know…not going to be alive anymore." She held up her hands in disbelief.

"I didn't write any note." Earl shook his head with conviction. "I had a men's choir meeting at St.

Boudreaux's this morning, and when I got home and pulled my car into the garage, I went to the house and noticed the doors were locked. Well, I'm pretty bad about losing stuff, and of course, I lost my house key last week, so I couldn't get in. I went back and sat in the car, waiting for Suzy or Beaux to get home and unlock the door. I must have dozed off while I was waiting. I haven't been sleeping very well since Jeb's death." He wiped away a single tear. "Next thing I know, you're giving me CPR on my back lawn."

Sunny sat back in her chair, her hands rubbing her eyes. This story was almost too weird to be believed.

"You're saying that someone came into your garage, saw you sleeping, turned on your car, left a suicide note, and then shut the garage door behind them, letting the whole place fill with carbon monoxide?" She felt like she was Alice on the other side of the looking glass. There was no way this was something that happened in real life. "I don't know if I can believe that, Earl." She gave him a pitying look.

"Believe what you want," he snapped. "It's true."

"But why would someone want you dead?" Sunny asked.

"Jeb is dead, and now Annie too. Of course, I'm next, Sherlock." He fiddled with the IV taped to his hand.

A voice sounded from the hallway. Suzy was back. Sunny stood, frantically looking for a way to escape. She grabbed a stack of charts from a table in the corner of the room.

"Don't tell anyone I was here," she whispered to Earl. "We need to find out who is trying to kill you, and we need to find out fast." She held the stack of files up to cover her face. Suzy opened the door.

"Darling, I'm back." She announced as she entered.

"Just leaving, ma'am." Sunny spoke in a lowered voice, quickly shuffling past Suzy and out the door.

Sunny was reeling as she drove to the Coconut. She needed to talk to the tikis about this. Could she speak to them twice in one day? Did the magic work that way? Was it magic? Was that the right word for it? She pushed open the tiki bar door and gasped.

The room was empty. The tiki spirits and everything else in the Cajun Coconut had been stolen.

Chapter 51

Sunny spun around the room, her mouth agog, not believing what she saw. Someone had broken into the Coconut and taken everything–the palm trees, the tiki lanterns, the fish floats. Chairs and tables were strewn across the room like a hurricane had hit. Bottles of rum and liqueurs were smashed into shards on the floor, the brown liquid puddling in stains on the tropical floral carpet. But most importantly, they had taken the tiki spirits. The spot where Cook stood was empty, a ring of dust on the floor in his usual place. Cora and Pearl were ripped from the wall where they hung, the empty nails that once held them a painful reminder of their absence. Barry and Vin no longer dangled from the ceiling on their bamboo perches.

"Who would do this?" Sunny cried. She didn't know what to do. "Call someone," she muttered as she reached into her purse. The only thing shaking more than her voice was her hand as it groped around for her phone. "I should call someone for help." But who? Her first instinct was to call Flo, and her heart smashed to the floor, broken like one of the rum bottles. Flo couldn't help her now. She hesitated before dialing Tony. She was still angry at him for what he had done to Flo. Her finger hovered over his number. "I don't have a choice. I need to get my tikis back," she sobbed and dialed the call.

"Police Chief Perez." Tony's voice was all business.

"Tony," Sunny began to bawl gut-wrenching tears, unable to speak.

"Sunny, what's wrong?" He dropped his stony exterior, his voice softened and filled with concern. "Are you in trouble?"

Sunny told him what had happened, and within minutes, three squad cars were pulling to a stop in front of the tiki bar. They took her statement and examined the bar for any evidence linked to the thief. When they found nothing useful, they returned to their squad cars and left Sunny and Tony alone in the empty bar.

"How long do you think it will take before we find who did this?" Sunny asked in a weak voice.

"Could take hours. Could take months." Tony shook his head. "Honestly, we might never find out who did this. But you have insurance, right?" His face brightened slightly. "You can make a claim and get all of this covered. Then you can go buy new decorations and open up again."

Sunny felt like screaming and crying again, but she knew it would do no good. It wouldn't bring her tikis back, and how could Tony understand that the unique magic of her tiki bar couldn't be bought at a store?

A knock came from the front door. Sunny opened it to find Marian standing on her doorstep.

"Marian," Sunny gave a small smile. "This is kind of a bad time, honestly. I've got a bit of a crisis on my hands." Her lips began to quiver as she swallowed down a sob.

"We know," Marian nodded as she reached out to give Sunny's shoulder a sympathetic squeeze. "That's why we are all out searching the town for your things." She smiled.

"We?" Sunny asked.

"I gathered a big group of people in town," Marian beamed. "Me, Rachel, Buzz, the ladies from book club, the Gary's diner triplets...even snobby old Julia Donahue is helping," she laughed. "We won't stop until the Cajun Coconut is restored." She clasped her hands in a prayer motion.

"Oh, Marian," Sunny started crying again in earnest. "I can't thank you enough." She hugged the librarian.

"Don't waste time thanking me." Marian returned the hug with gusto. "Get your skates on, girl, and let's go get your tiki stuff back!"

Sunny couldn't believe how the people of LouLou had come together for her. Every inch of the square was searched for the next several hours, and every local business owner was questioned. Sunny cried the whole time–partly out of sadness for her lost tiki friends, partly in gratitude for her newfound human ones. Sunny's phone buzzed with a text message.

I HAVE YOUR TIKI JUNK. COME ALONE TO 348

PELICAN COVE.

Chapter 52

Sunny knew she should have told the others where she was going, but the text had said to come alone. What if she showed up at the address with a group of people, and the thief did something rash like destroy her tikis? She would never forgive herself if they were gone forever, so she quietly slipped back to where her car was parked in front of the tiki bar and drove out of the square.

She plugged the address into her phone and followed the directions out of LouLou town limits, down a red dirt road that led deeper into the thick Louisiana wilderness. Sunny watched with worried eyes as the service bars on her phone disappeared one by one until she had one bar left. What if she needed to call for help? Would a call even go through out here? Several times, she almost turned back towards town, but the thought of her tikis locked up somewhere spurned her on. She had to get them back.

Something had been bothering her ever since she read what she originally thought was Earl's suicide note, and talking to him at the hospital made it worse. The wording of the note was so familiar. She knew if she could just place where she had heard those words before, she would have found an essential piece to the puzzle.

"In this town, we are Christians..." She repeated the words out loud. Suddenly, it all made sense. "I know who the killer is," Sunny whispered, her heart racing. Now, how was she going to prove it?

Up ahead, Sunny could tell that the bumpy, dirt road she had been following for at least twenty minutes came to a dead end in a clearing in the dense, swampy forest. She slowed the car, arriving at what looked like a storage unit facility. Three rows of blue metal storage sheds lined up one against the other. Sunny looked down at the text message again. Was she in the right place? Hesitantly, she exited the car and walked closer to the storage sheds. Which one had her tikis? She stepped closer, wondering how she was supposed to find them when all of the sheds were very identical and also very locked shut.

"Hello?" She called out. "Is anyone here? It's me, Sunny." She listened, but no one called back. "Look, I just want my tikis back. Give them back, and I won't say a word to anyone. I won't even file a police report. I just want them back." Her voice cracked, and she wiped away a tear from her cheek. She gasped. At the end of the third row, a shed stood with its doors wide open. Inside the shed, she caught a glimpse of her tikis. She ran, a cry of relief in her throat.

"Oh, I am so happy to see you guys." She wrapped her arms around Cook and hugged him tightly. "Now, how do I get you all back home?" She bit her lip. Her car was too small to fit everything in one go, and she certainly didn't want to chance making two trips. Suddenly, the door of the shed slammed behind her. She spun around and screamed, the space going dark.

"Who is there?" Sunny yelled. "Let me out!" She banged on the shed door, but it held firm. She pounded her clenched fists on the door again.

"Hold your horses." A familiar woman's voice spoke from outside the shed. Sunny heard the clanking sound of a latch being pulled, and she stood back as a small window in the shed door slid open. A woman with a black balaclava stood on the other side, peering in, a sneering grin on her lips.

"You can go ahead and pull that ridiculous mask off, Mary Kay." Sunny rolled her eyes. "I already know it's you."

"Well, well, aren't you smart?" Mary Kay Middleton yanked off her disguise and shook out her perfect blonde curls. If Sunny hadn't been so terrified of being trapped by a killer, she would have asked Mary Kay what cosmetics she used. Despite the balaclava and the heat of the day, her hair and makeup remained impeccable as ever. "Unfortunately, you aren't smart enough not to get yourself trapped in a storage shed in the middle of nowhere." She laughed.

"It all makes sense now." Sunny slowly shook her head. "You hated Jeb and Earl because of their relationship. You hated Annie for encouraging them to live their truth. But..." She held her hands up in disbelief. "Did you hate them so much that you had to kill them? Really? Why couldn't you just mind your own darn business? In what way did their love hurt you?"

"Oh, it didn't just hurt me." Mary Kay's eyes flashed with malice. "Those men and their illicit, unnatural, disgusting affair were on track to hurt the whole town!"

"How?!" Sunny yelled.

"I would have thought a fellow mother like yourself would understand," Mary Kay explained. "We are raising innocent, impressionable young men. Do you really want your son exposed to such sinful behavior? Jeb and Earl could have turned my son gay, and I'm not having it. I stand on the rock with my Lord and Savior." She squared her jaw. "That's why I took matters into my own hands."

"You snuck into my bar and put grapefruit oil in Jeb's drink knowing he couldn't ingest that because of his medication." Sunny's voice sounded braver than she felt, but she was desperate to keep Mary Kay talking. It would buy her time to find a way out of this jam. "My question is, how did you know that Jeb was taking statins?"

"Oh, please," Mary Kay pursed her lips. "Have you seen our town's native cuisine? Everybody over the age of forty-eight in Louisiana takes statins." She swatted at a mosquito that buzzed near her face. "Plus, Barbara was always nagging Jeb about his health." She began to imitate Barbara in a mocking tone. "*Take your medicine, Jeb. Eat a vegetable for once, Jeb.*" She choked out a bitter laugh. "I didn't have to be a rocket scientist to know how to take him down."

"But how did you get Suzy's car?" Sunny genuinely

hadn't worked that one out yet.

"It wasn't that hard." Mary Kay was clearly proud of her work. "I had been stalking Earl for weeks, which is how I knew where he would be that day in the garage. Don't think for a minute I plan on forgiving you for thwarting my little plan when you saved Earl's life." She narrowed her eyes. "I waited that night until Earl and Suzy had fallen asleep on the sofa in front of the TV. Then I snuck into their house, grabbed the car key from their kitchen counter, and took the car." She clapped her hands in satisfaction. "I knew Buzz had security cameras recording the back alley, so I parked where I knew the car would be caught on video. Everyone would watch the tape and think it was Suzy."

Mary Kay was really on a roll now. She didn't even need Sunny asking questions to prompt her further confessions. She knew Annie would eventually go to the police when she heard about Jeb's death. Mary Kay had been the woman harassing people at the Corner Pocket, and she knew Annie would make the connection. While Mary Kay went on and on, Sunny heard a slight whisper behind her.

"Call the police," Cook's voice hissed in the darkness. "Your phone...Call the police."

Sunny's stomach gave a leap. *That's right! I've got my phone in my pocket.* She wasn't sure if she even had cell service out here, but she pulled the phone as covertly as possible from her dress pocket and held it close to her side, dialing 911.

"911, what's your emergency?" The operator spoke on the other end. Mary Kay stopped talking and glared at Sunny.

"Naughty, naughty." She shook her head. "That

will never do. I'm going to need that phone now, missy." She unlocked the shed with a clink and opened the door. Sunny saw this as her only chance. She rushed at Mary Kay, throwing all her weight at the woman before her. Mary Kay didn't budge. She was built like a Barbie doll, but the woman had the strength of a linebacker.

"Hmm," Mary Kay sighed with satisfaction. "I will have to call my pilates instructor and tell her all the weight training is paying off. Now, give me that phone!" She reached for a baseball bat that leaned in the corner of the shed. With one successful wack, she took Sunny down.

"Nighty, night," Mary Kay's voice trailed in Sunny's ears as the world went dark.

Chapter 53

When Sunny opened her eyes again, it was to see the faces of Flo and Danny staring down at her. She rubbed her groggy face and looked around. She was in a hospital room, lying in a bed with an unsettling amount of wires connecting her to several beeping machines.

"What happened?" Her question sounded like a harsh, gritty croak. Her memory came flooding back, and she attempted to sit up in bed. Flo put a hand on her shoulder to stop her. "Mary Kay, she's the killer!" Sunny panted. "She trapped me in that shed with all of my tikis!"

"We know." Flo patted her hand. "How are you feeling?" She studied Sunny's pale complexion.

"Like someone whacked me on the head and left me for dead," Sunny winced.

"That's because someone *did* whack you on the

head and leave you for dead," Flo nodded. Sunny noted a touch of irritation in her friend's voice. "Why, oh why, did you go off on your own to meet Mary Kay? You could have been killed!"

"I got a text saying that if I wanted my tiki stuff back, I needed to go to the address the thief gave me *alone.*" Sunny closed her eyes as the room swam around her. "If I had shown up with a search party, who knows what Mary Kay would have done to my tikis."

"I'm sorry, but is a bunch of decor that could be easily replaced worth risking your life?" Flo shook her head, and Sunny stayed silent. How could she explain to Flo just how wrong she was? Cook, Pearl, and the others were much more than decor. Flo took a deep breath. "I'm sorry that I snapped at you. I've been sitting here worrying, and I let it get the best of me. I'm just thanking all of our lucky stars that you are going to be okay." She patted Sunny's hand again.

She explained that thanks to Sunny's quick-thinking call to the police, they were able to track her location to the storage shed, where they found her lying unconscious.

"After bringing you here to the hospital, they were able to catch up with Mary Kay. She tried to make a run for it, but they got her."

"Let's pack up and go home." Sunny tried to sit up again.

"Oh, no, you don't!" Flo stood to pour Sunny a glass of the iced sweet tea from a pitcher on the nightstand. "You've got a major concussion. The doctor wants to keep you here for at least a few more days." She handed Sunny the glass of tea.

"What?" Sunny complained before taking a sip,

wincing a little at how sweet it was. "Surely not. What about Danny?" She turned to her son. "You need me home, don't you?"

"I'm going to stay with Flo while you are here. I'll be okay. Plus, Flo's going to need my help now that she's got more mouths to feed." He smiled and took out his phone to show her a picture. "Look who had her kittens a few hours ago." He held the screen for her to see an adorable picture of Boo happily nursing her four sweet babies. Sunny cooed.

"I guess I can stay here for a little while longer if you are okay, Danny." Sunny put her tea glass on the nightstand and laid back in bed. "Oh, I almost forgot! What about my tikis? Are they still out in that storage shed?"

"Nope," Flo grinned. "When they heard the news, the whole search party went out and loaded everything into Buzz's truck. They should be at the Coconut as we speak putting everything back together."

"Really?" Sunny began to cry. It turned out the people in town cared about her after all. She decided right then and there that when she was strong enough, she would have one big luau and the whole town would be invited.

"Knock, knock." Tony Perez stood in the doorway, gently rapping on the open door. He held a large bouquet of yellow roses. "May I come in?"

"Sure," Sunny nodded weakly.

"We were just leaving." Flo stood. "Right, Danny?" She winked at Sunny before taking Danny's arm and leading him out of the room.

"Bye, Mom." Danny blew his mom a kiss, and Sunny raised one hand to catch it.

"We'll be back in a few hours with dinner," Flo called before leaving the room.

"May I sit?" Tony motioned towards the seat Flo had vacated. Sunny nodded.

"I'm sorry," they both blurted out at the same time.

"Let me go first," Tony said. "I'm sorry for the way I acted. I was under a lot of pressure from the state higher-ups to solve this thing, and I kind of panicked. See, I spent my days in L.A. solving some of the most horrific crimes imaginable. I thought moving to a small town would allow me to leave that life behind. Being wrapped up in a murder investigation just brought back all of the trauma. But it's no excuse for the way I acted."

"I'm sorry, too," Sunny said. "I shouldn't have gotten involved in the investigation. I know that now."

Tony rose and placed the roses on Sunny's bedside table.

"I know I told you mere seconds ago that I wasn't going to meddle in police business anymore, but…" She hesitated, but then continued, deciding she had a right to know. "Why would Mary Kay steal from the Coconut? How did that fit in with the murders?"

"She saw you poking around and asking questions, and it made her nervous." Tony returned to his bedside chair. "When she saw you go off with Annie at the Labor Day picnic, she knew she had to do something. Stealing your things was a way to lure you out where no one would find your body. She planned to get you out there and kill you." He shuddered at the thought.

"I'm lucky that you guys were able to track my location from my phone call." Sunny picked up the roses and put them to her nose, the light honey-sweet scent making her smile.

"That is something I wanted to ask you about." Tony frowned. "We didn't track where you were from your phone. Someone on the line with you told us where you were. It was a man's voice, but when we got there, you were the only one we found." He looked to her, hoping to find answers. "We searched the woods and the surrounding areas, but we never found anyone."

"A man?" Sunny puzzled. "There wasn't a man with me."

"Well, whoever he was, he's a hero. Not only did he tell us where you were, but he told us that Mary Kay was responsible. We were able to catch her before she got too far away."

"Visiting time is over in two minutes." A nurse called from the hallway.

"I better go." Tony stood. "Can I ask you something?"

"Sure," Sunny shrugged.

"Can we get a fresh start?" His eyes sparkled. "I think we had the start of something good when we weren't at each other's throats trying to catch a killer."

"Yes," Sunny smiled. "My answer is yes."

Tony grinned and left her room.

Chapter 54

"Two mai tais, please!" Bunny, the baker from across the square, ordered drinks for her and Julia Donahue before taking two tiki mugs to a table in the corner of the room. Sunny had been out of the hospital for two weeks, and while her head still hurt on occasion, she was feeling strong and healthy. She smiled as she looked around the packed room. It was the first night that the Cajun Coconut had been open since Mary Kay had lured Sunny to the storage sheds, and it seemed that the whole town had shown up to celebrate.

"You know what, Sunny?" Buzz leaned against the bar, clad in his usual biker leather, his blue polarized Ray Bans perched on the top of his head. "This tiki drink stuff ain't half bad." He took another sip of his fruity cocktail.

"Thanks, Buzz," Sunny said without the slightest hint of sarcasm. With the tropical music playing and the rowdy crowd chatting and laughing, Sunny could barely hear the clinking of the seashells on her front door as it opened. Even more friends walked in. Tony led the way with Earl and Marian following behind.

"Tony!" Sunny beamed. "I thought you had to work tonight."

"Wouldn't miss opening night for anything." He gave her a hug and kiss on the cheek before joining a table of his work friends.

"I'll take one mai tai, please," Earl said with a watery smile. Sunny realized that it must be hard for him to be so near the place where his loved one died. She mixed his drink and slid it across the bartop. Grabbing the glass of sweet tea she had been sipping all night, she held it high in front of Earl.

"To Jeb," she toasted, and Earl nodded, lifting his glass to clink with hers.

"Look what I've got!" Flo called as she and Danny entered the bar. "Two things that are too sweet for words." She placed her familiar Tupperware cake tin on the bartop and popped open the lid to reveal her famous coconut cake. "Who wants a slice?"

Everyone in the bar descended on the cake for their own slice of fluffy, buttery heaven.

"You said two sweet things." Sunny cocked her head to this side, her mouth full of cake. "Where's the second?"

"Right here," Danny reached into the pocket of his coat and pulled out a tiny, black kitten. He cradled the little ball of fur in his hands and beamed. "Flo said she's ready to come home with us. She can, right?"

Sunny looked at the kitten with its gleaming black fur and tiny green eyes that shone like specks of peridot gems.

"How could I refuse?" She took the kitten from Danny and snuggled it to her cheek.

That night after the last friend had left the bar, Sunny flicked off the neon sign in the front window with a tired-but-happy hand. She finished her closing up to-dos, wiping down the tables and bartop, stacking the clean tiki mugs on shelves, and balancing the money in the cash register. With everything done, she sat in one of the peacock chairs with a gratified sigh. This night had been the kind she had dreamed of ever since she stood in that run-down barn on the edge of the town square wondering if she could really turn the place into the tiki bar she pictured in her mind. That night the tiki bar had been filled with genuine friends, a real community. Sunny sighed. She was finally home.

"Cook! Pearl! Guys!" Sunny called and waited patiently as her tiki friends came to life.

"It's so good to see you, me girl," Barry squawked.

"It's been too long," Pearl agreed. "We could sense that you were okay, but we still worried when we didn't see you for weeks."

"I'm sorry about that," Sunny nodded. "I was really weak for a while. I feel much better now though."

"We are glad that everything worked out in the end," Cook said. "The whole situation was quite worrisome to be sure."

"We never had to worry about murderers when Aunt Edna was in charge," Cora complained.

"I wanted to talk to you guys tonight because I feel that I'm still alive because of one of you." Sunny turned to Cook. Ever since Tony's visit to the hospital, Sunny had wondered and wondered who was the man that had saved her life in telling the police where she was. She had finally worked out the puzzle. "Cook, you were the one who told the police where to find me." Tears began to well in her eyes. "I wouldn't have made it if it weren't for you."

"As long as we are here with you, we will do our best to serve and protect you." His eyes glowed a calming blue-green.

"We love you, Sunny," Pearl cooed. "We will do whatever it takes to keep you safe."

"Thank you." Sunny brushed away the tears. "I love

you all too, but don't worry. Mary Kay is going to be behind bars for a long time, and that was enough murder and mayhem for me. I won't need your protection anymore."

She smiled, completely unaware of just how wrong she was.

Recipes from the Cajun Coconut

One Killer Mai Tai

1 oz. white rum
1 oz. dark rum
1/2 oz. orange liqueur
1 oz. lime juice
1/2 oz. orgeat
A cherry and mint for garnish

1. Add white rum, orange liqueur, lime juice, and orgeat into a shaker with plenty of ice and shake.

2. Pour into a rocks glass or tiki mug.

3. Use a spoon to float the dark rum on top.

4. Garnish with cherry and mint.

Sunny's Rum Runner

1 oz. dark rum
1/2 oz. banana liqueur
1 oz. Chambord
2 oz. pineapple juice
1/2 oz. lime juice
grenadine to taste

1. Combine all ingredients into a cocktail shaker filled with plenty of ice and shake until icy cold.

2. Strain into your favorite tiki mug.

Flo's Famous Mac and Cheese

2 cups milk of your choice
2 tablespoons butter
1 tablespoon all-purpose flour
1 t salt
1/2 t pepper
3 cups hoop cheese, shredded
8 oz. elbow pasta, cooked

1. Preheat over to 400 degrees.

2. In a saucepan, warm milk on stove. Melt butter in another pan and whisk in flour, cooking for one minute.

3. Whisk milk into flour/butter mixture and cook until thickened. Add seasonings and 2 cups of cheese. Stir until the cheese is melted and then add the cooked pasta. Stir to combine.
4. Pour into a 9x13 dish and bake until bubbling and browned.

Made in the USA
Columbia, SC
27 April 2025

57134611R00207